Hunter's Edge

Look for these titles by
Shiloh Walker

Now Available:
Always Yours
Beautiful Girl
For the Love of Jazz
Playing for Keeps
Talking with the Dead
Vicious Vixen

The Hunters Series
The Huntress
Hunter's Pride
Malachi
Hunter's Edge

Print Collection
Legends: Hunters and Heroes

Coming Soon:
Print Collection
Taking Chances

To Aja

Hunter's Edge

Shiloh Walker

Get Hunted!

Shiloh Walker

A Samhain Publishing, Ltd. publication.

Samhain Publishing, Ltd.
577 Mulberry Street, Suite 1520
Macon, GA 31201
www.samhainpublishing.com

Editing by Heidi Moore
Cover by Scott Carpenter

First Samhain Publishing, Ltd. electronic publication: May 2008
First Samhain Publishing, Ltd. print publication: April 2009

Chapter One

Age 8

"I'm gonna marry you."

Kelvin Saunders blushed beet red as all his friends started to laugh. It was the kiss of death for an eight-year-old boy, having some girl come up and say something like that in front of his friends.

Part of him, that embarrassed part, jeered at him to say something to her, make fun of her, anything to get the kids around them laughing at her—instead of him.

But Kel couldn't. He wasn't even really sure why. But he just couldn't.

He knew who she was—her name was Angelica something or other. She was new in town, had moved into a house not too far from where he lived. A thin strip of trees separated their neighborhoods—that, and a lot of money, according to Jill Baker, the fifteen-year-old who watched him on Friday nights when his parents had date night.

Angelica gazed at him with eyes the same pretty blue as the September sky, her hair pulled back into two neatly braided pigtails. She wore a pink T-shirt with a pair of spotless white shorts. Man, Kel couldn't wear anything white without getting dirt all over it. The new girl, though, she looked all shiny, neat and clean. Even her tennis shoes looked brand new. She smiled at him, showing perfectly straight teeth, and her nose crinkled.

Denny Mayhue punched Kel's arm. "You got a girlfriend, Kel?"

Defensively, Kel snapped, "No." But then he looked back at the girl. She was embarrassing him, big time, but as much as

7

he wanted to retaliate, he couldn't do it.

He couldn't do something that would hurt her feelings.

She gave him a secretive smile, a smile that said she knew something nobody else did, and maybe, just maybe, she wanted to tell him. "My name's Angel..." She rolled her eyes and made a face. "Actually, it's Angelica, after my dad's mom. She died before I was born. I really hate being called Angelica and she did, too, or that's what my dad says. So he calls me Angel. And Mom hates it."

She prattled on, ignoring the boys who were still grinning at both her and Kel, and the girls who had been behind her when she announced she was going to marry him. They'd started giggling but now, as she ignored them, they wandered off. Kel's friends lost interest, heading for the basketball court, leaving him alone with Angel/Angelica as she talked.

And man, did she talk. She talked fast, she talked about everything, and she didn't even seem to care that he wasn't talking back. Scuffing his feet in the dirt, Kel told himself he needed to just go find his friends and maybe play basketball for a few more minutes. Recess didn't last forever and after this, he still had two and half hours before school let out.

But he realized he couldn't quite pull himself away.

Even when Mrs. Gumble blew her whistle, announcing the end of recess, Kel didn't want to walk away. It wasn't until she grinned at him and said, "I'll talk to you tomorrow," that he could even move.

He was still puzzling the girl over in his mind as he lined up to go back into school. She lined up in Mrs. Romero's line and gave him a sweet smile.

Denny nudged him from behind. "You got a girlfriend," he said again.

But Kel just ignored him.

Age 14

"You've got to learn to ignore people, Kel," Angel said, sighing and shaking her head as she touched her fingers to his swollen black eye.

He batted her hand away. "Stop it, Angel. That hurts."

8

"Why did you get into a fight this time?"

Shrugging, he turned away and went to study his face in the mirror hanging over the back of the couch. They'd gone to Angel's house—her parents both worked pretty late—and he'd hoped he could have a few minutes to think up some believable line for his mom.

So far, no luck. And there was no way she wasn't going to notice his shiner, either. Still fuming, he glared at his reflection.

The mirror showed a tall, lanky boy with dark brown hair that curled if he didn't keep it cut close, green eyes surrounded by long, thick lashes that he hated. Days spent in the sun had turned his skin a deep, golden tan and streaked his dark hair with lighter strands. If he wasn't so damn pissed about the fight—and worrying about how his mother was going to freak— he might have taken a minute to admire the black eye. His face that had gotten him called pretty boy more than once.

Much as he hated that, he could ignore it easy enough.

If he could have ignored it when Denny started making fun of Angel, he wouldn't be in this mess. But...

"Kel." Angel's voice, soft and patient, jerked him back to attention.

Man, he hated when she talked like that, all grown up and polite and persistent. Scowling, he turned around and stared at her with his hands shoved deep in his pockets. "That jerk-off Denny said you were weird. I told him to shut up. He got in my face. I hit him."

"Kel...I am weird."

"No, you're not," he snapped, his hands clenching into fists. He hated when people talked about her like that—hated when she did it herself. Angel wasn't weird—she just wasn't... She just wasn't like everybody else.

She wasn't like anybody else.

Angel grinned at him and said, "Just because you say it doesn't make it true, Kel." Then she shrugged. "Kel, I don't want you getting into fights over me. You keep it up and you'll get in trouble with your folks. Or worse." Her lip poked out a little and she murmured, "I don't want you getting in trouble."

Man...

She climbed off the couch and walked over to stand in front of him, near enough that he could smell the cherry lip gloss she wore, close enough that he could just barely see the shadow of her bra strap through her T-shirt. Angel was tall for a girl, almost as tall as he was, and Kel wasn't short. She leaned and kissed him, quick and soft. Blood rushed to his face but before she could move away, he reached out and caught her hand, tugged her close.

It was scary, the way he felt about Angel. It had been like this ever since he'd met her. *I'm gonna marry you.* He hadn't ever forgotten those words. And even though she hadn't ever said them again, Kel had a feeling she was right. It was almost creepy even thinking about.

He wrapped his arms around her and she snuggled against him with a happy sigh. "I don't like people talking about you," he said, his voice cracking a little.

"Ignore them, Kel. I don't care what people say. I really don't."

Age 15

The pain hit him square in the chest, like a ton of bricks. Or worse, like his wrestling coach had decided to let the heavyweights use him for target practice. It woke him from a dead sleep, pressing down on him so hard, he couldn't breathe, could hardly move. Rolling to his side, he shoved his arms under him and managed to force himself onto his hands and knees.

"What the..."

Another spasm hit him and when it passed, Kel didn't have to ask what again. He knew. It was Angel. He could feel her. It was crazy, the way they were so in tune with each other, the way one seemed to know when the other was hurting or mad.

This was unreal, though, vicious enough to make him want to puke from it. "Angel..."

Almost like she heard him, some of the weight on his chest eased, just enough that he was able to get out of bed and drag on whatever clothes came to his hands. He probably should try to go out the bedroom window—if his parents heard him leaving the house again, they'd freak.

10

But he didn't trust his shaking hands or legs enough to climb down without breaking his neck, so he shuffled through the house as quietly as he could. When the door closed behind him, he breathed out a sigh of relief.

"I'm coming, Angel." His friends would think he was crazy—hell, half of them thought that already anyway. Rain started to fall as he took a well-worn path through the trees. Their subdivisions backed up against each other and only about a half a mile and a bunch of evergreens, maple and oak trees separated him from Angel. Usually, the walk was a breeze, even at night. Right now, it was taking forever.

When he emerged from the trees, he wasn't surprised to see Angel sitting on the back deck, wearing one of his T-shirts, a pair of panties and not much else. With her knees drawn up to her chest, she sat there, shaking and crying. He mounted the steps slowly and when he held out his arms, she came to him and the quiet tears turned into harsh, ugly sobs.

Holding her close, he rocked her. His chest ached in sympathy with the force of her sobs—he felt them as though it was him crying. When the storm of grief finally eased, he had tears of his own running down his cheeks. She looked up at him, her pretty face drenched with tears, her eyelids puffy and swollen.

She sniffed a little, tried to speak. It took a couple of tries because her voice kept breaking. "It's my dad," she whispered, snuggling up against him, burying her face against his worn-out fleece jacket. "My dad's dead—he had a...car...wreck."

No words were going to take that kind of pain away and Kel didn't see the point in trying. Instead, he picked her up and settled down on the deck stairs and held her as she started to sob again.

As night slowly bled into dawn, Angel fell asleep in his arms. She shivered a little, but if he tried to get her inside, he worried she'd wake up. Instead, he managed to unzip his jacket and pull it off, covering her up as best he could.

That was how his dad found him. Jacob Saunders came through the trees and when he saw Kel sitting there, holding Angel while she slept, all Jake did was sigh and shake his head. Kel sat there as his dad climbed the steps and settled on the step below them.

"Sheriff Rogers just called me with the news. Wanted me to come and sit with Angel. Her mama..." Jake never had a mean word for anybody. Even when he was madder than hell at Kel, he managed to keep his voice level. The disappointment Kel would see in his dad's eyes was worse than the yelling anyway. A minister at the local church, Jake was kind, considerate—too kind and considerate to say the truth out loud.

"Her mama is probably off whining and wailing and doesn't give a da—crap that she left Angel here alone," Kel said, quietly. He couldn't keep the anger out of it, though. Ann Mathis-Pierson cared about exactly one person in this world—herself.

"Now Kel, her husband is dead," Jake said quietly, glancing down at Angel's face.

Angel slept like the dead, though, and Kel knew she wasn't going to wake up any time soon. She was like a limp dishrag in his arms, her breathing soft, slow and deep, her body warm against his under the cover of the jacket he'd draped over her.

"Yeah, her dad is dead. So why was Angel here alone? In the middle of the night?" Kel demanded.

Angel stirred in his arms and automatically, Kel lifted a hand, brushed her hair back from her face. Lowering his voice, he asked, "Do you know what happened?"

"Troy tells me that Paul was heading home—outside of Nashville. Kid was driving along beside him and changed lanes, didn't see him. Ran him off the road—Paul most likely died instantly."

Though she was sleeping, Angel started to whimper. Bending down, Kel kissed her forehead. "Shhhh. It's okay. I'm here, Angel." Her face eased and she sighed, settled deeper into sleep.

He was quiet for a minute, but the ugly words had to come out. He couldn't keep them inside anymore—they were choking him. "Her mother wasn't here when they came to tell her, was she?"

The look on his dad's face was answer enough.

Ann hadn't been home, probably out screwing somebody. When she wasn't working past nine or ten, she was usually shacked up with some guy. Working as an attorney would definitely call for long hours—Kel knew that. His mother was also an attorney, although she worked in the district attorney's office, unlike Ann, a high-priced defense attorney. They'd come up against each other in court and although Kel's mother, Meredith, hadn't ever said anything, Kel knew she didn't like Ann.

Ann was hard to like. Kel knew that. For Angel's sake, he'd always been polite to her, but it was going to be hard now. Very hard.

"She doesn't have anybody now," Kel whispered, closing his eyes. Her dad had been a great guy. A bit of a pushover, Kel had always thought, for putting up with his wife. Still, Paul had been great. He'd adored Angel and he did his best to make up for the fact that Ann wasn't worth shit as a parent.

"That's not true, Kel." His dad reached up, patted him on the shoulder.

Sliding his dad a sheepish look, Kel rolled his eyes. "I'm not exactly talking about God, Dad. Not trying to discount Him, but it's good to have a person to talk to, one who will answer."

With his characteristic, understanding smile, Jake replied, "Oh, God always answers, son. But I wasn't talking about God, either. I was talking about you. And your mom and me—you know we love Angel like she was our own." He squeezed Kel's shoulder. "She'll be all right, son. She's too strong not to be."

Age 18

This had to be the most embarrassing conversation of his life. Kel sat at the kitchen table, his arms folded across his chest and his chin tucked low so he didn't have to see his father's face. He didn't have to see his father's face to know that his dad was blushing.

"Dad, I told you, Angel and I aren't having sex," he repeated, trying to cut the conversation short.

"And I told you that I believe you," Jake replied, snapping a little.

His voice was sharp. That was odd enough that Kel glanced up. His dad hardly ever raised his voice, it just wasn't in him. Kel met his eyes and Jake pushed back from the table, stood up and started to pace, long jerky motions like he couldn't quite coordinate his arms and legs. "This isn't much fun for me,

13

either," Jake said, sending Kel a look that reminded him of a hound dog, all long-faced and sad-eyed. "I thought we'd moved past the stage of talking about the birds and the bees, and why you should respect yourself enough to wait until you find the right person."

I already found her, Kel thought, but wisely, he kept his mouth shut.

Jake laughed. "You really need to work on that poker face." He sighed and rubbed a hand over his face. "Look, I know what you're thinking. You're thinking about Angelica—I know you love her. I know she loves you."

"Don't go telling me that I'm too young to really understand love, Dad. I don't want to hear that."

Gently, Jake said, "Now that's exactly what I'm not going to tell you. Kel, I met your mama when I was eighteen. She was sixteen. I knew right away that I wanted to marry her." He came back to the table, but instead of sitting across from Kel, this time, he took the seat right next to him. "Sometimes, it does happen like that. When it does, it's a wonderful gift. I thank God every day of my life for your mother, for you. I didn't have to go half of my adult life trying to find the right woman—she was already there. I didn't suffer the loneliness, I didn't have all those unasked questions."

He reached up, awkwardly patting Kel's shoulder. "I think what is between you two is real. Angel, she's a special girl, a bright one." Jake grimaced and added, "Sometimes too bright. I swear, sometimes it's like there's a forty-year-old woman trapped inside that girl's body."

The chair creaked and Kel heard his dad's knees pop as he stood up. From the corner of his eye, he watched his father shove his hands deep into his pockets, watched him shuffle his feet a little more. "But your mother and I just felt maybe I should have this talk with you."

"Why?" Kel demanded.

"Because we love you. We want what's best for you—and for her. Kids don't always think about the future and we want to make sure the two of you have the best, the brightest future possible. Decisions made in the heat of the moment—" At that, Jake's face flushed beet red and it was a wonder he managed to talk at all, considering how tight his voice sounded.

"Sometimes, those decisions can have consequences."

Kel shifted uncomfortably on the chair, focused on the clear plastic box in front of him. It was a corsage, an orchid with a pale blue bow. Angel had told him she was wearing light blue, and he'd told his mom that, so she told him he needed to make sure the corsage would go with her dress. He'd rolled his eyes and muttered, "Girls..." But he'd made sure he told the florist that his prom date was wearing light blue. Focusing on the silly flower made it a bit easier to speak, a lot easier than looking at his dad while he spoke. So he stared at the flower like it held the answers to the universe. "Dad, Angel and I aren't really in any rush to...to... Well, you know." *Liar*, a voice in his head jeered. Kel was in a big damn hurry to *you-know* with Angel, but talks like this one were burned on his brain and Angel wasn't ready. He knew it, without even having to ask her.

So he didn't push.

Desperate to get this conversation over and done with, he rushed the rest of the words out. "Angel isn't ready. I don't want to rush her." He deliberately left off commenting about whether he was ready. Kel didn't lie to his dad and he wasn't interested in making this take any longer than it had to.

Kel was going to marry Angel.

He hadn't asked—they never talked about it. But they both knew it. He was even saving some of his money for a ring. It was a few years off, and Kel seriously hoped she wasn't planning on making him wait until then before they did it, but he could wait until she was ready. Angel deserved that much.

Risking a quick glance up, he saw the relieved smile on his dad's face and shrugged restlessly. "Stop worrying about me so much, Dad. I love her. I'm not going to do anything that will mess that up."

Age 19, May

"Your parents are going to wonder where you are," Angel said softly. She had her legs drawn up to her chest and her arms linked around them. She rested her chin on her knees and focused on the flickering firelight.

Kel shrugged. "I doubt they'll wonder too much." Yeah, they would. He knew that. He might be nearly nineteen years old and finishing up his freshman year in college, but in the eyes of his parents, he was still a kid. They might wonder, they would probably worry, but Kel wasn't in any hurry to leave just to suit his folks.

Especially not right now.

Something was bothering Angel but she wouldn't tell him what it was. He could feel it, an ugly, nasty weight on his chest and until she opened up and talked to him, he wasn't leaving. They'd driven to Tennessee to do some hiking and before they'd left, Kel had told his parents he'd probably be back pretty late.

Angel hadn't said much of anything to her mom, but it wouldn't matter. On that front, nothing much had changed in all the years Kel had known Angel and her mother—Ann still didn't concern herself with her daughter. As far as Ann was concerned, Angel was kept clothed, fed and sheltered. That was the extent of her parenting worries.

Unless Angel was gone long enough that it interfered with Ann's life, the woman would never notice. When she came looking for Angel to run some errands, to make some phone calls, then maybe Ann might notice Angel wasn't there.

That was it.

Ever since her dad had died, things at Angel's house had gotten worse and he knew she was literally counting down the days until she graduated from high school. She'd turn eighteen in July and on her eighteenth birthday, she was getting one whopping sum of money. Paul Pierson had a very large life insurance policy and Angel would receive the largest part of it. A certain amount of money had been set aside to pay off any final expenses and pay off the house so Ann wouldn't need to worry about that.

But the rest of the money was set aside for Angel. It came with some restrictions, things like she'd get so much on her birthday, so much for college, and the rest of it upon her college graduation.

And it was a lot of money. Enough money that she could pretty much pick her college and it was all but paid for. Enough that she wouldn't have to work a part-time job, that she didn't have to worry her mother wouldn't help her out. Paul might have been a pushover, but he'd known his wife and he hadn't wanted Angel to suffer should something happen to him.

Propped on his elbow, Kel stared into the fire and wondered if Angel was going to spill or if he was going to have to drag it out of her. The fire crackled and popped and a shower of sparks went flying into the air as one of the flaming logs split into two parts.

"Mom's getting married."

He glanced up at Angel and then looked back into the fire. "That's what you've been worrying about?"

She made a face at him. "I'm not worried—exactly." Shifting around, she moved her shoulders in a restless shrug. "Dad's been gone four years now. And it's not like she ever really loved him. Hell, the day we buried him, she acted like it didn't matter he was gone. She went and redid the whole damn house less than a month after he died. Now she's getting married and I'm expected..." Her voice trailed off and she shook her head. "Forget it."

"Expected to what?" Kel asked, narrowing his eyes. He didn't like that look on her face, the grim cast to her gaze.

"You're going to get mad."

Shoving himself upright, he drew his legs up and braced his elbows on his knees. "I'm already mad and I don't even know what it is you're talking about."

Her pretty mouth twisted in an ugly smirk. "She's kicking me out, Kel. Naturally, not until I'm eighteen, but she's already told me that she wants me gone before her new husband and his kids move in." With a loose, easy grace, Angel shoved herself upright and started to pace around the fire. "I don't know why in the hell I'm surprised. And it's not like I won't be okay. Dad made sure of that."

Rising to his feet, Kel followed her and when she turned around, she plowed straight into his chest. Gently, he reached up, closed his hands around her arms and studied her face. She was crying. Firelight flickered off the tears on her face and Kel felt his heart break a little. "Angel..."

"I've lived in that house since I was seven years old, Kel. The summer I turned thirteen, Dad painted my room and he did everything exactly the way I wanted. And now I have to leave it."

Brushing her hair back from her face, he dipped his head and kissed her. "I'm sorry, Angel."

She slid her arms around his waist and snuggled in closer. "She doesn't care about me at all." It was a flat, emotionless statement—there wasn't any self-pity in it and Kel knew she wasn't feeling sorry for herself or trying to make him feel bad for her. Although he did—he was pissed off, hurt and disgusted. But just like Angel, Kel knew what she said was the simple truth.

Ann Mathis didn't love her daughter. She'd dropped the Pierson from her name as soon as her husband was buried. She hadn't loved her husband and she didn't mourn him.

And when Angel left that house, Ann probably wouldn't even miss her only daughter.

Cradling the back of her head in his hand, he held her close, breathed her in—Angel always smelled of honeysuckle. Even in the dead of winter, she smelled like summer and he loved it. He nuzzled her neck, stroked a hand up her back. She snuggled in closer and Kel gritted his teeth when her lower body pressed up against his.

"Kel..."

He lifted his head, forced a smile. She slid her hands between them, tugged up his shirt. Her hands were cool against his flesh. Kel stared at her face, his heart beating so hard he thought it might explode out of his chest as she slid her fingers along the waistband of his jeans.

But when she went to his belt buckle, Kel caught her hands. His body was going to make him pay for this, he knew it. Still, he caught her hands, lifted them up. Dipping his head, he kissed her knuckles.

She tugged against his hold, a strange light shining in her eyes. Whatever their weird connection was, it wasn't anything that let him know what she was thinking, just what she feeling. Right now, there was a weird desperation inside her.

Desperation...and determination.

It was enough to lay Kel low, feeling the hungry need inside her, knowing she had made a decision he'd been praying she'd make soon. And it was an unlucky sucker punch, because there was no way Kel was going to let their first time happen when she was miserable.

"No, Angel," he whispered, dipped his head and kissed her

lips. "Not when you're pissed off at your mom, or when you're hurting."

"Why not?" she demanded, jerking back. She grabbed the hem of her shirt and jerked the navy blue cotton up, over her head. Letting it fall to the ground, she reached behind to unhook her simple white bra.

Kel swore and turned away, but the image was burned in on his mind. It wasn't just seeing her stripping naked. They hadn't had sex yet, but they'd come close. She was so pretty, soft white curves, golden curls, pink nipples that had gone hard and tight in the cool night air.

"Because it's not how this should be," Kel said, shoving his hands in his pockets. He hoped he wasn't going to do something embarrassing—like come inside his shorts just from looking at her. "We haven't waited this long to do it because you're pissed off at your mom and you're hurting and you need to know somebody loves you."

She came up behind him, slid her arms around his waist, pressed her naked breasts against his back. "I know somebody loves me—you love me. I'm doing this because you love me and because I love you and because I don't want to think about anything but that."

Kel caught her hands as she once more started to tug at his belt buckle. Turning in the circle of her arms, he wrapped his arms around her waist, lifted her up. "I'll make you stop thinking—but we're not doing this tonight," he said gruffly. "When we do this, it's going to be because you're already thinking of nothing but us. We deserve that much, Angel."

July

Kel found Angel at the top of the stairs, staring into the huge room. It didn't look that big right now, considering it was packed with boxes, Angel's bed and a couple other pieces of furniture. Along the western wall was a small kitchen area and there was a bathroom just behind the staircase.

"Not bad, Angel." He smirked and added, "It's a hell of a lot better than my dorm, that's for certain." Of course, a shoebox might be an improvement over his dorm.

His freshman year at Georgia State University had been the

first time he'd spent so much time away from Angel. She was a year younger than he was, and while she was finishing up her senior year, he'd been an hour away, only able to see her on the weekends.

It had been hell.

She glanced over her shoulder at him, a faint grin on her lips. "I don't even know where to start."

His arms were full of boxes and he took a minute to lower them to the ground before going to her. He stood behind her, linking his arms around her waist and resting his chin on her shoulder.

Angel laid her arms on top of his and leaned back into him with a sigh. "I don't think I'm going to be the type to move around a lot. I hate this."

"You could have let your mom hire those movers," Kel said, grinning.

"And let her kick me out that much sooner?" She wrinkled her nose. "Nah. Besides, I hate letting other people touch my stuff."

Sliding one of his hands up over her waist, he teased, "Hey, I touch your stuff all the time."

Angel arched, pressing against him as he cupped one breast in his hand. "Hmmm. You're welcome to touch anything you like."

Kel groaned and dipped his head, nuzzled her neck. "Don't tell me that."

Turning in the circle of his arms, she slid her hands up and linked them behind his neck. "Why not?" she whispered against his lips.

Kel cupped one hand over the back of her neck and angled her head back, taking her light, teasing kiss deeper. He circled the outline of her lips with his tongue and then teased her until she opened for him. Trailing the fingers of his free hand down along her side, he slid a hand under the hem of her T-shirt, curving his fingers around the soft, warm weight of her breast.

Caught up in her warmth, in her heat, Kel slid his lips down her neck and bit her softly. Angel shuddered in his arms, lifted her hands to his waist. Sliding them under the worn fabric of his T-shirt, she touched him, running her palms over his sides, up over his back—then up in between them, pushing against his chest until he fell back a step.

With a wry grin, Kel started to respond, "That's why not."

But the words ended up drying to dust on his tongue as she reached for the hem of her shirt, dragging it off. Under it, she wore a white bra dotted with little red flowers.

"Why not?" she murmured, stepping back up against him.

"Angel?" he asked hoarsely.

She tipped her head back, smiled at him and then as he stood there, she fisted her hands in the bottom of his T-shirt and stripped it off, tossing it down on the floor beside hers. That secretive little smile on her lips told him everything he needed to know. For a minute or two, Kel didn't know if he could even move.

Terror wrapped a fist around his throat, blood roared in his ears and Kel couldn't quite manage to take a breath. Nerves had his hands turning hot and sweaty and he knew, he just knew, he was going to end up doing something that would totally humiliate him.

But then Angel leaned in, pressed her lips to his jaw and whispered, "I love you..."

Her soft, familiar voice soothed the tangled nerves wreaking havoc on him, and the feel of her body pressed against his own took care of the rest. Abruptly, he picked her up and when she giggled, a foolish grin spread over his face as he carried her to the bed.

It was bare, not even a sheet on it yet, but neither of them cared. Settling back on his heels, Kel untied her tennis shoes and tossed them on the floor. Her socks, then her jeans followed. Then he slid off the bed to stare down at her as he took care of the rest of his clothes.

The panties matched the bra.

For some reason, the sight of her wearing those skimpy white panties dotted with red flowers turned him on even more than if she'd been completely naked. And a naked Angel was probably a damn fine sight. He wasn't in any hurry to see that picture just yet, though. They'd seen each other wearing pretty damn little and even if Kel didn't have a vivid imagination, he could have easily filled in those small gaps just fine.

21

But he wasn't ready to see her naked yet. Once their clothes were gone, it was pretty much all over with for him. He already knew it.

Still wearing a pair of boxer-styled briefs, Kel crawled back onto the mattress and knelt between her legs, staring at her. Those red flowers were going to kill him, he thought. Especially the ones on her panties. There was one that was just where he was going to be in a couple of minutes and he lowered his head, pressing his mouth against it. His penis throbbed demandingly and he had a bad feeling he wasn't going to last very long at all once he did get inside her.

Kel was still a virgin—he thought about sex plenty. What nineteen-year-old guy didn't? But he was also a nineteen-year-old guy in love with a girl who seemed to know his every thought—a girl he had loved and adored for years. Even during the past school year when he'd been separated from her, he hadn't thought about messing around. He wanted it so bad, wanted it to the point of obsession, thinking about it when he was supposed to be working, thinking about when he was supposed to be studying, sleeping...

Seemed like he thought about sex all the time. There'd been a couple of times he'd get to his dorm room and his roommate would be making it with some girl, and a couple of times, the girl would bring a friend along, thinking Kel would be looking for action.

Kel wanted action, all right.

But he didn't want it with some coed he didn't know. He wanted it with Angel. Up until now, she hadn't been ready and Kel would have chopped off an arm before he did something to hurt her. Until she was ready, thinking about sex was about all he'd do.

Well, think about it. Dream about it. Jack off—a lot. And listen to friends from school. Listen quite a bit. Listen, read about it. A couple of times he'd gone to a friend's room to study and there would be a porn flick on. It had left him feeling kind of dirty—his strict upbringing, no doubt.

But there had been things in those flicks, things that he might not really care to watch, but things he was dying to do with Angel. Like kissing her through those white cotton panties, like pulling them aside and staring down at the pale blonde

Hunter's Edge

curls covering her, licking her there and grinning when she bucked against his mouth.

Turned out that imagination and dreaming about sex could come in pretty damn useful, because she was wet and hot under him when he finished. Panting and whimpering. She lifted her arms to him and he started to crawl up her body— only to freeze and swear. "Damn it, Angel, I don't have anything..."

But, just like she so often did, Angel knew what he was thinking. She smiled. "There's something in my jeans."

Something turned out to be a couple of foil-wrapped condoms and Kel slid her a look. "You planned this."

"Yep." She sat up, glanced at the condoms in his hand and then down between his thighs. He blushed a painful shade of red, but she was too busy staring at his erection to notice his blush. "You know how to put that on?"

"I think I can figure it out," Kel muttered. His fingers trembled as he tore it open and he had a feeling all his nerves wouldn't be so damn acute if she wasn't watching so closely. But Angel was going to watch, no matter what—and he wasn't about to wait until he wasn't so nervous about all of this.

Nineteen years without sex was plenty long enough, he figured. So he tore open the foil packet and as Angel watched, he fumbled with it, dropped it once, but managed to get it on. The nerves faded then, as he lifted his gaze and stared at her.

It was like tunnel vision—Angel became his entire existence as she lay back and reached for him. Her long blonde hair, those soft blue eyes, all those pink and white curves and the wispy blonde curls between her thighs. Those blonde curls hid soft, wet pink flesh. Touching her, Kel hissed out at the feel of her, silky wet and hot, so hot. "Am I going to hurt you?" he asked hoarsely.

"Probably. I don't care."

And he did—by the time it was over, she was crying, soft, gasping sounds that tore at him. Guilt ate a hole inside him as he rolled away from her. How could something that made him feel so good hurt her like that? How could he enjoy it?

"I'm sorry," he said into the silence.

Angel rolled over and nestled up against him. "I'm not." She

23

lifted up on her elbow, tears still damp on her face, and gave him a wobbly smile. "We knew it would hurt."

Wiping away her tears, Kel said, "I didn't know I'd end up making you cry over it."

Angel shrugged. "If it just hurts a little bit the first time, then so what? You're not sorry, are you?" When he remained silent, Angel lifted a brow. Propping her cheek on her hand, she watched him. "Are you?"

Rolling his eyes, Kel muttered, "No." He pulled her naked body onto his, her hair falling around them like a blanket. With his voice muffled against her neck, he muttered, "But you didn't like it at all. I should have made you like it."

"I liked it just fine." Angel kissed him. "I love you. That's all I needed..." Then she lifted her head and grinned down at him, wagging her brows comically. "At least this time."

September

Kel held the phone to his ear, pretty sure he'd misunderstood. "You're what?"

Angel sighed. "Babysitting."

"You're babysitting. Angel...we're supposed to go out."

"Yeah, I know." She sounded a bit pissed off. "But Derek asked me and I had a hard time saying no." Her step-dad wasn't half bad—another pushover as far as Kel was concerned, considering he'd married Ann and actually thought she was going to be faithful.

Derek also had two kids and Kel had to admit, they were cute kids. One was eight and she could ramble on for hours. The other was a four-year-old boy who made monkeys in the zoo look tame. But as cute as the kids were, he couldn't believe he was being ditched for them.

"You're mad."

Kel sighed and raked his fingers through his hair. "Not mad, really. Just aggravated." They hadn't seen each other in nearly a week. School had started and although they both attended Georgia State, the campus was huge. He got to see Angel more often than last year, but not enough. Not for him. They rarely got to see each other during the week and it was worse now that Kel had picked up a part-time job at nights.

"You know...you could come over."

Kel laughed. "Yeah, that's exactly how I planned to spend Friday night...you, me and two shrieking kids."

"Actually, it's three. Lindsey has a friend spending the night."

"Even more exciting." Leaning back against his desk, he propped the phone on his shoulder and crossed his arms over his chest. "So after they go to bed, can we make out on the couch?"

"I was hoping you'd ask. You still have to work until nine?"

Kel eyed the clock on the wall as he answered, "Yeah, and I'm going to have to get going or I'm going to be late. You got any idea how late Derek and your mom will be?"

"He said by eleven or so. Knowing Mom, that might not happen. But maybe we can try to grab a movie or something after."

Kel grinned. "I vote for the or something. At your place." Another reason why they couldn't see each other as much—he still lived on campus, but Angel had her apartment, nice, private. All hers.

Much as he loved his folks, he definitely enjoyed the freedom that came from not living at home. But damn, there was even less privacy in the dorm than at home. Unlike his roommate, both the one from his freshman year and this one, Kel had no desire to take Angel to his dorm to make love to her. He preferred privacy, thanks.

The couch at her mom's house wasn't the same as the bed at Angel's, but it was better than nothing.

"Or something, huh?" Angel said. Her voice softened, becoming a low, husky purr that sent shivers down his spine. "Hmm...like the sound of that. And we can do that no matter how late they get back..."

Shooting a glance at the clock, Angel wished Kel would

hurry up and get here. It would probably be another half hour, easy, before he made it, though.

Still, it didn't keep her from sending the clock another look before five minutes had passed. She was jumpy. Uncertain of the reason, she made a pass through the house, checked all the locks, checked the windows. Everything was locked up, shut down and the kids were having the time of their lives upstairs.

No reason for her to feel like she was going to crawl out of her skin... But she did. Trying to make herself relax, she settled down on the couch and turned on the TV. She found an episode of "Law and Order", the only new show worth watching as far as she was concerned.

But Lenny wasn't doing much to distract her tonight. When the phone rang, she jumped and just barely managed to keep from yelping in alarm. Feeling like a moron, Angel hit the mute button on the TV and grabbed the phone. The caller ID read Unknown Number and she laid it back down without answering.

It stopped after ten rings—then a heartbeat later, it started again. This time, Angel sighed and answered, "Hello?"

But nobody replied. All she heard was heavy breathing.

Part of her wanted to be amused.

But the other part... Now she understood what was wrong, why she was so jumpy, why she'd felt so edgy ever since she'd shown up at the house where she'd grown up.

Evil...

It whispered through the air, chilled her flesh, and deep down inside her, she felt cold. All her life, Angel had known she wasn't normal. She heard whispers in the night, she saw things before they happened—like with Kel. She'd been all of seven when they first met. But when she looked at him, one of her weird little flashes hit and she'd seen them—not kids like they had been, but older, all grown up. She'd been wearing white, he'd been wearing black and she'd heard *You may now kiss the bride.* From the time she was seven, she'd known she'd marry Kel.

If that wasn't weird, Angel didn't know the definition of the word.

That weirdness was on her now, and riding strong as she

lowered the phone down. Her hand shook and it took two tries to get the phone to hang up. She glanced at the clock hanging over the fireplace. It was just after nine-thirty. Kel was off work, heading her way. But it would probably be close to ten before he got to Greenburg.

Upstairs, she heard mad little giggles and the occasional shriek of laughter. Slowly, she rose from the couch and headed for the stairs, following the sounds of play with the knot of cold fear lodged in her belly.

Halfway up the stairs, the phone started to ring again. There was a table on the landing and it held another extension. Coming to a stop by the phone, she eyed the caller ID display. Unknown Number.

She grabbed the phone and lifted it to her ear, keeping her voice down as she said, "What in the hell do you want?"

A low, nasty chuckle came through the line. Angel shivered as it seemed to wrap around her, echoing through the air. Not possible, the man was on the other end of the line and not in the house.

But she could feel the laughter. It turned her blood to ice and then he spoke.

"You, sweet baby girl. I want you."

The phone went dead.

Abruptly, the noise from the second floor died. The laughter stopped, the TV went silent and the house was as cold and silent as a tomb. Clutching the cordless phone in her hand, she raced up the stairs, towards her step-siblings' rooms.

Joey was laying in the hall just around the corner. So still and quiet. Kneeling by him, she laid a hand on his chest, felt the steady beat of his heart. But he didn't so much as flinch when she touched him and when she called his name, he didn't waken.

Carefully, she lifted him in her arms and carried him into Lindsey's bedroom. After laying Joey on the bed, she went to shut the door, dialing 911 as she went. Leaning back against the door, she lifted the phone to her ear and waited for an answer.

But no answer came. No answer. No dial tone. No ring. Nothing but dead air. She disconnected and checked for a dial

Shiloh Walker

tone. Nothing. Her breath started to come in shallow, harsh pants.

Lindsey and her friend Sloan were sprawled on the floor in the same boneless way she'd found Joey. Their chests moved in a slow, regular pattern. The TV screen continued to flicker, but there was no sound.

It was so quiet in the house that when the eerie laughter started a few minutes later, Angel jumped. Terror made her sluggish. It was like moving through Jell-O as she turned and pressed her ear to the door, listening.

That strange, eerie laughter continued and now it seemed to echo all around her, not just out in the hall. A dark ugly cloud wrapped her mind and Angel had to concentrate to think past the fear. But the more she focused, the easier it became. The cloud seemed to lift from her mind and once more, the laughter came from one clear direction, instead of from everywhere.

"My...you're a strong one, aren't you?"

Through the door, Angel demanded, "What in the hell do you want?"

"I already told you that, baby girl. I want you."

Although he made no sound, she knew it when he touched the door. She could feel it. Cold seeped through the sturdy, white-painted wood and she almost took a step back. Scared to death, she looked back at the three sleeping, helpless kids. "What did you do to the kids?"

"Nothing, baby girl. They just sleep...for now." The man dropped the friendly tone and his voice went hard-edged as he snapped, "But if I don't get you tonight, I'll take them."

Angel swore she could feel her throat close up. Black dots swarmed her vision and the world danced around in dizzying circles. *Don't you dare pass out!* she screamed silently. Catching the inside of her cheek between her teeth, she bit down until she tasted blood and focused on the pain of that. The blackness receded, just a little, and she sucked air in through a tight throat.

Staring at the door, she backed away slowly.

The pure evil waiting on the other side of the door was unlike anything she'd ever experienced. Not even in her

28

dreams—and she had some seriously weird dreams—had she experienced anything like this.

The fine hairs on her arms and neck stood upright and her skin all but crawled from the tension in the air. Tension—no, that didn't describe it. This wasn't tension. It was cloying, thick and noxious. It was like the man's malice had taken corporeal form. Every so often, she almost glimpsed some dark, hazy mist snaking in under the door, through the cracks in the side.

Reaching for her.

"What do you want me for?" she asked, her voice so faint, she barely even heard it herself.

But he heard it. Laughing that bone-chilling, ugly laugh, he answered, "Don't you know? Hmmmm...that mind of yours, you got power, girl. So sweet...so clean—I want it."

His voice turned hard and cold again, like knives made of ice. "Open the door, girl. You don't really want me to come in and get you, do you?"

Desperate, scared, she looked at the kids. They lay still, sleeping—no, it was deeper than sleep. They were totally unaware of what was going on and she was thankful for that much. An overwhelming sense of helplessness swamped her. There wasn't any way she could protect them if she got hurt—and that was exactly what was going to happen.

In her gut, she knew it.

Just like she knew there was nothing she could do to protect herself.

"Open the door!" This time, his voice was so loud, so deep and powerful, it hurt her eardrums. He struck the door and it rattled its frame. Little splinters of wood went flying.

Angel swallowed, took one step towards the door. She was crying, whimpering in her throat, but she didn't even realize it. Her hand shook as she turned the doorknob and opened it, just far enough that she could slip through, and closed it behind her—*as though that would keep those kids safe.*

Don't look up, don't look up, don't look up, she told herself. She wasn't sure why, but she couldn't look at that man. Keeping her chin tucked low, she breathed fast, shallow. Another wave of dizziness swamped her and she swayed. A pale hand appeared in the field of her vision and she cringed, jerking back and pressing her back up against the wall.

"Look at me, sweet baby girl... Let me see those pretty eyes." His voice was an oily, insidious whisper but the command inherent in those words was almost too strong for her to resist.

Angel resisted. Refusing to look up, she inched down the wall. She couldn't see more than that pale hand, still reaching for her, and his feet as he mirrored her steps, following her down the hall.

"There is no point in fighting this, girl," he murmured, his voice softer now, almost gentle. Almost sweet. But it was underscored with that same malice she'd sensed earlier and it sent shivers racing down her spine. "You can't possibly hope to get away."

His fingers brushed her averted cheek and she bit her lip, jerked away. If she could have disappeared inside the wall, she would have. She was so desperate to get away from his touch, from his taint. He laughed, and thanks to her gift, she knew he was amused by her fear—aroused by it. Instinctively, she darted a look up at his face and even as she did, she wondered what in the hell she was doing.

It was like looking into the gates of hell.

Lust glittered in the depths of his eyes—eyes that glowed faintly red. Hunger burned there, but it wasn't just a hunger for sex—without understanding how she knew, Angel knew he wouldn't just use her body and walk away. Horrifying as that thought was, he wanted more.

He had harsh, oddly handsome features, his face planed down to hollows and angles, compelling brown eyes and a mouth that looked too full, too red for his pale skin. His hair was dark, matte black against his milky complexion, and long, framing his face and hanging down past his shoulders.

There was something familiar about him, but Angel couldn't figure out why. He smiled, slowly, and Angel's heart stopped for the briefest second. Then it started to race inside her chest and a surge of adrenaline rushed through her.

"Come here, girl," he purred, holding a hand out, palm up.

Oh, yeah, like I'm gonna do that, she thought, half

hysterical. She shook her head, backing away from him, one careful step at a time, keeping her back pressed to the wall. From the corner of her eye, she could see the stairs.

His body tensed—a half second before he moved to grab her, she ducked aside and then lunged, leaping for the landing. She missed, hit the second-to-last step and fell the rest of the way. Adrenaline numbed the pain and she sprang up, dashed down the rest of the stairs—*outside, get outside, see if he'll follow you.*

Away from the kids. That was what she wanted—*oh, shit.*

She plowed straight into his chest. How had he...?

He smiled down at her, pulling her struggling body close, totally unaffected by her attempts to fight. "I knew you'd be sweet..."

He dipped his head—it was almost like he wanted to kiss her. Angel turned her head to the side and finally, the scream trapped inside broke free. He fisted a hand in her hair and jerked her head to the side—then he bit her.

A sharp, piercing pain—there, and then gone. She struggled, whimpering, crying, but he continued to stand there, holding her pinned against him, his mouth at her neck. She could feel the pulling draws of his mouth. Revulsion snaked through her as an inkling of idea formed in her mind.

Was he... He was... The guy was drinking her blood. Angel could all but feel it flowing out of her. Time slowed down, stretched out. She was acutely aware of every little thing. Against her chest, his heart started to pound, hard powerful beats, but oddly slow. Hot tears burned their way down her cheeks and she felt each one. His hand tightened in her hair and his body shuddered against hers.

Angel shuddered as well, but it was revulsion that had her trembling. He was turned on—completely turned on by her fear and the more she cried and whimpered and fought, the more it turned him on.

"Sweet little pet," he crooned after the longest time. He lifted his head and licked her. She flinched, trying to jerk back, but the bastard was strong and she was so damn weak. "I think I'd rather like to keep you."

He moved with a blurring speed that had her already dizzy

head spinning, turning her around so that his front cuddled up to her back. Using one steely arm to both restrain and support her, he lifted his free hand. From the corner of her eye, Angel could see him moving, although she had no idea what he was doing.

Not until he suddenly shoved his bloodied wrist in front of her mouth. "Take it, baby girl."

She clamped her lips shut, averted her head.

His voice hardened. "Take it—or what I just did to you, I'll do to the children upstairs. They haven't a chance in hell of resisting me." His cold hard voice softened to an evil, menacing purr as he added, "And children, they are so soft, so frail...so easily broken. So weak... You can survive this. They cannot."

Images rolled through her mind, but they didn't feel like her own thoughts. It was more like watching some sick, twisted movie that she couldn't turn off. Her stomach revolted while under her breath, she whispered, "No, no, no, nononono!"

"Yes." He nuzzled her neck, nipped her ear with those wicked sharp teeth. "They might not offer me the feast you'd provide, but youth and innocence—it's a sweet treat, all the same." Once more, he shoved his wrist to her mouth. Her throat closed up and the blood pooled in her mouth, thick, cloying and vile. Instinctively, she tried to spit it out but his hand clamped over her mouth, covering her nose until she either had to swallow or choke.

She started to swallow and immediately, she began to retch. Vomit rushed up her mouth, through her nose, but the man still had his hand over her mouth and she started to choke on it. Dimly, she heard him swear and then he threw her. She hurtled through the air and crashed into the railing at the head of the stairs. Gasping for air, she shoved up on her hands and knees and started to vomit. Blood, bile and the remains of the dinner she'd shared with the kids came rushing out. She puked until she'd emptied her stomach and still she continued to heave.

He made no noise but she could sense him approaching. On impulse, she cringed away but there was no place to retreat. The splintered wood of the railing cracked and groaned as she huddled against it. She wiped the back of her hand across her mouth and slowly looked up.

Eyes that glowed red burned down at her. His hand shot out, grabbed the front of her shirt and hauled her off the floor. "That mind of yours is stronger than I thought," he murmured. He trailed his fingers down her cheek, almost gently, and then said in a queer voice, "I'll have you, though. Regardless. I don't care if I need to drain you to the brink of death to do it."

He pulled her against him again and this time, she was so weak she didn't have the energy to struggle. His teeth pierced her neck again, on the uninjured side. It barely even hurt. The slide into oblivion was slow and easy this time and Angel wasn't even aware of it as she drifted into unconsciousness.

The low-level burn in his gut had Kel speeding down the expressway with the gas pedal pressed to the floor. His eyes kept straying to the digital clock on the dashboard and each minute that ticked by seemed to last an hour.

All damn night, something had been driving him nuts. Edgy, anxious, itchy, but he couldn't quite put his finger on it. Then twenty minutes ago, he'd known. The itch had bloomed into a low-level burn and he'd known.

Angel.

Something was wrong with Angel. She was in trouble.

He turned off the expressway, five miles to go. That low-level burn wasn't low level anymore. It was a high-octane explosion and he could feel Angel's fear, her terror—and pain. She was in pain. She was hurt. His neck burned in sympathetic pain as he took a left on Mulberry and then sped down the street, veering onto the shoulder to go around a slow-moving minivan. The driver laid on the horn as Kel cut back onto the road.

The Estates of Whispering Oaks took up several hundred acres of land along Deermont Road. The fourth and last street was the street where Angel had lived most of her life. Kel took it at a speed that had his tires squealing and as he hit the brakes in front of her house, he realized he couldn't feel that fear any more, or the pain.

He couldn't feel Angel at all. Even when he tried to reach out, tried to sense her, he couldn't feel her—it was something that had never happened. For a good eight years, from the time he was eleven—Angel had been in a narrow strip of trees behind her house, playing in an old tree house built by the previous owners, and she'd fallen, broken her arm. Nobody had heard her scream but Kel had been in his room, grounded because of a C- he'd brought home on a project for science.

Something had been wrong. He'd felt a burning pain in his arm, and he'd known instinctively it was Angel. From that time on, he'd always been able to reach out and just feel her—he knew when she was happy, when she was scared. But now, he couldn't feel her and that scared him more than anything else.

Logically, that drive took thirty-four minutes—he kept track of every last one. Those minutes were endless and when he pulled up in front of the old colonial house where Angel had grown up, he left the keys in the ignition and the engine running. Leaping up the steps, he knelt down in the flower bed and grabbed the little rabbit statuette, wiping the soil away from the false bottom and digging the key out.

He got the door open and dimly, his mind registered an electronic beeping—part of him seemed to recall the alarm system, that he needed to reset it—it was weird the way his mind cataloged all those minute details even when his heart was rushing like an express engine and his breathing coming in hard, rough pants.

As he passed by the narrow console table in the main hall, he grabbed a silver letter opener. It looked delicate but felt damn solid in his hand. The blade was thin and not meant for cutting, but the point of it was damn sharp. Not much of a weapon...

Fuck.

He saw her now, up on the landing between the first and second floors—at least he saw her hair at first, the long, pale golden sweep of it hanging down. The rest of her body was obstructed by a big, mean looking bastard who held her clutched against him.

The man shifted a little and Angel's arm swung into view. Kel saw red. Literally—and physically. Thin streams of blood flowed down her wrist, down her slack fingers to drip down onto the floor.

Time seemed to freeze, yet speed by in an incredible blur as he tore up the stairs and rushed them. Angel was unconscious. Kel saw that almost right away as the man turned towards him, startled.

His eyes—the dude's eyes were seriously messed up. Glowing a funky shade of red and his pupils constricted down to mere pinpoints like he was drugged. He blinked, once, twice. Like he couldn't quite understand the fact that somebody was charging towards him with bloody murder on his mind.

He blinked a third time, kept his eyes closed a few seconds, precious seconds that allowed Kel to close the distance.

"Let her go," Kel snarled.

The man's eyes opened, and although they still had that weird reddish glow, the dazed, drugged look was gone. He glanced down at Angel's slack body. She hung in his arms like a rag doll, eyes closed, her lips parted. "Hmmmm. But I don't want to, boy. She's quite precious. Go on now."

The words vibrated—rippled, flowed through Kel and over him and as they faded, Kel had to fight the urge to do just as he'd been told. But it didn't take much of a fight—just a glance at Angel's face, just the memory of the fear he'd felt coming from her—and his complete inability to feel anything from her now.

Louder, Kel repeated, "Let her go."

The man cocked his head, narrowed his eyes as he studied Kel—kind of like he was examining a bug under a microscope. "How odd. Two of you. In one night." He glanced down at Angel and then smiled, stroked her hair. "I'm not done with you, precious. But the rest of this will keep...for a bit."

Like she was so much garbage, he threw her on the ground and stepped over her, smiling at Kel. Blood stained his lips. "It's too bad I'm only in the mood for one kind of sweet, boy. You'd be even more fun than she is—you'd fight harder." He edged near Kel, but didn't come at him head-on, circling around and away, that weird smile still tugging at one corner of his mouth. "All I had to do was mention the sweet little kiddies and she caved. A female's soft spot, every time. You'll fight, though, as long, as hard as you can, just hoping you can save her from me."

"Shut the fuck up. Get the hell out. Now," Kel snarled.

He laughed. With Angel's blood staining his lips and her lying on the floor in an unconscious slump, the bastard had the nerve to laugh. Kel's control snapped—he rushed him, fist closed tight around the letter opener. Lifting it high, he brought his arm down hard. The man jerked back but the tip of the letter opener caught his cheek, slicing him open.

He hissed, pressed a hand to his cheek. Wide-eyed, he looked at Kel and then at the letter opener.

For one brief second, Kel thought he saw fear in those strange eyes. The reddish cast grew stronger and the air in the house went cold. Kel could have sworn it dropped a good twenty degrees in five seconds flat.

The cut was bleeding, but it wasn't the rich, vibrant red Kel would have expected to see. It was darker, a strange reddish black. And—shit—the sliced flesh seemed to be smoking. Little tendrils of smoke curled away from the man's face in wisps.

"That was a foolish thing to do, boy," the man rasped. His gaze zeroed in on the letter open. "Drop it."

This time, the words didn't wash over him, didn't slide through him in a teasing, coaxing suggestion. They crashed into him, weighty with a command that didn't want to be ignored. Kel almost staggered under it, but he didn't drop the letter opener.

Weird—it wasn't some big, lethal-looking blade and it sure as hell wasn't some kickass gun that could turn the guy's brain into Swiss cheese. But the man continued to stare at it with his face bleeding and skin smoking. Kel tightened his fingers around it. He didn't waste his breath talking. He just lunged for the man again.

But the man was prepared. He slid away like oiled leather, moving silent as a whisper, quick as a snake, circling around. He moved quicker than Kel could even track and Kel spun around, trying to keep his eyes on the man. He felt like he was being toyed with, like some giant cat playing with a mouse.

A hand came up between his shoulder blades, shoved him. He went flying face first to the floor. He just barely missed taking a header down the stairs as he landed on his hands and knees—the letter opener still clutched in his fist. Angel lay two feet away, her head turned from him. Her neck was exposed— he could see the ragged, ugly holes and the blood that hadn't yet clotted trickling down.

"I don't really want to bother with you now, boy." Hard, steely fingers curled around the back of Kel's neck and he lifted him, hauled him straight off the floor. "I've got something a bit more pressing to deal with now. So if you want to live...just drop that paltry silver thing and run on."

Instead, Kel swung out, caught the man's neck—a shallow slice when what he'd tried to do was bury the silver inside the bastard's jugular. But the cut, shallow as it was, made the man scream and throw Kel across the landing. Plaster and dust drifted down when Kel hit the wall and then slid to the floor. Spinning away, the man screamed.

When he turned back, the narrow gash on his neck was smoking. More of that dark blood flowed. "Stupid human!"

Head reeling, Kel pushed himself upright. "Damn straight." He took one stumbling step towards the man standing at the head of the stairs, just a few feet away from Angel's body. Kel tightened his hand around the letter open. Adrenaline began to pump through his body, numbing the pain, clearing the fog in his brain—and giving him the energy he needed to rush across the hall, tackling the maniacal bastard.

The two of them went crashing down the stairs, Kel stabbing and slicing with his makeshift weapon while the man roared. The stink of burnt flesh filled the air as Kel managed to pierce skin again and again. Brutal, inhumanly strong fingers closed around Kel's wrist and the man squeezed. Over his scream, Kel heard bone crunch.

And the wail of sirens...

"*Shite!*"

The man shoved upright, wobbled as he shot a look upstairs and then at the front door. It was still open. Already red and blue lights were splashing and Kel heard footsteps as the cops came rushing towards the house, heard them with startling clarity.

"Little fucker..."

He grabbed Kel just as the cops appeared in the doorway.

Kel thought the man had moved fast before but nothing could have prepared him for the speed he moved with now as he threw Kel over his shoulder and flew towards the back of the house. The man might not have wings, but he certainly seemed to fly, navigating the halls, the furniture and hurtling through the glass doors that opened out on the patio. Literally hurtling through them, the glass shattering as he lunged straight into it.

Glass stung Kel's eyes as he struggled. Weak struggles, though. His shattered wrist screamed with pain and his vision was red and blurry. Wind danced along his skin and he tried to see but the world spun by at breakneck speed.

The sirens faded away into the distance and soon, the only sound he heard was his own harsh breathing.

Then laughter, ugly, mean laughter.

His head struck something hard as he was flung to the ground and automatically, Kel tried to roll upright, using his elbow and his good hand. Vicious pain exploded through him as he was kicked, once, twice, three times in the gut.

"Little bugger. You had to interfere, didn't you?" Steely fingers, ice cold and brutal, dug into his neck and once more, Kel found himself dangling in the air.

Pain blistered through him, a black veil threatened to drop over him as unconsciousness beckoned. Desperate, struggling for a breath, he clawed at the fingers wrapped around his throat.

"Congratulate yourself, boy. You saved your little bitch. At least for now. No fucking way can I go after her anytime soon—I don't wish to draw that kind of attention to myself. But I wanted her—you got in my way. For that, I'm going to kill you, boy," the man whispered, slowly lowering Kel until his feet touched the ground. "It's going to be slow...and oh, so painful. Nobody interferes with what is mine." With each word, he squeezed tighter and tighter. Kel's oxygen-starved lungs felt like they'd explode—

And then he went crashing back to the ground. He sucked in a breath through his abused throat, gagged, tried to take another breath. Dark, red-tinged rainbows danced before his eyes. Each breath was painful, but he welcomed it. He tried to get to his feet only to get knocked back on his ass. Another brutal kick to his ribs—this time, he heard bone break. By now, even adrenaline and fear couldn't numb the pain, but he couldn't manage to scream either. His throat felt swollen, his tongue thick.

In that moment, Kel knew he was going to die. Too weak, hardly able to breathe, he couldn't even find the strength to pull away when the man crouched down behind him, laid those icy cold fingers on Kel's shoulders. Through the thin cotton of his T-shirt, he could feel those cold, strong fingers and that chill spread through him until he ached from head to toe with the intensity of it.

"The Change is so very unpleasant. Your frail mortal body may not even survive it, but if you do..." The man's words made no sense to Kel. Struggling to breathe, to see, to think past the pain, he wobbled on his knees and would have crashed forward onto his face if cruel hands hadn't caught him and held him.

"If you make it through, the sun will rise on your new body, you will burn. Suffer every bit of the pain...and think on how you could have just walked away."

Walk away...from what? Kel thought.

With that inhuman strength, the man grabbed Kel and jerked him backward. Pain flared in Kel's neck, ripping, burning, tearing—distantly, Kel realized the man had bit him and through the pain, Kel could still feel the man's wicked sharp teeth, his icy mouth—and blood. Kel's blood, hot as fire, flowing over his chilled flesh.

The man rode him to the ground under his greater weight, crushing him. Face pressed into the dirt, unable to breathe, Kel was helpless.

When finally the man pulled away, the gray cloud of oblivion beckoned but there would be no escaping into it. He was turned over. His uninjured hand grabbed at the dirt beneath him, fingers digging into it. As his fingers closed around something thin, rough, the man crouched by his side, lifting a wrist.

"Your little bitch fought when I tried to bring her over—I wonder how much fight you've got left." He sank his teeth into his wrist, tore the flesh and then fisted a hand in Kel's hair, jerking him up and forcing Kel's mouth to his wrist. "I'll think of you when I get my hands on her—and she'll suffer for it. Die knowing that."

Like hell. As the bitter, thick blood trickled down Kel's swollen throat, he swung out.

It was a scream that no mortal creature, man or animal, should be able to make. It echoed through the night, rebounding through the trees and as Kel slipped into oblivion, his last sight was that of a stick, not much bigger than a butter knife, protruding from one of the man's eyes.

"We're too late." It was a grim, angry voice, made all the more nerve-wracking by the fact that it came from a big man who carried a long, curved sword in his left hand.

Rafe watched as his wife, Sheila, knelt down by the boy and touched him.

"He's cold," Sheila murmured.

In the air, Rafe could smell the taint of a feral vampire, the rage and the violence. And the blood. "He fed him—just enough to start the Change, I'd bet, so the poor kid would die out here in the open as the sun came up."

Sheila's soft blue eyes went wintry with fury but her hand was gentle as she wiped some of the still-tacky blood away from the boy's face. "Rafe, he's just a kid."

Stroking a hand down Sheila's hair, Rafe said, "We'll take care of him, Belle. Come on...we need to get—"

His voice broke off abruptly, a breath hissing out between his teeth. His head went back, his eyes closing. "Damn it— bastard's still close. He's looking... Oh, shit. Ain't that a son of a bitch." He looked back at Sheila and his dark brown eyes had a weird reddish glow.

Recognizing the look, Sheila sighed. Smiled. "Go on, slick. I can get this one to the car okay." She narrowed her eyes. "You are going to have to leave me the car. I can't carry him indefinitely."

Rafe turned over the keys to his '57 Bel Aire without batting an eyelash. That, all by itself, told Sheila how strong the urge was riding her husband. Rafe didn't turn over those keys very easily at all—and never without a number of promises that she take care of his precious car.

Okay—maybe Rafe didn't call the car precious, but it amounted to the same thing.

All Hunters felt these urges, an impulse that could drag them out of bed, drag them miles through the night to find whoever was pulling at them.

In this case, it had dragged them quite a few miles. Hundreds, in fact. Rafe and Sheila lived in Memphis, Tennessee, and usually, they stayed in western Tennessee. Rafe hadn't ever felt anything pull at him in such a way, at least not until now.

Sheila hadn't ever seen him under such a strong grip. Not once. It had scared her, bothered her enough that she had demanded he take her with him. He hadn't wanted to, so she'd just settled her ass in the Bel Aire and refused to get out.

Rafe knew her well enough to know better than to argue, so instead of arguing, they'd left the enclave in the hands of Rafe's lieutenant, Dominic, and hit the road. The first few hundred miles sped by in silence, Sheila sensing nothing but the urgency rolling off Rafe.

But then Sheila had started sensing it. Sensing them, this man who seemed too damn young, and a vampire. The vampire wasn't one that Sheila could identify. Vamps had a feel to them, almost as individual as smell or a set of fingerprints. But it was a psychic thing and Sheila's psychic skills were nothing to brag about.

Rafe, though? Rafe was a Master vamp, powerful enough to feel this call from so far away. Strong enough to feel the feral, too, from wherever in the hell the bastard was. And despite what Rafe said, it wasn't that close. Sheila wasn't a strong Hunter, but if there was a feral anywhere close, she'd feel it, too.

Close. It was all relative, she guessed. Rafe glanced at her, at the kid sprawled on the forest floor, pale as death, his heartbeat weak and slow. "Can you get him to the car okay?"

Sheila smiled. "Yeah, slick. I think I can handle one kid."

Rafe didn't wait another second. He disappeared into the woods on swift, silent feet and Sheila sighed, whispered, "Be careful."

She set about getting the kid thrown over her shoulder. He wasn't as light as she would have expected—some seriously solid muscle on him, even as lanky as he was. He groaned, a soft, tortured sound. Sheila winced in sympathy. "I'm sorry, sugar." He had to be hurting. Already, he was going through the Change, but it was at a slow rate. She could feel it burning through him, moving at a crawl.

The Change was usually a hell of a lot quicker. Sheila remembered her own Change. When you were going through it, it was slow, sheer agony. But she'd watched others go through it and the Change actually moved pretty damn quick. It took three days, but during those three days, the mortal body changed. The digestive system altered. Fangs formed and cut through. Bone and muscle became tougher, stronger. Senses were heightened.

All within a mere seventy-two hours.

But this kid, if he lived through it, was probably going to be stuck in the Change for close to a week. Some blood would help. Once she got him someplace safe, she'd feed him a little, but a major feed would have to wait until Rafe showed up. A baby vamp needed stronger stuff than she had in her veins.

You are what you eat.

Snorting, Sheila muttered, "Yeah, with us, that's a fact." She continued to talk, not because she expected him to really hear her, but she knew the sound of a voice was a comfort. So she talked.

"You want to be strong, first feed has to come from the strong." Finally, she broke through the trees and emerged where Rafe had parked the car. In the moonlight, the baby-blue paint was colorless, the chrome reflecting the silvery moonlight back at her. "Here we go, sugar. Just a few more minutes…"

She shot a glance towards the horizon, but it was still dark. The edgy anxiety riding her wasn't coming from the sun's approach. It was this totally bizarre situation. Her husband was out there Hunting a feral and Sheila had her arms full of a baby vamp who looked like he'd gone a few rounds with a heavyweight boxer—and lost.

"Wonder how old you are," she said, trying to keep up an endless flow of words. "Don't look much more than seventeen or eighteen. God, please, at least be that old…"

Manhandling him into the back, she settled him on the bench seat as gently as she could. Hard, though. He was a long, lanky bastard and she had to plop his big feet on the floor board to close the door. Shoving her hair back from her face, she muttered, "Rafe gets to have all the fun."

It was nearly dawn before Sheila sensed his return.

Her blood went hot, feeling the echo of the adrenaline that pulsed through him. Even though he hadn't even reached the hotel room yet, she could feel the wildness. Shoving off the bed closest to the door, she went to meet him, smiling a little.

Her smile faded, died away as she saw Rafe's face, though.

"You didn't find him."

His dark, sexy face was set in grim, harsh lines. "Yeah, I found him, right as he was getting ready to kill some stupid teenager. He felt me coming, crushed the kid's larynx—I had a choice, either go after him, or help the kid." His mouth twisted in a snarl.

"You did what you had to do, Rafe." She stroked a hand down his face.

Blowing out a breath, he shoved a hand through his short, dark hair. "Yeah, I'm sure that's going to be a real comfort when he kills again." Glancing over her shoulder, he studied the new vamp and said softly, "And it won't be a comfort to him, either."

Rafe closed his eyes, lowered his head. Wide shoulders slumped. When he looked back at her, there was a screaming hell in his eyes. "There was another one hurt, a girl." Rafe jerked his chin in the direction of the bed. "I won't know what happened until I talk to him, but I could smell the feral and the boy there. Police all over the place, I couldn't get too close. But I heard enough. There was a girl attacked, probably right before this kid—I think he must have interrupted."

A fist closed around Sheila's heart. Unconsciously, she rubbed the heel of her hand over her chest. "What's going on with the girl?"

Rafe shrugged, but the motion lacked his normal grace. It

was jerky, stiff. "She's alive. Low on blood. Unconscious."

"Think the feral will go after her again?"

Rafe sighed. "Hell, I don't know. Not if he's halfway sane. She's in a hospital, surrounded by people. No vamp wants the attention it would attract if he went after her there. But since I didn't find and kill that fucker, I'll have to get somebody in to watch her."

He started to move past her, shucking the long leather coat he wore. Sheila stopped him by stepping in front of him and sliding her arms around his waist. "You're not Superman, slick. We aren't guardian angels and we aren't miracle workers."

A small smile tugged at his mouth. Cupping her face, he rubbed his thumb over her lower lip. "I got an angel of my own, only seems fair everybody gets one."

Snickering, Sheila said, "I'm not an angel." Then she grinned, pushed up on her toes. "But if I am...sweetie, don't take this wrong, but I don't want you being an angel for anybody but me." She kissed him until she felt some of the tension drain out of him. Pulling back, she skimmed her lips down his neck. "If he's around here, we'll find him. Dawn's coming... He'll be doing the same thing we're doing, finding some place to hole up. We got time for now."

"Time." Rafe sighed. He rubbed his mouth against hers and then stepped back, finished stripping his coat off. "Yeah. Time to feed some poor kid that oughta be home having wet dreams about his girlfriend. Watch him like a newborn, try to keep the Change from killing him."

Grimacing, Sheila folded her arms around her waist. "That might be easier said than done."

Hooking a hand over the back of his neck, Rafe rotated his head one way, then the other. "Tell me about it."

Sheila urged him to sit down on the edge of the bed. "Do you want to have Dom come out here?"

Shooting her a glance, he asked, "Why?"

Digging her fingers into the stiff muscles of his neck and shoulders, she worked out some of the tension there. Rafe hated it when his prey got away. Hated when they didn't make it in time to help, and neither of them were pleased with the fact that they'd saved the new vamp from sunlight...but not from having the Change forced on him. "Because we're going to have our hands full getting this one to Excelsior. You don't want to let this feral slip away from us, do you?"

His muscles had started to loosen just a little, but then bunched up and Sheila sighed, watched as Rafe shoved off the bed and started to pace the narrow hotel room. "Yeah, we can call Dom. But he can help you get the kid to Excelsior and I'll track the prick down."

It wasn't a suggestion that surprised her, but it was one that wasn't workable. She shook her head. "That won't work. You need to feed him and he'll need another feed here in the next few days. We both know it will be better for him if it's the same vamp guiding him over. And he can't wait until Dom gets here to feed." Lifting her hands, she shrugged helplessly. "I gave him some, but I'm not strong enough to get him anchored, much less get him through this."

Rafe went still, still as death, still as the night. In a low, furious voice, he muttered, "Damn it!"

"Rafe...call Dom. He can handle the feral, but that kid needs you now."

Scowling, Rafe shoved a hand through his hair and then nodded. "Fine." Stalking to the phone, he grabbed the receiver. Abruptly, he slammed it back down. "You know who in the hell I'm going to have to leave in charge?"

Tucking her tongue into her cheek, Sheila tried not to smile. "Yeah."

"Hell, no."

She couldn't fight the grin any more. "There's no choice, baby. Josiah is the only one who can run things if both you and Dom are gone."

Swearing, Rafe once more grabbed the phone. "I need more people. Shit."

Sheila laughed. Yeah, leaving Josiah in charge was going to be interesting.

Chapter Two

Kel shoved his arms into a worn-out blue jean jacket and his feet into a pair of worn tennis shoes. Hunger gnawed at his stomach like a vicious beast and his gums ached, throbbed. Automatically, he ran his tongue over them, pressed it against one of the narrow-notched depressions just behind his regular teeth. His fangs throbbed and burned, ready to push down, to sink into some soft neck and feel the sweet fire of blood as it flowed down his throat.

"Easier said than done," he muttered, shoving tumbled brown hair out of his eyes.

"You need to go feed, damn it. Why do you have to fight it so hard?"

He could see Sheila's pretty blue eyes, see the worry there, the sympathy. He hated her. Hated those soft blue eyes, her long blonde hair—she reminded him too much of Angel. Even after twelve years, he couldn't see a blue-eyed blonde without thinking of Angel. He'd loved her—still did.

And he'd lost her. He couldn't ever have her back.

Again, his hunger screamed at him and he heard the nagging echo of Sheila's voice from the past day. Go feed, Kel. Feed. Go feed off some woman who'd get all soft and needy, who'd press her body to his, who'd rub against him. His body wouldn't listen to him—it would respond, and he'd want.

If he was weak at the time, or especially lonely, he'd give in. Then after it passed, once the hunger was sated and his body was satisfied, he'd be miserable.

Would be easier to go on like this if he could just get Angel out of his head. He knew she was out of his reach now, but he couldn't quit thinking about her. Couldn't quit dreaming about her. Couldn't quit wanting her.

It would be impossible, considering that weird connection between them had become ten times stronger than it had been back before he'd been Changed. Before that, Kel's psychic abilities had been nil. It had all been on Angel's side, her natural gifts had formed a bond between them and their feelings for each other had augmented that bond, letting them feel each other, sense each other.

It had been that bond with her, Kel suspected, that had kept the feral who had Changed him from working his vamp mojo on Kel. Even now, twelve years later, he remembered the innate urge he'd had to leave when the feral had suggested just that.

Kel was stubborn, always had been, but it hadn't been his stubbornness that enabled him to resist. The strength had been born from their bond, a bond that wouldn't have existed without Angel's psychic abilities.

But vampirism was a weird thing. It created a mind-reading ability. While it wasn't exactly psychic abilities, it made a vamp able to sense a person's thoughts. Usually just prey, whether a woman's secret fantasies would make her that much easier to seduce, to fuck and feed, or the fear of those who preyed on others.

"It's a Hunter's calling," Kel had been told. Told time and again, but he didn't have any desire to be a Hunter, to be some altruistic defender of the innocent. Part of him knew it was because he blamed them. Blamed people like Rafe and Sheila, not only because they'd failed to save him and not even for the failure to save Angel.

No. He blamed them for saving him. Now he was stuck in what looked to be one long-ass life, a life where he was able to feel, hear, dream about Angel, but never to touch her again. Never to see her.

A life where she'd grow old and die—without him.

She was still the only woman he'd ever loved, and the time that stretched out between them didn't change that. Neither did the fact that she wasn't even aware he was alive.

Thanks to their bond, Kel was acutely aware of her, aware of her happiness. Aware of her sadness. Aware of the triumphs she'd had over the past ten years, and the losses. Aware of all the dreams she'd had about him, and how she'd wake from time to time, crying into her pillow and whispering his name.

When his family had a memorial for him after, she'd wept and he'd felt every damn tear as though it was his own. As they'd lowered an empty coffin into the ground, he'd felt the rose she'd gripped, felt the thorns digging into his flesh as though he'd been the one holding it. He could smell the scent of the flowers bedecking the empty box, and he could smell Angel.

Every damn day, he felt her, heard her voice. And those nights when she woke in tears, he felt the ache of her loneliness as strongly as he felt his own.

This existence was, plain and simply, pure hell.

The only comfort he had was in knowing that while he might be condemned to feel Angel's every need, wish and hurt, he could keep her from feeling his. During those first few weeks after the Change, while his body adjusted and his grief and rage spiraled out of control, he'd almost driven her insane.

When he awoke hungry and craving blood, she'd done the same, without understanding why or even realizing it wasn't her hunger, but his. When he slept like the dead throughout the days, waking only after the sun had set, she did the same.

Every new, hated experience was shared with her. Poor Angel. She'd thought the blood thirst, the rage, the sleeplessness was hers, something manifested out of her grief and fury.

When he fed, she'd believed she was hallucinating.

Her urge to sleep throughout the day, her insomnia, she'd thought it was all on her.

But it was him and he hadn't known.

Then, abruptly, some witch at the school where they'd sent him realized what was going on. How, Kel didn't know.

He hadn't wanted to be at the school, but he'd been too messed up in the head to think about leaving. He'd thought, more than once, about taking a walk in the sunlight, but his body's survival instinct was stronger. Each time he'd tried to take that daylight walk, his body had refused to cooperate.

One of the older vampires, a teacher whose name escaped Kel, had taken him out for a Hunt in the forest. They'd been tracking a deer, the vamp making Kel track the animal by scent. Saliva pooling in his mouth, his fangs throbbing and his gut a screaming, empty knot, Kel had all but been out of his mind and then the witch had come.

Her name was Kelsey. She'd been the healer who'd come to him those first hellish nights and the sound of her voice registered before he recognized her face. His instinct had been to run. It wasn't her fault. She hadn't done a damn thing to him, but hearing her voice had reminded him of all the shit he'd tried to forget.

If he could have, he would have run away from her.

But something about the way she'd looked at him had frozen Kel in place. When she'd sent the other vampire away, Kel hadn't known what was going on, hadn't known what she wanted from him. All she'd done, at first, was watch him with compassionate eyes.

That compassion hadn't done him a lick of good once she started to speak. Once he realized what he was doing. He'd always known Angel was different, had always known that the two of them had some weird connection, but he hadn't thought it would backfire like this. Even after he'd come out of his Change, realized what he was and that he couldn't ever go back home, he hadn't thought about how this could affect Angel.

His selfishness still made him sick. Even after all these years. Angel had spent a good two months in hell because of him—and not just because of natural grieving. By the time any of the Hunters had figured out what was going on, Angel had all but retreated inside herself, convinced that her grief was driving her crazy.

With help from Kelsey and some of the vampires at Excelsior, the school he'd been sent to, Kel had managed to get it under control and block Angel out. Time passed, allowed her to grieve, and eventually to heal.

She even tried to forget.

She didn't succeed.

But then again...neither could he. No matter how hard he tried to forget, he couldn't.

He couldn't forget.

He couldn't even begin to heal.

After a while, he'd stopped trying.

He heard the footsteps coming his way before Sheila even knocked, could smell her even though she wasn't in the room. "Come on in," he said when she knocked. He didn't raise his voice, but then again, he didn't have to. In addition to the increased strength and speed, the Change heightened the senses too.

Sheila came inside, wearing a floor-length pink skirt and a soft white sweater. She didn't look a damn thing like a vampire. No. She looked like a soccer mom, a PTA mom. She looked like somebody who ought to be making cookies, rocking babies and helping her daughter deal with her first crush.

She might bake those cookies, although she didn't get to eat them. They got eaten by the resident shape-shifters and the lone witch who lived within the enclave. Instead of being mama to a bunch of kids, Sheila played mama hen to a Master vamp's enclave. She fussed when any of the motley crew living there didn't feed or take care of themselves.

But she didn't just play mama hen. Once he'd come back here, Sheila had been one of his trolling partners. New Hunters weren't allowed out on their own and she'd been one of the few partners who hadn't outright refused to Hunt with him after more than one or two weeks.

He knew from experience that Sheila might look soft and sweet, but she could kick ass just like any other Hunter. She didn't think much of her abilities and Kel knew it wasn't just an act. She wasn't one of the strong ones, she'd told him. Over time, he figured out what she'd meant.

The strong ones usually ended up seeking out their own territory, driven by some instinctive need. They would be their own Master and they wouldn't have to fight some overbearing urge to submit to a stronger vamp.

Rather like Kel had to do here with Rafe.

Another thing Sheila was good at—playing mediator when her hard-ass husband got too domineering.

Which happened a lot. Might be a trait of Master vamps, or might just be because the guy was an arrogant S.O.B. She was the wife of the vampire who had saved Kel, a Master by the name of Rafe. At times, arrogant didn't even come close to describing Rafe.

For the longest time, Kel had hated that man. Rafe had known too. And from the sympathy he'd seen in the man's eyes a few times, Kel knew the guy understood. Sucked when even the meanest vamp around could see Kel's misery—and sympathize.

That sympathy didn't make it easier at all.

"You didn't feed yesterday," Sheila said. Her voice was soft, but he heard the accusation all the same.

Lifting a shoulder, he said, "I'm fine. I'll feed when I need to."

Lifting a golden brow, Sheila studied him.

Kel knew what she saw, a man who could stand to put on some weight. He often looked gaunt since he went too long between feedings. A too-young face and world-weary, old eyes. Kel had been nineteen when he was Changed. Until the day he died, he would have the face of a young man. Heavily lashed green eyes, thick, wavy brown hair he rarely bothered to cut, it all added to the pretty, young package.

Some guys would probably love to have an eternally young face and never have to worry about going bald. The face he had, coupled with the lean, rangy body and that hated vamp appeal drew women like honey drew bees. Most of the women didn't give a damn that he could stand to put a few pounds on.

Yeah, some guys would love it. But Kel hated it.

"You look like you need to now."

Need to what? he almost asked. Then he remembered. Feed. Yeah, she was here to nag him into feeding. Again.

Instead of answering, he bent down, tied his tennis shoes and then stood. Tension had every muscle in his body knotted and out of habit, he rolled his neck in an attempt to relieve the tension. It didn't help.

His wallet was on the plain, utilitarian dresser, along with the keys to a motorcycle. It looked like an ugly piece of crap, but that bike could move. It all but growled and rumbled with power when he revved the engine. Sometimes, when he went speeding down the highway with the speedometer edging up over 120 m.p.h., 130 m.p.h., 140 m.p.h., he could feel his heartbeat speed up, just a little, as adrenaline flooded his system. For a few minutes, he'd almost feel alive.

But when he went to scoop up his keys, he saw the fine tremor of his fingers. Swearing, his hand clenched into a fist. He heard her moving behind him, but he didn't move away quick enough to evade her hand as Sheila reached out and grabbed his wrist.

His freaking bony wrist. Until that moment, when Sheila's slim, small hand easily encircled his wrist, he hadn't realized just how pathetic he must look.

"You're not fine," Sheila said, a thread of steel edging into her soft Southern drawl. She squeezed gently and then let go, eying him with a mix of frustration and disgust.

"You're not doing yourself any favors by starving, Kel."

"I'm not starving." But as if to countermand his words, a wave of hunger washed over him, hitting him with an intensity that nearly drove him to his knees. Sheila said something else, but he didn't notice. The only thing he was aware of was that she'd fed recently, that somebody's blood, hot and potent, was pumping through her veins.

Her lips moved but he was fascinated with the sound of her heartbeat. Sheila's sweater had a cowl neck that hid the ugly scars on her neck, scars she'd received when she'd been Changed. Kel found himself staring at her neck, envisioning how her soft white flesh would look, how she would feel, how she would taste.

The deep, booming voice was an intrusion, one Kel really didn't care for. He was focused on the ripe pulse of life flowing through Sheila and he wanted it—wanted it with an intensity that would shame him later—although it wasn't her he wanted.

But the intrusion wasn't going anywhere. If he could have swatted it away, he would have. It pushed between him and Sheila and Kel was more interested in going around the obstacle. When he tried, the obstacle moved with him, blocking him yet again.

His lips peeled back from his teeth in a snarl as the hungry beast inside him rose a little closer to the surface.

Then the obstacle grabbed him by the front of the shirt and

jerked him forward. Reality came crashing down and Kel found himself literally nose to nose with one very pissed-off vampire.

The crushing, oppressive weight of Rafe's will as the Master forced Kel's hunger back into submission and his attention away from Rafe's wife.

Fury glittered in the black depths of Rafe's eyes but when he spoke, his voice was soft. "You're feeding tonight if I have to drag you out of this house and find a woman for you, kid. You got me?"

Fear, the need to submit and do whatever the Master demanded, rode hard on Kel's shoulders, but his own will kept him from meekly agreeing. He dropped his gaze to Rafe's hand, still fisted in the front of his T-shirt, and then he looked back up at Rafe and gave him a mocking smile. "Gee, Dad, can I pick out what I eat or are you going to do it for me?"

Behind him, Sheila snorted. Rafe sent his wife a narrow look and then slowly loosened his grip on Kel. Common sense screamed that Kel should back away now, back away, get the hell away from Rafe and do what he'd been told. But Kel had stopped listening to common sense years ago. So instead of backing away and getting at least the pretense of safe distance between them, he remained where he was, not even an inch away from Rafe.

The two men settled into a staring contest and Kel's misery, his rage, even his hunger fueled him, letting him meet the older, stronger vampire's glare with his own. It was Rafe who ended it, falling back first one step, and then another. But not because Kel had backed him down. Kel wasn't delusional enough to see that happening any time soon. Ever. No, Rafe backed away because he felt like it, and for no other reason.

Knowing that pissed Kel off even more than the smirk on Rafe's face. "I don't know why in the hell I like you so much," the older vampire muttered, shaking his head.

Instead of responding, Kel turned away and headed out of the room. Behind him, Sheila gave Rafe a warning glance and he just rolled his eyes, but fell into step behind Kel silently.

Rafe might have been the local Master, but there was little question about who really ran things in the enclave. Soft, pretty, with a deceptively sweet face and that slow Southern drawl, Sheila was one of the weaker Hunters and she'd never be a Master.

But she had Rafe wrapped around her little finger.

She had him so wrapped, he'd never get untangled from it and Rafe knew it. He adored her with all his heart and soul and losing her would kill something inside of him.

"You plan on following me around all damn night?" Kel demanded, shooting Rafe a narrow glance as he mounted the stairs.

"No. Just until I see you feed."

Kel's eyes narrowed. But he kept whatever he wanted to say to himself as he moved through the house. The main level was mostly quiet. The other vampires living in the enclave were either out Hunting, feeding or doing whatever they preferred when they weren't on rotation.

Most of the shifters, by preference, preferred to sleep through the night. The only shifter awake now was Toronto, but that was nothing new. The shape-shifter tended to live a very nocturnal lifestyle.

But he didn't show his face as Rafe followed Kel through the library, the dining room, on through the kitchen to the back of the house. A huge garage had been added since Rafe had taken over this piece of land, housing the vehicles of the Hunters living here.

He didn't head for the garage, though, just slipped between the hodgepodge collection of buildings. A gym, a greenhouse, the grouping of smaller, recently built homes for those who didn't want to live in the main house. They weren't big, designed just to sleep one or two people. Sooner or later, when money allowed, Rafe planned on adding a few more.

Kel slid past all the houses, bypassed the utility shed at the far end of the grounds and disappeared behind the tree line. Rafe kept right behind him and tried not to get too irritated over the fact that he was babysitting one of his Hunters when he could be back at the house and making love to his wife.

Even as that thought circled through his head, guilt surged through him. When the night was over, Rafe would return home and crawl into the bed with Sheila, hold her soft, sweet body against his as they slept.

While Kel spent the daylight hours alone and caught in the

daytime prison-like sleep that came over the younger vamps, unable to fight the dreams that would come on him. And knowing when he woke, the memory of those dreams would still be there to haunt him.

Rafe couldn't imagine the hell Kel must be going through. Kel never talked about it, but the kid had the shitty luck of living in close quarters with the type of people who didn't need him to say a word for them to feel his misery, taste it or scent it on the air.

Every emotion had a unique feel, a unique taste, a unique scent. The scorching scent of rage, the sweet tang of joy or amusement. The bitter taste of rage, coupled with the acrid burn of misery, they hung around Kel so thick, so strong, the only time they eased was when his hunger spiraled out of control.

Rumors circulated around Excelsior about the girl who Kel had bonded with, a girl who nearly went crazy after Kel disappeared from her life. Feeling his hunger, his bloodlust, his depression—falling into the death-like sleep of the newly Changed.

A soul-mate bond, Rafe suspected, one forged between the two mortals before Kel had been yanked unceremoniously out of his normal, happy life. Sometimes, he was amazed the two of them had survived. Rafe had heard rumors of soul-mated pairs among non-mortals who'd lost their mate and ended up dying shortly after. Death by loneliness, he could get.

Sheila had left him once. Each day she'd been gone, he had felt as though he died a little more inside. But he hadn't physically been fading away. Neither had she.

He loved his wife, but theirs wasn't a soul-mated love. If it came right down to it, he preferred it that way just because it meant they were together because they loved each other.

Not because they had to be.

The star-crossed, soul-mated deal was a bitch as far as Rafe was concerned. Hell, look at what it had done to these two. The pretty lady Kel had been forced to leave behind almost went crazy because of their bond.

Kel had spent the past twelve years miserable and alone. Rafe had given up on him ever getting over the girl.

Shit, the girl. She was another responsibility he didn't want, and a human one, no less. He had his hands full with his enclave and watching his territory, but that hadn't kept fate from dumping the welfare of one Angel Pierson in his lap.

The feral who had attacked Kel had never been caught. Slimy bastard had slipped away and disappeared. Rafe wasn't the optimistic sort and he knew the vamp was probably still alive and preying on innocent people, but he hadn't ever come close enough to set Rafe's radar off. Without that radar, he had no way of tracking him, no way of finding him and killing him.

No way of getting justice for what had been done to Kel or Angel.

Not that justice would help Angel much. Because of the attack on her, she was vulnerable.

Vulnerable in a way that could get her killed if they didn't watch her and if Kel hadn't damn near pushed her straight into madness, none of them would have known.

A few months after Kel's Change, word came down from the Council that there might be some trouble brewing for the girl left behind. By an unspoken code of the Hunters, Rafe had been charged with checking on the girl.

She'd been close to the end of her rope, hanging onto sanity by a thread. What Rafe had seen upon his reluctant visit to Greenburg was a woman who would most likely find death a sweet release. She was so filled with pain, so tormented by what she thought were hallucinations, Rafe wouldn't have been surprised if she'd already tried to end it a half dozen times over.

It had been coming. Rafe had sensed that without any trouble, at all. The older man who intervened was the reason she was still alive, of that Rafe had no doubt. It hadn't taken much work for Rafe to learn that the older man was Kel's dad. Angel, the poor girl, only had a mother who didn't really give a damn and a step-dad who barely knew her.

If it hadn't been for Jake Saunders, Angel probably would have just ended it.

And that would have been on them. On him. Rafe hated realizing how close he'd come to letting some innocent girl grieve herself to death.

Hunters ended up stepping in on a lot of lives, he knew

that. Trying to help, sometimes succeeding, but sometimes coming too late, like in Kel's situation. Rafe was an arrogant bastard, but he knew he couldn't take on the welfare of every single human life that might somehow come in contact with his Hunters...even on the fringe side.

But the families of the victims, when he failed, they were his responsibility. Angel had been a responsibility and he'd failed her. It wouldn't happen again. That was a promise he'd made himself, standing in the shadows and watching as a middle-aged mortal helped a young woman place one foot in front of the other, walking down a pretty, flower-lined path. She'd signed herself into a mental health facility and it hadn't come soon enough.

Rafe could still remember how painfully thin the girl had been, how grief-stricken, and the look of utter dejection on her face.

Beyond that driving pain, though, Rafe had seen something else, something that made him feel that much more a failure.

Shooting Kel a dark look, Rafe wished the kid would at least speed up his pace a little. Long-ass walks like this through the woods made for entirely too much thinking time.

Angel had been attacked that night too. Kel still wouldn't talk about it, but Rafe figured Kel had walked in on the attack and by either divine intervention or just plain dumb luck, he'd distracted the vampire before he could drain Angel. Which would piss off any predator. Taking away a predator's meal could make you the replacement. Rafe figured that was what had happened with Kel.

For all Kel's attempts to save his lady, he hadn't been able to stop something from happening to her. Angel hadn't emerged from that night unchanged. At some point, between biting her and attacking Kel, the feral had also forced some of his blood down Angel's throat.

From time to time, some vampires outside the Hunters took on a regular feeding companion. It wasn't exactly forbidden— the Hunters couldn't damn well police every single non-mortal in the world. They were charged with watching those who were a threat to humanity. They weren't there to babysit each and every last vampire, witch, shifter and were in existence. Just the ones that were a threat.

The problem started when a civilian vamp took a regular feeding companion and shared blood. That, in and of itself, posed another problem. The risk of exposure was too damn high. The typical vamp had the common sense to wipe away, or at least alter, any memory of a blood sharing. But there were idiots everywhere and vamps weren't excluded.

With a few minor exceptions, the few times there had been a decent risk of exposure, they'd been able to move in time, sending in a vamp with enough power to wipe away memories whether the mortal wanted it or not—and dealing with the vampire dumb enough to get caught in the situation.

Those exceptions were, from time to time, seen in tabloids or on websites, places where nobody would give it much attention. But sooner or later, Rafe suspected it was going to happen to somebody who could garner attention from some place other than tabloids or some of the Goth communities.

It was part of the reason he forbid any vampire in his territory to have a regular, mortal feeding companion unless the mortal was somehow already aware of their existence. The Council had resisted trying to forbid it among the general population, but they left it up to individual Masters to decide how they'd police their territories.

It was a problem Rafe didn't need or want, so the few times it happened in his land, the offending vamp ended up getting a visit he'd rather not get.

But how he ran his territory wasn't going to make a lick of difference to what had happened to Angel. Sharing blood didn't automatically make a mortal a vampire. Some mortals could take a sip or two of vamp blood and it wouldn't do much of anything to them. Others, like Angel, underwent a change of their own, and usually one they weren't even aware of.

Vampire bait.

For some mortals, something about the blood-sharing altered their makeup, made their blood that much more enticing. Over the past few years, there'd been a couple of scientific types among the non-mortals who were bent on figuring out answers to centuries-old questions.

Why the Change killed some and not others.

Why some were born with magick and others weren't.

Why they were even real creatures, instead of myth.

Those science-minded types had a theory. Not all mortals who shared blood with a vampire were going to end up vampire bait. Not all of them would have their blood and genetic makeup altered in the least. It only happened to a fraction of them.

The theory was that those who ended up altered—or vampire bait—were mortals more likely to survive the Change, if a vampire made the attempt to bring them over.

Rafe didn't know, didn't care about the science or the answers, unless it offered a solution. Because vampire bait was a problem. They took on an otherworldly appeal and it wasn't one the weak could easily ignore.

That was the danger. In the hundred plus years that Rafe had been a Hunter, there had been a few accidental deaths when one of these altered humans crossed paths with a vampire who couldn't resist temptation. Draining them to true death, taking so much that the mortal died before the vampire even realized they'd taken too much.

Couldn't even try to Change them at that point—dead bodies can't swallow the blood needed to jumpstart the Change. A vampire could kill in self-defense and while it was frowned upon, it wasn't a violation of Council law. But if a vampire killed outside of self-defense, that was all it would take to trip the internal radar of whichever Hunter was nearby. Whether the mortal death was accidental or not, it ended in a death sentence for the offending vampire.

Over time, most of the civilian vampires decided it wasn't worth the risk. Blood sharing was seen less and less.

Too damn bad nobody had bothered to inform the ferals.

Angel's life had been turned upside down by that attack in so many different ways. One fucked-up night. Violence so rarely affected just a few, but that night had been for the books.

Because of that night, Angelica Pierson was permanently on their watch list. Not because she was a threat, but because too many of their kind might prove a threat to her. The feral that had attacked her probably intended to Change her, but he was interrupted before a full blood exchange was done. Instead, he'd forced enough of his blood down her throat that it had altered hers. She was now vampire bait and that pretty much painted a huge, glaring neon target over her head and now the vampire population, both the good and the bad, presented a threat to her.

A threat she didn't even know existed.

Even Rafe, so in love with his wife he hurt with it, had felt a siren's call when he looked at Angel. Just before she'd disappeared into the hospital for a voluntary commitment, he'd felt it.

She was too damn thin, too damn weak, as pale as a ghost and what he should have felt was a need to protect her, a need to fix the damage he'd unwittingly allowed to happen. But instead...he'd felt hunger.

Despite her weak, obviously unwell physical state, he'd looked and he'd hungered. She had a surreal quality, the scent of her blood was like ambrosia and even as laden as she was with grief, the pulse of life inside her was entirely too tempting. Entirely too sweet. She all but shone with it.

Vampire bait. No vamp could possibly look at her and not have the compulsion to feed. Compulsions could be ignored, but walking away from Angel had taken an act of will. He hadn't even understood the why of it until later.

The next day, in fact, trapped inside a hotel while the sun burned overhead, he'd been beating himself up, half-sick with guilt and confusion and then it had come to him. Rafe knew himself. Damn well. He loved his wife. Full stop. All there was to it. Loved her blindly, completely.

In all the years since they'd married, he hadn't once felt tempted. Oh, he'd noticed women. His eyes worked just fine. But the urge to take something he had no right to take? That was new and until he'd laid eyes on Angel, he wouldn't have seen it happening.

He knew it wasn't normal for him, craving something he couldn't and shouldn't have...so he'd made himself look deeper. At Angelica Pierson, and at his unexpected response. The following night, he'd figured it out. She'd been asleep, but finding her inside the hospital had been easy.

It was almost like something had guided him there, and that in itself was another clue.

Bait. It wasn't the man who had responded. It was the

vampire, that dark, surging force inside him, that craved.

Any and every damn vamp who saw her was going to have the same visceral response and not all vamps were the nice type who would just admire, wish and walk away.

So Angel was watched. Treated just like one of the kids the Hunters watched from a distance, the kind who possessed a latent power, the kind of power that called to the evil in the world.

Watched and protected.

Watched. Protected. Hell, just like her sweetheart. The sweetheart in question was still walking on, heading towards town with single-minded focus.

Rafe sighed, shoved a hand through his hair and wished he'd sent Toronto after the kid.

Kel stopped dead in his tracks and turned around to glare at Rafe. It was a moonless night and under the trees the darkness was thick and weighted, but they both saw the other fine.

"If I tell you that I'll feed before I head back tonight, will you leave me the hell alone?" Kel demanded, his voice harsh with aggravation.

A familiar light gleamed in the younger vamp's eyes, but Rafe wasn't about to give Kel the fight he was so desperately looking for. "No. You want me off your ass, you'll just shut the hell up and find somebody. After you feed, I'll leave you alone."

Eyes narrowed down to slits, Kel said, "I can handle this on my own."

Rafe snorted. "Sure you can. But you aren't. You never do. So tonight, I'll make sure you do. And if I have to do this on a regular basis with you, fine. Until you get it in your head that you can't ignore the hunger like this, I'll just play babysitter."

The kid was looking for a fight. Even though he was weak from hunger, Kel was in the mood to brawl. Par for the course. Happened regularly enough that everybody in the enclave knew the signs. For some, they took them as a signal to give Kel a wide berth until he'd either fed or got the fight he was looking for.

And the others had no problem giving Kel that fight.

Better one of their own than having Kel look outside the enclave for a fight. When that happened, the cleanup got messy. He never went after people who couldn't handle a pissed, heartbroken vampire, which meant he either went on the Hunt or searched out their own kind.

He'd picked plenty of fights that he would have lost, and lost in a big, rather final way, if he hadn't had others watching out for him.

But Rafe was getting tired of making his Hunters play babysitter when Kel got into one of his moods. He was tired of doing it himself, and he was tired of dealing with the cleanup end when Kel's inner rage took control. This shit seriously needed to stop.

Kel took a step forward, his chin angling up. Rafe was tempted to just plant a punch right there, nip this mess before it started. But until Kel fed, he'd be hanging onto control by a thread. Could be that punching him would just delay the mess. Sure as hell wouldn't prevent it.

"What you going to do, spoon-feed me or something?" Kel gave him an obnoxious smirk.

"If I have to." Rafe looked at Kel, focused—watched as the younger vamp's pale features contorted in a grimace, a muscle jerking near his temple as he fought Rafe's control.

Wasn't too pleasant for Rafe, either, but Kel had to get a grip on reality. Had to accept his life for what it was. If he kept fighting it, it was going to kill him.

Of course, maybe that was what he wanted.

He maintained control over Kel's mind for long, tense moments, forcing the younger vamp into a submissive silence that probably rubbed him raw. Self-disgust tangled with the need to do whatever was necessary to protect his territory, his Hunters.

Including protecting Kel from himself.

Slowly, he released the control and watched grimly as Kel staggered away, swearing at Rafe in a ragged voice.

"I can make you feed, Kel. You know I can."

Angry eyes cut towards Rafe, anger, shame, misery. Did the kid ever feel anything else? Ever let himself? "You son of a bitch, you got no right doing that."

Shaking his head, Rafe said, "You got that wrong. You took a blood oath when you decided to come here. You made vows. You signed onto a life where you protect people...and right now, you need to get it through your skull that we also have to protect them from us."

Kel slashed a hand through the air. "When have I ever hurt somebody innocent?"

"It hasn't happened...yet. But if you keep doing this, you keep starving yourself, pushing yourself to the edge of your control, it's going to happen. All of us can break, Kel, especially when you're hanging onto control by the threads."

Kel's lips peeled back from his teeth. "I wouldn't hurt somebody who didn't deserve it." His fangs glinted in the faint light, an indicator of just how ragged his control was. If he'd been in control, the fangs wouldn't show unless he was feeding.

"I hate this." Kel turned away from Rafe but didn't continue on towards town. Instead he paced.

"You think I don't know that?"

Kel shot Rafe a dark look. "I don't fucking want this. I don't want to give some blood oath to anybody, least of all, *you*. I don't want to live this life. I don't want any of it."

"Again, you think I don't know that?" Rafe sighed and passed a hand over his face. He circled as Kel paced, keeping him in his line of sight. "It's a shitty thing that happened to you, I get that. I'm sorry for it. Even shittier is the fact that you can't even make an attempt at a normal life because you feel the same damn drive I do—you're a Hunter, whether you like it or not. It chose you and there's not a damn thing you can do about it. Flat out, it sucks."

Kel stopped dead in his tracks and turned, staring at Rafe. A bitter smile curled his lips. "It sucks? Come on, is that the best you got? This goes a little deeper than sucks."

Returning Kel's bitter, ugly smile, Rafe said, "Yeah, so does having to deal with a half-suicidal, heartsick Hunter who's bent on self-destruction. But you're under my watch and I'll be damned if I risk the consequences that may result from that self-destruction."

Resentment burned through Kel, sizzled inside his veins, in his head, threatening to spark him back into one of his rages. He knew that was why Rafe was still trailing him as he headed towards Beale Street.

It chose you and there's not a damn thing you can do about it. Flat out, it sucks.

Talk about being a master of understatement.

But the bitch of it was that he knew exactly where Rafe was coming from, especially after the fucking weird deal that happened to him earlier when he was talking to Sheila. He hadn't once looked at that woman like that.

His heart was pretty much dead inside his chest, although his body hadn't shut down. But he hadn't ever come close to falling under his body's control, falling under his hunger's control—and it was because he hadn't fed.

Rafe didn't trust him to stay in control. None of them did, but Kel knew he hadn't exactly proven himself on that front. Every time he got like this, he told himself he wasn't going to do it again. He wasn't going to end up so close to the edge again.

But the problem with that logic was the solution. Feeding. Regular feeds, from a living, breathing human and for some fucked-up reason, Kel couldn't stand to feed from a male. It filled him with a revulsion that turned his stomach. He knew from experience, puking up blood was a disgusting experience.

So if he wanted to keep himself from going off on a hair-trigger rage, he had to feed regularly—from women. Feeding for a vamp was altogether too damn sexual and even if he didn't give in, just the arousal left him all but sick with guilt.

Sick with guilt because the woman wasn't Angel. Sick with guilt because even after twelve fucking years, he was still so hung up on a woman he couldn't have, hung up to the point of obsession.

That obsession was killing him.

As he got closer to Beale Street, the music became louder and louder. Soon, it was loud enough to drown out the near-soundless footsteps following him, but Kel knew Rafe was still back there. He bypassed the first three bars, looking for a little hole-in-the-wall that tended to attract a certain crowd.

Memphis had a huge paranormal population. Witches, vamps and shifters flocked to the city. Whether it was because they knew it was under the protection of the Council, the governing force of their kind, or because they just liked the tourists, the nightlife, Kel didn't know. Didn't really give a damn, either.

Hell, maybe they just really liked Elvis.

The civilians fit in with the mortal population fairly well. They worked, they paid their bills, some of them even tried to marry amongst mortals, hiding the darker part of themselves from their friends, their family.

But here, this was a place where none of them had to hide who or what they were.

Although lights shone all around, spilling out of the clubs, from the streetlights over head, this part of the street was dark. Kel had no trouble finding the door, though. Some weird kind of magick colored the air and although Kel hadn't ever asked, he'd pretty much figured out what purpose the magick served.

It was a "go away" signal. On a subconscious level, it came through loud and clear to mortals. None of them wanted to approach this particular door and most of them would quickly edge by, as though they couldn't stand to be too close.

A pair of eyes gleamed at Kel from the darkness and he dug into his pocket, pulled out a twenty. It wasn't accepted, though, and he knew why as Rafe edged a little closer. Narrowing his eyes, he glared at Rafe and then looked back at the big, broad bastard watching the door.

Can't go taking money from one of the Hunters, now can we? This wasn't the first time it had happened and for the most part, it was something he didn't give a damn about one way or the other. He could pay or not. Didn't matter.

But tonight, it dug at him, reminding him once more how set apart he was.

Leaning forward, he shoved it into the guy's shirt pocket and then stomped inside, ignoring Rafe, ignoring the people gathered near the door.

Ignoring everybody and everything except the bar.

65

One thing Kel could still stomach besides blood was alcohol and right now, he needed some. No. A lot. He needed a lot of alcohol to fog his brain and keep him from thinking about what he had to do.

If he got drunk enough here, he might be able to handle what came next.

Elbowing his way through the crowd, he focused on the bar. When he finally got to the crowded bar, he stood there less than five seconds before a couple of guys off to his left vacated their seats. He shot Rafe another sour look and settled down on one of the stools. Rafe joined him, propping his elbows on the stained, scarred oak.

"Would you leave me the hell alone? Or go play Lassie on the other side of the bar?"

With a smirk, Rafe shrugged and asked, "Why? You think me going away is going to keep people from looking at you and knowing what you are?"

"Shit." Tearing his attention from Rafe, and the truth of what he'd just said, he signaled to one of the bartenders.

"This really what you need?"

Instead of answering Rafe, he just watched as one of the bartenders headed his way. She was new. Slim, almost petite with dark, kohl-lined eyes and moon-pale skin. Her short cap of hair framed elfin features and when she smiled at him, her teeth gleamed white. She had ruby red lipstick on, the exact same shade as the closely fitted top she wore. It looked more like a corset than a shirt, Kel decided, cupping each small breast and elevating it.

Tinkerbell does Goth.

For some reason, he realized his mouth was watering.

She leaned against the bar across from him and he tore his eyes away from her tits, made himself look at her face. She wasn't the kind he wanted. He wanted—

Angel.

Can't have her, he told himself bitterly. No. Couldn't have her, so he'd settle for somebody he could pretend was her. Tink wouldn't work.

"What's your pleasure?"

She had a soft, breathy little voice that suited her Goth-Tinkerbell appearance.

"Jack Daniels. Bring the bottle."

She turned, walked away, and Kel found himself staring at her ass, snugly encased in black leather. There was an energy shimmering in the air around her and he pegged her as a shape-shifter with no difficulty. Shifters were like that, throwing off energy so it was like the air around them was electrically charged. Vamps had a quieter feel, fitting, in Kel's mind, since every damn one of them should be staked, burned and their ashes scattered to the winds.

Including himself.

Rafe remained silent as the bartender appeared in front of Kel, leaving the bottle and a glass. A smile curved her lips and she said, "I'm told there's no charge."

Kel snorted. "Of course not." Sending Rafe a sidelong glance, he wrapped his fingers around the glass but before he could reach for the whiskey, she was there, opening the bottle, filling Kel's glass a third full. She lifted a brow and he tapped the rim of the glass. More splashed in.

"You look like you need a drink or two," she murmured, leaning in. The rest of the bartenders were rushing around behind her like a bunch of ants on a picnic blanket, but she looked like she had all the time in the world. With her elbows propped on the bar, she smiled at him, leaned in, treated Kel to a very nice view of her breasts. The corset was cut low, just barely hiding her nipples.

His voice was rough as he murmured, "At least."

She dipped a finger into the whiskey and slid it between her lips. "Then maybe you should drink this," she suggested after she licked her finger dry. Using the same one, she pushed the drink closer to Kel.

Hunger, that hated hunger, flared to vibrant life. It burned inside him, turned every last inch of him from ice to flame. Desperate to chill it a little, he grabbed the drink and emptied it. She took the bottle, poured him another. He drained it just as quick. After the third one, she pushed the whiskey off to the side.

Nobody in the place blinked as she hopped on the bar and

swung around so that she sat spread-legged in front of Kel. The leather pants couldn't quite hide the scent of hot, hungry female. She bent down, placed her lips next to his ear. "You're not going to find what you need inside a bottle, handsome. But I can give it to you."

Bitter, Kel shook his head. He hadn't drunk enough to fog the brain, fog his need. "You can't. Nobody can."

Her lips, hot and silken, traced along his cheekbone, brushed against his mouth. "Try me..."

He wanted to pull away from her. Wished he had the strength to do it, wished he wasn't so damn weak, so tempted. Easing back, he stared into her eyes. They were a warm, wicked brown, full of life and seductive welcome. When he eased back, those pretty brown eyes went dark, her mouth turning down in a frown. Quick as a wink, though, she was smiling again.

Try me...

Abruptly, he reached out, cupped the back of her head in his hand and jerked her against him. She came to him eagerly, all but climbing up his body, unconcerned by the fact that there were easily two hundred people in the bar, and not one of them blind. Reaching out, Kel closed his hand around the bottle of Jack Daniels. With his arms full of woman and whiskey, he slid off the seat.

"To the back," she whispered in his ear, but it wasn't necessary. Kel could follow the scents of blood and sex easily. The back of the club was marked off from the main room by a plain door, guarded by a big black man with dreadlocks hanging halfway down his back. He opened the door for Kel and the girl without any of them saying anything and when Kel passed through, the door was closed behind him.

The music fell to a muted roar. She lifted up, gazed down at him. "End of the hall, there's some stairs. I've got a room on the second floor."

The largest part of him didn't want to find some quiet room. He just wanted to fuck her here, in the hall, where anybody could see. Fuck. Feed. Walk away.

But for reasons he couldn't explain, he searched out the stairs. Walked up them, staring into her face—pretty, not beautiful. Tinkerbell does Goth, he thought again, as her ruby red lips pressed up against his. She licked his lips and he opened for her, kissed her. Her taste was darker, more exotic than Kel had expected.

Not sweet. A rich wine. "There," she whispered, pulling back a little and nodding to the left.

He didn't look away from her as he entered the room—if he did, he might start to think and he couldn't risk thinking. Once he finally decided to give in and feed, the hunger had risen out from its hiding place, a sleeping beast, and he had to sate it.

Sate it now.

But the blood-hunger wasn't the only thing demanding satisfaction. His cock throbbed, thick, hard and aching. He kicked the door shut behind them and leaned back against it, watching as she reached down, took the whiskey from him. Kel watched, mesmerized, as she dribbled the liquor along the tops of her breasts.

"Take what you want." Reaching out, she threaded her fingers through his hair and tugged him closer. She tightened her knees around his hips, gripping him and steadying her weight as she slowly straightened so that his face was level with her breasts.

Kel licked the droplets of whiskey away. Each lick, each taste of her fanned the fires of his hunger and he got rougher, rougher—his fangs dropped and he raked one soft swell. As the taste of her blood filled his mouth, he swore and tore away.

"No!" She urged him back, whimpering, rocking against him. Blood welled against the ivory of her skin. Lost, Kel licked the drops away and then sealed his mouth over the wound. She healed quick, too quick—shifters, like vamps, always did—and when he lifted his head, his hunger screamed at him.

"Do it again," she rasped.

And again...

And again...

Kel let himself get lost in her, lost in the dark, wild ride, feasting on her sexually, feasting on her blood. A shifter's blood had a stronger kick than a mortal's. It wasn't something he'd had much of, but now he wondered why. So easy not to think past the high her blood gave him. So easy not to feel anything beyond the way her slender, delicate body moved against his, meeting strength for strength. So easy not to think about anything but how wild, ripe and exotic she was.

The hours grew late, ticking by without Kel even realizing. By the time he collapsed between her legs one final time, head buzzing and his body all but limp with satisfaction, it was past two in the morning.

She purred deep in her throat, sounding like a cat.

"What's your name?" he asked abruptly. Almost instantly, he wished he hadn't. He never wanted to know their names. Never wanted them to have a name—all he wanted was for them to be Angel. Just for a little while. Just long enough to take what he needed.

But it was too late to take it back and he couldn't pretend she was Angel, anyway.

"Phoebe." She hummed under her breath and slid her hands over his shoulders. "I know who you are. You're one of the Hunters. Kel...right?"

Shit. Disgust started to pulse through him. A groupie? He'd run into them on occasion, female vamps or shifters who seemed to think that fucking a Hunter was pretty much the ultimate hobby. He hadn't quite caught that off her.

Still...

Lifting his head from between her breasts, he saw that she was smiling. It was a sad, understanding smile.

"Relax," she teased. "I'm not going to go cut a button off your jacket or anything."

"I wasn't wearing a jacket."

Phoebe shrugged. "You know what I mean." She reached up, traced his lips with her finger. "I knew you were a Hunter, yeah. But I don't care. That wasn't why I wanted to be with you." Holding his gaze, she reached down, trailed her fingers over the curve of her breasts and murmured, "This is why."

Looking down, Kel found himself staring at her breasts with something caught between horror and fascination. Dried blood streaked her soft curves. Blood he'd put on her as he nicked her silken flesh time and again.

"Son of a bitch," he muttered, almost sick with disgust.

Phoebe placed a finger under his chin, guiding his gaze

back to hers. "Don't. I like the edge," she said in a calm, level voice. "I knew you could take me there. And I knew you needed...something."

Something. Yeah. He needed something. Shaken, he pushed away from her and stared down at his own body. As drained as he was, he wouldn't heal as quick. Even with her potent blood pulsing inside him, it would take him a little longer. So the scrapes, scratches and bite marks on him hadn't faded away into nothingness like hers had.

They'd left marks all over each other.

Yeah. He needed something. He needed his head examined. Phoebe, like she knew what he was thinking, laughed.

"Stop looking so tormented. We didn't do anything that can't heal. And...if you'll let yourself admit it, what we did felt good. I bet that's the most alive you felt in years."

Good. Shit. Yeah. It had felt damn good. "That's not the point," he said, his voice gritty and rough. He settled down on the edge of the bed and studied the room. Their clothes were tangled up in a line between here and the door. The room looked like something out of a war zone and he wasn't entirely convinced it had looked like that before they got in there.

He was pretty sure just about every flat surface, horizontal and vertical, had been pressed against one of them at some time during the night. He'd taken her bent over the bathtub, pressed against the reinforced windows, sprawled facedown on the floor near the bed.

The bed itself was a disaster, the sheets twisted and stained with sweat, semen and blood.

"Not the point," he muttered, dropping his face into his hands.

"No? What is the point?" She sat up, trailed her fingers over his shoulder. When he looked back at her, she smiled. "What's the point? Both of us are miserable. I saw that on you even before I realized what you were. Neither of us are going to get to have what we want in life."

Startled, he shoved up off the bed and grabbed his jeans. "What in the hell are you talking about?" he demanded.

A humorless smile curled her lips. "You know what I'm talking about." She slid from the bed in a smooth, sinuous motion. She moved across the floor in a glide of silken skin and sleek muscles, bending down to grab a T-shirt from the floor. She tugged it on, the hem falling down to cover her delicate curves.

Kel felt a little better as the simple white cotton hid those curves and the faint traces of blood, lingering reminders of what they'd done to each other. Reminders he really didn't need. His gut was already a nasty mess, from guilt and from the overpowering urge to grab her, push her down to the floor and start it all over again.

Tearing his eyes from her body, he watched as she shoved a hand through her short, spiky hair. "Broken souls recognize each other, Kel. I look at you and I see a man with a huge, gaping hole inside him. Not many things leave that kind of hole. That kind of hole is caused by loss. Losing the one you love, losing your family." She slid him a look over her shoulder. "Which one did you lose?"

He didn't answer her. Not even when she approached him, staring into his eyes and she reached out touched the gold chain he never took off. Not for Hunting. Not for fighting. Not for anything. It was a simple rope chain and it had a gold ring on it. The diamond on it wasn't much, although that wouldn't have mattered to Angel. He'd bought it the weekend before it happened. It was why he'd been busting his ass working those extra hours, hours he could have spent with her.

The ring was a mocking reminder that it had all been for nothing and now he had the rest of his life to think about everything he'd missed.

Phoebe slipped a finger under the chain and lifted it, staring at the ring. "Who did you lose?" she asked again, her voice soft, but determined nonetheless.

Protectively, he reached out and took the ring away, closing his hand around it. His voice was rusty as he replied, "Everything. Everybody." A hollow ache settled in his throat. "My mom died two years after...after this. I never got to tell her goodbye, couldn't go to her funeral. But—"

He broke off, shaking his head.

Phoebe watched him with knowing eyes. "Losing your folks didn't put that pain in your eyes."

"No. It was a woman—*the* woman. Losing her is what..." He trailed off, unsure what to say. Yeah, he missed his dad, and wished a million times he could have had a chance to tell his mom goodbye, that he loved her.

His dad was alone now. It had been twelve years since he'd seen the kind, gentle man who had raised him, helped make him become the halfway decent guy he'd been before he'd been Changed. Kel had thought about going to see his dad... Not visit, but just to look at him without letting the old man know he was there. Visit his mother's grave.

Just once. To say goodbye.

But their absence, missing his mother's funeral, or knowing his dad was alone, none of that was responsible for killing something inside him. It was Angel.

"She's the one who put that hole inside you," Phoebe finished for him.

"Yeah." And she was the reason he wouldn't let himself go back home. There was no way he could look at her from a distance. If he was close enough to see her, he'd have to touch her, have to hold...have to make love to her.

Vampires couldn't have sex without feeling the urge to feed and he wouldn't do it. Wouldn't risk it. Not with Angel. He wouldn't damn another person to this life, least of all her. Since he couldn't trust himself, he wouldn't risk it.

A hole... Yeah. That pretty much summed it up. Kel had a huge, gaping hole in his useless heart, a place Angel had filled inside him.

"Hmmm. I get that." Phoebe turned away and padded on silent feet across the room, kneeling down in a front of a dark wooden chest. The metal hinges squeaked as she opened it, gently, carefully easing the lid back. Something about the way she handled it told Kel it was important to her. She smoothed a hand along the front of it, touching it with reverence. Reaching inside, she said, "My parents have been gone a long time...a real long time."

Glancing at him, she gave him a forced smile. "Really long. Probably longer than you've even been alive."

Curling his lip, Kel said, "I ain't been alive in more than ten years."

Phoebe shook her head. "You're alive, Kel. You're just different now." She lowered her gaze, staring back into the trunk.

Curious, he edged closer, but she shifted her body, shielding him from seeing inside. She pulled out one thing and eased the lid back down before she stood and turned around. Whatever she'd pulled out was pressed against her middle, shielded from him. "Not too many of us come into this life happily," Phoebe said, her voice soft, faraway. "And most of us fight it. I know I did."

"Do you hate it?" Kel rasped, his hands opening, closing, the impotent rage inside him fighting to break free.

"Now? Not as much as I did then. Now...now, I guess I just get by. But back when I was first Changed, yeah, I hated it." Taking a deep breath, she looked down and stared at what she held in her arms. "If I wasn't such a coward, I would have ended it a long time ago."

It was a picture frame, Kel realized, even as his mind processed what she'd just said. Ended it. His brows dropped low over his eyes as he stared at her face. "You mean..."

Phoebe laughed, a sharp, cynical sound that sliced through the air like a knife. "You know damn well what I mean. Can you tell me you haven't ever thought of it? Hard not to think about it, when you've lost everything. When you have nobody."

Abruptly, Kel found himself remembering a night more than fifteen years earlier, when a sharp, harsh pain had jerked him out of his sleep. The night Angel's dad had died, how he'd gone to her, held her until she cried herself to sleep. His dad emerging from the darkness to sit beside him as Angel slept in his arms.

She doesn't have anybody now. He'd said those words to his dad on that long ago night, but he'd been wrong. She hadn't been alone then. She'd had him. And his family.

Hopefully, she still had his dad. Kel sure as hell didn't. In an unconscious echo of her words, he murmured, "Yeah, I get that."

She sighed. In that moment, she looked so sad, so desolate. The thick black eyeliner smudged around her eyes, her tousled black hair, even the T-shirt hanging from her shoulders added to the air of lonely grief. "They've been gone from me now for more than fifty years. It still hurts."

"Yeah. It does." Fifty years? Kel reached out and gently tugged on the picture frame, unsure if she'd let him see it or not.

But she let go easily, averting her face as he studied the grainy black and white family portrait.

It was Phoebe in the portrait. She was easy enough to recognize even without the short, gamine haircut and the Goth-girl makeup. In the picture, she had one of those beehive-looking hairstyles and a dress that would have done June Cleaver proud. The man at her side wore a suit and tie, resting his hand on her shoulder and giving the cameraman a stiff smile.

And sitting on Phoebe's lap was a little kid. A boy with his mother's dark hair and his dad's eyes. Kel's already battered heart ached with sympathy. "Both of them." He lifted his eyes to stare at her. Without realizing it, he reached up and closed his fist around the engagement ring he'd never been able to give to Angel.

Phoebe stood with her back to him, staring out a narrow window and swaying back and forth in a slow, unconscious manner. "Yes. Tommy wanted to take our son fishing. They'd left when he got home from work on Friday and they were going to camp out in a tent and spend all day Saturday on the lake. Saturday night came, and they never showed up. I got scared and worried. The lake where they'd gone fishing was a few miles away so I went to a friend's across the street to see if somebody could drive me out there." She broke off and when she spoke again, her voice was hoarse and thick with tears. "It was too late. Even if I'd gotten there earlier..."

"Werewolves."

"Yes." She nodded. "I was walking around, looking for Tom and Robbie, calling them. I heard this howl. Then a scream. They killed my friend, Tina. I heard her screaming and I ran, but by the time I got there, she was already dead. And then they came for me."

He'd always sucked at this part. Hell, as far as he was concerned, he sucked at all of it. But this was the worst, comforting the victims when he had nothing warm or comforting inside him to offer. And even though it had been a good fifty years, Phoebe was definitely still a victim. In a tight, rusty voice, he said, "You have to know there's nothing you could have done to help them."

"That doesn't make it any easier." She sighed, rubbed a hand across her chest as though it hurt.

Kel imagined it did. Broken hearts weren't just about emotional pain, but also physical. That was a lesson he'd learned in spades. "No." His voice was hollow as he responded, "No, it doesn't." Looking back at the picture he held in his hands, he rubbed a finger across Phoebe's image.

She looked happy.

In love.

Complete.

A whisper of sound drifted to him. Slowly, he lifted his gaze, watched as she turned around and stared at him. "I've been dead inside for longer than you've been alive," she said softly. "Am I wrong?"

Kel shook his head. Even though he could argue that he wasn't alive anymore, he didn't see the point. She must have been born sometime in the 1940s. Hell, his parents hadn't even been alive in the '40s. Shit, he'd just fucked a woman who technically was about the same age his grandparents would have been, if any of them had been alive.

Crossing over to him, she moved with a slow sinuous rhythm that called to mind the predator that lived under her skin. Eyes bright and half-wild, she said, "You look like you're in the same place as me. Alive on the outside...but in your heart, you're dead." Gently, she took the picture frame from him and set it aside before reaching up and curling a hand around his neck, pulling him down with surprising strength. "I can't feel guilt or shame over this, Kel. I won't let you make me. This is the only time I feel alive. So I like a little pain. A little blood. At least I'm still capable of feeling something. And at least I never turned into the kind of monster that did this to me, to my family."

Her eyes glittered with a queer light. His slowed heart skipped a few beats, sped up as they stared at one another. Then, abruptly, she shoved him away and said, "You better go.

Dawn isn't too far away."

Chapter Three

The alarm blared into the silence, the hard, driving sounds of classic Aerosmith blaring from the speakers. Rolling onto her side, Angel Pierson smacked at the snooze button and she ended up knocking her iPod off the docking station.

"Shit." Eyes gritty with fatigue, her entire body aching from head to toe, she rolled upright.

The iPod lay face down on the hardwood floor, numerous little dings and scratches on the shiny silver back attesting to just how often she subjected it to such treatment.

Angel was not a morning person.

There'd been a time when she'd loved mornings and sunrises, but it was so long ago, it was almost like another life.

Hell, it was another life.

A life with Kel. The way her life was supposed to be. Like a mirage, she saw the memory of old visions flicker before her eyes. A happy life. One where she married the man she loved, the only man she ever would love.

That life was a fairytale now, something that would never happen. She didn't want another man. She didn't want to fall in love, even if she could. She'd spent her life alone and she was just fine with that. Even if it meant growing old alone, because nothing was worth risking the agony she'd experienced when Kel disappeared. Nothing.

Besides, deep inside, in a place that went even deeper than what she felt in her heart, she knew that she was only meant to fall in love with one man. Trying to make any sort of relationship with another when Kel was all she could think about, how fair was that?

For years, she'd deluded herself into believing that maybe one day, Kel would come back to her. But that had been just another fairytale.

He'd been officially declared dead five years ago and his case remained unsolved. The few clues had been worthless to the police, a blood trail that police dogs had followed into the woods a good five miles from Angel's childhood home, and then the trail went cold. The dogs had searched the woods for a good twenty-four hours trying to find a trail, but there was nothing.

Inside her house, there'd been plenty of physical evidence that had given the cops hope, but most of the blood had come from her or Kel. She'd learned later, months later, that there had been trace evidence, most likely from the intruder, but somehow every last bit of it had disappeared from the lab, leaving the cops empty-handed.

No eyewitnesses—not even Angel, because she couldn't remember much of anything from that night. Neither had her step-siblings or the girl who'd spent the night with Lindsey. The three kids had slept through the entire attack, waking in the morning with no memory of anything.

Angel's own memories were so vague, so unclear, they hadn't been any help. Memories of fear. Memories of pain. Then Kel's face. Waking in the morning and feeling...something. It wasn't that he had felt gone, exactly, but she couldn't feel him the way she'd always been able to, either.

It had been that feeling that had lulled her into believing Kel would come back to her, that he'd show up someplace, hurt...but alive. But the first week passed, then the second...by the third, she'd fallen into a fit of depression so severe, she'd ended up hospitalized over it.

The night Jake had found her, he had no idea how close she'd come, no idea that when he knocked on her door, she'd been standing in the kitchen, holding a knife and admiring the way it glinted under the light, wondering how it would look if she pressed it to her wrist and slashed.

Blood... It called to her and she'd been obsessed with seeing how it would look trickling down her skin, how it would smell, how it would feel.

When she wasn't thinking about blood or fighting a deep inner rage, she was caught up thinking about Kel. Thinking about him hurt so much, she'd been willing to turn to anything, just to get away.

Even her compulsive obsession with blood had been better than the pain. But then, like it had just been waiting for her, that obsession got stronger, stronger, and eventually, it overtook her thoughts. She couldn't make herself quit thinking about it.

It had started when Kel disappeared.

Months later, her obsession with blood had damn near caused her to slit her wrists. Not so much to kill herself, she didn't think...at least not at that moment. But to see the blood.

She dreamed of it, both awake and asleep. She dreamed...vivid, consuming dreams of blood, thoughts and needs that felt so alien, intruding on her, overtaking her, overwhelming her until they were all she could think about, all she could see. She'd wake craving the taste of it and with every passing day, she drifted further and further away from sanity.

It was nothing short of a miracle that she'd come back.

By the time she had finally gotten herself steady, Kel's case was all but dead in the eyes of the law. It hadn't been officially closed then, but with nothing but dead ends, Angel had known. Even without the cops coming right out and saying so, she'd known.

A rash of violence had plagued Greenburg for the two days following Kel's disappearance. Another teenager nearly died of blood loss after something attacked her and tried to rip her throat out. Outside of town, the police found the body of a dead hitchhiker.

But after those two days, it had all stopped.

Just like her life, it seemed.

A cold, wet nose brushed against her bare calf and she looked down to see a pair of soulful brown eyes gazing up at her over the rim of a blue plastic food dish. "Hey, Rufus," she murmured, reaching out to scratch the dog behind his ears.

Rufus was a big, ugly mutt, but as lovable as the day was long. She spent many a night cuddled up against him, her face buried in his thick fur as she cried herself to sleep. He was also a present from her current employer.

Jake Saunders.

Sometimes she wondered why she tortured herself like this, working for the father of her dead lover. It wasn't like she couldn't find another job. A better-paying one. It wasn't like she needed the heartbreak.

But he needed her.

Kel was gone, and less than two years after Kel had disappeared, Meredith had been killed. In the past twelve years, the man looked like he'd aged fifty years. He'd just turned fifty-five a month ago, but he looked like he was in his seventies. Frail, stooped and bent.

After a debilitating stroke two years ago, he'd retired from the church where he'd preached for nearly thirty years. The stroke kept him from driving, but not from walking, not from talking.

Not from hoping.

Being face-to-face with that hope almost every day was destroying something inside Angel, in what little remained of her heart. But she couldn't turn away from Jake. She owed him her life, as pathetic as it was, because he'd reached her just before she lost herself completely.

Even though it was a lonely, miserable life, it had to be better living it as a rational—or mostly rational woman, instead of locked in some mental facility. Or dead.

Angel was too stubborn to let herself contemplate how much easier things would be, how the pain would have stopped long ago if Jake hadn't pulled her back from the edge. She might not love her life, but it had a purpose.

Even if that purpose was just caring for Kel's dad.

All in all, it was as good a reason to go on as anything. Jake needed help, and Angel would give it. Because he was Kel's dad. She couldn't have walked away from this any easier than she could have stopped loving Kel—dead or not, it didn't matter. She still loved him.

Still dreamed of him.

Still cried for him.

Still hurt for him.

Because she loved him so much, she knew she couldn't walk away from his father. For as long as Jake needed her, she'd be around. Kel wasn't there to take care of his dad, but Angel was. So she would.

Driving him to the store, to the doctor's office, helping him with his physical therapy, transcribing his dictated notes onto the computer. Whether or not Jake would ever try to publish the long, rather sad story of his life, she didn't know.

But telling it was therapeutic for him. She knew that.

She just wished it was as therapeutic for her, plunking out details about Kel's life, from his birth to a death that came way too early. Pair that with the fact that Jake still had hopes that Kel was alive, that he'd come back—shit, it hurt.

Rufus whined and nosed her leg again. Sighing, Angel muttered, "Yeah, I know." Shoving out of the bed, she shuffled to the bathroom.

It wasn't even seven in the morning, way too early for her to want to be awake. But if she stayed in bed too long, she'd never make it to Jake's before the old man decided to try his hand at making breakfast again.

She shuddered, recalling the last attempt. Since the stroke, Jake had a problem with short-term memory. He would start breakfast and then wander off. It wasn't until the bacon would burn, the biscuits turned to charcoal and every smoke detector in the house was going off that he'd remember he'd left the oven on.

The last time it had happened, she'd walked into the kitchen with Rufus just as a grease fire was starting. Thinking about how close Jake had come to setting his home on fire, Angel had made the decision to start taking care of breakfast, as well as lunch and dinner.

Sundays tended to be her only days off. God love them, the women's committee at Jake's old congregation had settled into a routine where one of them would come for Jake in the morning for breakfast and then church, followed by lunch and usually dinner.

You should come with us sometime, Angel. It would do you a world of good.

No, thanks.

Angel believed in God, but she completely lacked Jake's steadfast patience. After losing her dad, then Kel...then

Meredith, watching as Jake grew old, sick and feeble, Angel decided she was too pissed off at God to consider stepping foot inside a church.

Not to mention that half of the women there had some freaky idea of trying to pair Angel up with the young preacher who had taken over Jake's position. Seth Roberts was a nice guy, pretty nice to look at, but he left her cold.

Every man did.

With a flick of her wrist, she turned on the shower. As steam started to billow out, she stripped out of the T-shirt and panties she slept in. She climbed into the shower and lifted her face to the spray, let the water sluice over her and wash away the cobwebs.

Cold. That pretty much described how she felt damn near all the time. The only time she felt warmth was in dreams she couldn't quite remember. Even now, with the hot pulse of water beating down on her, she was chilled.

What she wouldn't give to feel warm and safe again. It was a comfort that had been denied to her since awaking in the hospital to find Kel's parents at her bedside, watching her with tearful, hopeful eyes.

She'd dashed those hopes when she told them she didn't know what happened, that she couldn't remember the attack, or anything about Kel. She couldn't explain the blood loss, she couldn't explain her bruises.

Her attack was another mystery because she'd been admitted to the hospital for massive blood loss, treated for blood loss—responded to that treatment—but there hadn't been hardly a mark on her. A couple of punctures at her neck, but nowhere near the jugular and certainly not deep enough to explain the blood loss.

She didn't have any answers about her attack or about what had happened to Kel.

He'd tried to save her. She didn't need the memory to know that. He'd tried to save her from...something...whatever or whoever had attacked her and it had gotten him.

Because of her, he was dead. Cold, lonely misery was the least she deserved.

Slumping against the shower wall, she wrapped her arms

around her body and started to rock. "Kel..." Sinking down to the floor, she huddled there and whispered his name again.

Images that she couldn't quite make sense of flashed before her eyes. Someplace dark, the pulse of music throbbing, a woman's face—

Blood.

Her mouth watered and for a few moments, the bathroom faded away and she was someplace dark. Someplace warm. The taste of blood filled her mouth...

Outside the shower door, Rufus barked.

Jerking herself back into awareness, Angel shoved to her feet and hurriedly washed her hair, her body. The spray of water went cold before she finished but it didn't matter. She was already so chilled it wouldn't make a difference.

Nobody knew the bizarre hallucinations that had plagued her after Kel's death had never completely gone away. Back in the black days that separated her old life from the life she lived now, those dark, awful days plagued by inhuman urges and hungers, the hallucinations had seemed too vivid to not be real.

Now they weren't so strong, but the fascination was still there. She'd wake in the night to the sound of her own heartbeat, or at least it seemed that way, so painfully aware of the sound. She could be walking through a store and realize she was staring at the throats of the people around her, thinking about the rhythm of their pulse, the warmth of flesh.

Mindful of how hypnotic those unwanted thoughts were, Angel had taken to wearing a thick rubber band around one wrist. When she realized she was daydreaming about blood, almost running through the woods, chasing after some unknown prey, she'd snap the rubber band. That small, sharp pain helped her clear her head, helped her focus.

There were days when she'd have red welts on her wrist from it.

It had been really bad the past few days. Seriously bad. Even the sight of somebody's throat was enough to have her mouth watering. She'd promised herself last night if it got worse, she was going to make an appointment. She'd stopped going to therapy years ago, but when she found herself this close...

Oddly enough, though, this morning, it was better.

Easier.

Her mind seemed more like her own as she stepped out of the shower and went to inspect her pale, wan face. Her eyes were puffy from her crying jag, but that was nothing new. Sometimes she could go days without crying.

But then others...

Time heals all wounds.

"Not in my book," she muttered. Time hadn't healed her.

She'd never quite managed to get her appetite back after Kel had disappeared and she was still reed-thin, too thin. The ache in her heart hadn't ever gotten easier to handle and even the years she'd spent taking antidepressants hadn't helped.

It was like she just wasn't capable of letting go.

And after twelve years, she didn't expect that to change.

Chapter Four

Age 32

The cool air drifting through the open window dried the sweat on his body. It wasn't his—but Phoebe's. Vampires didn't sweat. They also didn't get cold too easily. They never got hot. He did like the warm feel of Phoebe's small, delicate form plastered up against his cooler body.

"Happy Birthday," she whispered, her voice soft, drowsy.

A faint smile curled his lips. "I don't count birthdays any more," he reminded her. He'd told her that the first time she'd asked him about his birthday, and the second, and the third...and when she'd finally snooped in his wallet and found the fake ID he carried, she'd asked him if that was his real birthday.

Pretty much every Hunter had a fake ID. They came in handy. They tried to keep the facts as close to their own personal data as they could, and when somebody at the enclave had gotten the fake ID for Kel, they'd used his birth date...minus ten years. There was no way he could pass for somebody in his thirties. He'd be lucky to pass for twenty-five.

"It's the day I was born, but I don't celebrate birthdays," he'd told her. Birthdays were for the living...not dead men walking. And no matter what Phoebe said, that was how he saw himself.

It didn't have so much to do with the vampire crap, legends of the undead or any of that shit. At least not as much any more. He just felt dead inside. He didn't look forward to the beginning of a new day, or the end of one. He didn't look forward to feeding, he didn't look forward to sex, he didn't look forward to life.

He didn't have a life.

Unless he was on the Hunt, speeding down the highway on his bike, or tearing up the sheets—literally—with Phoebe, he felt dead inside.

It wasn't really even Phoebe who made him feel alive, either, and she probably knew it. It was the way they pushed each other, hovering just on the edge of sheer madness, the way they used pain to bring that false sense of life.

After nearly a year of this, Kel had managed to stop feeling so guilty every time he gave in and came to her. She'd become his regular feeding companion, or as much as he'd let himself have one, although he still never came over more than once a month. More often than not, he had to force himself to do it even then, although once he got here and she put her hot little hands on his body, urging him on, he did grow a bit more enthusiastic.

Kel was still young enough as a vamp that he needed to feed once or twice a week if he wanted to keep the hunger under control, but those feeds were quick and anonymous. Finding a lonely woman in a bar, buying her a few drinks, having a few dances and then coaxing her into the shadows. One thing about Phoebe was that time he spent with her was enough to keep his sex drive under control.

Under control so that he no longer feared feeding as much because he knew his need for sex wouldn't get the better of him. He wouldn't close his eyes and pretend he was making love to Angel, and then drown in the instinctive surge of guilt once he'd satisfied himself, guilt over making love to a woman who wasn't Angel, guilt over using some anonymous woman and pretending she was somebody else.

They never remembered him come morning. A vampire's bite healed quickly thanks to the enzymes in their saliva. Although the bite itself wasn't gone in the blink of an eye, it healed quicker than wounds generally did and a lightly placed compulsion kept the woman from even thinking about the bite, had her hiding it without understanding why until even the faintest mark was gone. Generally, it just took a few days.

No harm. No foul. They didn't get used for anything other than a few sips of blood they'd never miss, and he didn't walk away from it feeling like a man betraying his wedding vows.

Not that he had ever gotten around to asking Angel to marry him. He hadn't had the chance... Closing his eyes, he reached up and touched the gold chain around his neck. But it didn't matter in his heart. Heart and soul, he belonged to Angel Pierson and making love to another woman was wrong.

What he did with Phoebe wasn't about love—hell, half the time he didn't even think it was about sex. It was about meeting a need that could destroy him if it wasn't satisfied. Since he'd met her, Kel hadn't fallen back into one of his black moods that lasted for weeks on end, and he hadn't made Rafe or any of the others so fucking mad they ended up going at each other like mortal enemies.

Regular feeds had put some seriously needed weight on his lean frame. Even if he still had an eternally young face, at least he didn't have that awful, stretched-out gaunt look any more.

The regular feeds, the regular sex made his existence a little less miserable. And sometimes Phoebe even made him smile. Made him laugh.

He didn't love Phoebe. She didn't love him.

But he did care about her.

Cared about her enough to see the faint hurt in her eyes as she pushed up onto her elbow and saw him toying with the ring he'd bought for Angel. He let go of it, but didn't apologize. She met his eyes and forced a smile.

"You really should get rid of that," she said, her voice soft, gentle.

A muscle ticked in his jaw. Instead of jerking away the way he wanted to, he put his arm under his head, pillowing it on his palm as he met her gaze dead on and replied, "You still keeping those pictures tucked away in that trunk?"

A grimace twisted her rosebud lips. "Guilty." Sighing, she lowered her head and rested it on his chest. "But I don't carry them around with me day after day. I don't look at his face while I lay next to you after we've made love."

Made love...

This time, Kel couldn't stop himself from pulling away. He jackknifed out of the bed and walked away, not looking back at her until he'd put the length of the room between them. Slowly, he shook his head. "We don't make love, Phoebe. We fuck each other's brains out, we hurt each other."

Phoebe slid out of the bed, a strange smile on her lips as she stalked him across the room. But there was no other way to describe that predatory prowl or that predatory look in her eyes. "Yeah. We do, and you love it."

"No. I don't love it—but I do need it."

"Need it...need me. Can't you even admit it?" she asked.

What in the hell... He didn't know where this was coming from. Phoebe came to a halt before him, slicking her tongue across her lips, sliding her hands up over her hips, her sides, until she could cup her breasts in her palms. As she squeezed her nipples, she stared at him and her smile turned decidedly wicked as his cock stiffened, hardened.

"You can't do without this," she whispered. "No more than I can. You need it...you need it to forget about her, whoever she was. Let her go, Kel. Whoever she is. She's not meant for you, not anymore."

She leaned into him, but instead of kissing him, she pressed her mouth to his shoulder and bit down. Sharp teeth pierced his flesh and Kel groaned, battling back the surge of lust, fighting the need to grab Phoebe, shove her to her hands and knees and take the little wildcat until she was too busy screaming to talk.

But something inside him was sounding an alarm bell.

Phoebe had been acting...off ever since he'd showed up at her door two days ago. Off enough that he'd changed his mind about spending the weekend with her, but when he'd started getting his stuff together a little before dawn, she'd slid up behind him. In her hand, she'd held the reinforced cuffs Hunters carried on patrol and when she'd put them on his wrists and then went down on her knees in front of him, he'd stopped using his head to think and let his dick handle things.

Bad mistake.

Gritting his teeth, he reached up, laying his hands on Phoebe's shoulders, trying to ease her back. She wasn't in any hurry to take her teeth out of him though and he ended up fisting a hand in her short dark hair and jerking. She bit down harder as he pulled her away and pain slashed through him.

"Damn it, Phoebe."

She smiled up at him, his blood staining her mouth. "You know you need it..."

The alarm bells turned into a siren's screech. Shouldering past her, he grabbed his jeans from the back of the chair but before he could jerk them on, Phoebe lunged for him, tearing them away.

"What the..."

Dropping the jeans, she swiped out, her eyes narrowed. Kel saw where she was looking and he deflected her arm with one hand as he closed his free hand around the chain. "Phoebe, what in the hell is your problem?"

"My problem?" she asked, stopping in her tracks and staring at him like he was speaking another language. "My problem is that I'm tired of seeing you touch that damn ring when you're laying in bed with me, still wet with me, my blood inside you and my body still aching from what we did to each other."

Her words sent a hot stab of guilt shooting through him. Keeping an eye on her, he grabbed the jeans she'd dropped and dragged them on, pulling them up over naked hips. He could smell her on him...but the scent of her didn't appeal to him. It didn't bother him exactly, but it didn't feel right.

It...

It felt wrong.

This is wrong. It was an abrupt realization and not one he cared for. He'd thought... Hell, screw what he'd thought. Yeah, he had feelings for Phoebe but they wouldn't ever be anything more. He liked her. Yeah, from time to time, she made him laugh, made him forget his misery for a short time. His life had been a little easier since he'd met her.

But he didn't love her—he couldn't love her. He'd thought she was in the same messed-up boat, but something about the way she was looking at him had him damn uneasy.

"You knew pretty much from the get-go that I was a mess, Phoebe," he said, trying to keep his voice soft and gentle.

He really didn't want to hurt her. But, as he stood there and stared into her eyes, he realized he wouldn't be able to avoid it.

The bitter, acrid scent of her pain stung his nostrils and he watched as she rapidly blinked away tears forming in her eyes. She sniffed, moving her shoulders in a small shrug.

"I'm not asking you to tell me you love me, Kel."

But something about the way she looked at him made him doubt the truth of those words.

That, accompanied by the way her heartbeat spiked, the way the scent in the air around her changed ever so slightly. She gave him a wobbly smile, holding out a hand.

"I...I just want you to actually be here with me...not thinking about her."

Instead of reaching for her hand, Kel reached out, cupped her cheek. "Phoebe, I'm sorry." He sighed, rubbed his thumb across her cheekbone, stared into her dark, turbulent eyes. "I know what you want me to say—or what you're hoping I might say sooner or later. But it won't ever happen."

Phoebe flinched, jerking away from him. "You can't know that."

Shoving his hands into his pockets, he watched as she started to prowl the room, pacing it with slow, measured paces that wouldn't have been so disturbing if it wasn't for the way her eyes kept going back and forth between human and—not.

Shifters always threw off a lot of energy, but Kel realized he hadn't been with Phoebe with the full moon so close. Two days away. A lot of pent-up energy compressed into that small package—a lot of emotion and precious little control.

Hell, if given a choice, he'd rather deal with a pissed-off werewolf two days away from the full moon than a woman who'd convinced herself there was something deep between them.

He didn't know where all that emotion was coming from and he didn't know how to handle it. He couldn't give her the pretty lie she seemed to want, though.

Almost like she was aware of every last thought trolling through his mind, Phoebe turned and met his gaze. That sexy, challenging smile curled her lips and she shifted her focus. From her anger and whatever else was driving her...to him. Her large, dark brown eyes suddenly glowed a pale gold and when she smiled at him, her teeth glinted white and sharp—sharper.

Longer, decidedly so.

"I didn't think I could say it either, Kel. Not until you. Not until the past few months," she whispered, pacing towards him, placing one foot in front of the other, her hips moving with an exaggerated sway, like every last move she made was intent on seduction.

But Kel knew it wasn't an intentional thought. Phoebe, for whatever reason, had it in her head that she'd gone and fallen in love with him. She was acting on instinct and trying to respond to those urges.

"Everything about you is different." Her gaze dropped and she stared at the necklace around his neck, anger flickering in those dark brown depths—and for the briefest moment, there was a flash of red.

Mother *fuck.*

Her gaze slowly lifted back to his and that anger he'd glimpsed was gone, replaced by yearning. Her voice was husky soft as she murmured, "Every day I see you, I want more from you, of you, from us."

Falling back a few steps, Kel curled a protective hand around the ring at his neck. "I can't give you any more, Phoebe." He shook his head as she moved to him and laid a hand on his cheek.

"Sure you can. Just..."

Kel reached up and closed his fingers around her wrist, easing her back. "There is no just. Just taking some more time won't do it. Just not thinking about it won't do it."

With a care he rarely showed her, he lifted her wrist and pressed a kiss to the soft skin on the inside. "Goodbye, Phoebe."

She flinched as though he'd slapped her and then jerked back. Her hands balled into fists as she stood there and glared at him, her body vibrating with fury.

"Goodbye?" she repeated, her eyes wide.

Kel didn't bother saying it again. Instead, he grabbed his shirt and shoes and headed for the door. But Phoebe got there before he did, staring at him, enraged.

"Goodbye?" She snarled at him and when she spoke again, her voice was disturbingly deeper. "You can't just walk away like this, Kel. Damn it, you need me. Don't you remember how fucked up you were before you found me? I made you live again."

In a soft, quiet voice, he said, "Phoebe, don't do this."

He saw the intent in her eyes and didn't bother to move away. Unintentionally or not, he'd hurt her. Somehow, he'd given her reason to think there could ever be anything more between them. So when she struck out and slashed her hand down his chest, he stood there and let her.

Rage was taking control of her, evidenced by the fact that her nails were no longer nails—more like short, wickedly sharp claws, sharp enough that she tore flesh and drew blood. It trickled unchecked down his chest and abdomen and he watched as her gaze dropped low, eying his bloodied chest with greed.

"You need this. *We* need it." Phoebe licked her lips and reached for him. "You need me, Kel...admit it."

He caught her wrists and held her back when she would have pressed her mouth to his chest. "I can't tell you what you want to hear from me, Phoebe. I can't give it to you."

Her body shuddered. Her head dropped. Kel didn't let her go though. The air around her rippled and a powerful sense of foreboding washed over him.

She threw her head back and when she stared at him, her eyes had gone black. Black and pupilless in her pretty, elfin face and as he stared at her, she started to shift. Changing under his hands. Smooth, soft skin rippled, almost like it was melting—then it stiffened, expanded and short thick hair spread across her flesh. He could hear her bones cracking as they realigned.

She grew, her slim form becoming large, bulky until she stood tall enough to stare him square in the eye. It was a quick shift, although the seconds seemed to tick by in slow, unending agony for Kel.

He let her go but didn't back away as the shift completed. Kel hadn't seen her shift before and for most, the big, hulking brute of a wolf-creature standing so close would probably be as intimidating as hell.

But all Kel felt was guilt and a faint sense of self-censure.

Partly for not recognizing just how fragile Phoebe's state of mind was. And partly for not realizing he'd been running this risk and not even thinking twice about it.

She cocked her head and stared at him. Her face looked like a badly rendered version of a Hollywood movie monster. But then, werewolves in this form weren't the prettiest creatures in his experience. She breathed out and her breath whispered over him in a scalding hot caress.

She lifted a hand, reached out, touched his chest, but it wasn't with the intent to hurt. Kel would have been happier if she had. He reached up and caught her wrist yet again. "I'm not into the furry sex scene, Phoebe."

"You need me."

Even in that deeper, growling voice, he would have to be deaf not to hear the plea. Even in her altered form, he'd have to be blind not to see the loneliness and pain in her gaze. It was so damn clear to him—*now.*

Why hadn't he been able to see it before now?

"We're not doing this," he said, shaking his head when she eased forward. Although her body was larger, obviously more powerful, it was still clearly female, her torso covered by a pelt of short, fine fur before thickening out on her limbs.

"We aren't normal people anymore, Kel. We can't *have* normal lives. We can't *have* normal things." Stroking one clawed digit down his chest, Phoebe rasped in her changed voice, "But we can have each other. We can have this."

Kel's fingers tightened around her wrist. In this form, it was easily three times as wide, probably as thick around as his own. The fine, silky fur was incongruously soft and on the deadly black curve of her claws, he could see the remnants of the blood-red polish she loved to slick on her nails.

Keeping his voice as gentle as he could, Kel said, "But I don't *want* this." He eased her wrist away and she jerked back, recoiling a few steps. Her shoulders slumped, her head bowed.

She stood there, utterly dejected.

For a moment, he thought it was done.

Turning, he headed out the door, his shirt and shoes still in hand. Out in the hall, the music from the club floor was louder, more vibrant, a hard, driving beat. He'd just made it back into the club when a whisper of warning danced along his spine. Her rage flooded the air and as though the rest of the bar's occupants sensed the rage, on the other side of the door, the music ended abruptly.

Talking ceased.

In the doorway, he stilled and turned, one hand resting on the doorjamb as he looked back. Still in the wolf-creature form, she rushed him. He evaded her first attack, dropping his shirt and shoes to the ground, and turned to meet her. "I don't want to do this, Phoebe."

"Too fucking bad—you don't want to do what *I* want. So we do this," she snarled. Her words were thicker, even deeper than they had been moments ago. Fury wrapped around her, tainting everything.

Tainting her.

"I don't like hurting women, Phoebe," he said, keeping his voice soft and low. It was nothing more than the truth. It wasn't unavoidable but it never failed to leave him with a bad taste in his mouth.

And this was worse.

"You think you can *hurt* me?" she jeered. "Fucking stiff. Only been one of us for ten years... I've been this way longer than you've been alive. And you think *you* can hurt *me?*"

Kel didn't bother wasting his breath explaining something that was obvious to him. He was a Hunter. He didn't *think* he could hurt her. He knew he could.

Some enterprising soul apparently felt sorry for her. The guy who pushed between Phoebe and Kel was on the short side, balding, with a friendly smile. "You don't want to pick a fight with a Hunter, kid," he said. He shot Kel a nervous glance over his shoulder and then looked back at Phoebe. "Nothing but trouble doing that."

Phoebe snarled at him and struck out, attempting to knock him back. "Mind your own business." She went around him and the good Samaritan gave her a faintly pitying look before melting back into the background.

Stalking up to him, she moved to strike again. As before, he slid away, sidestepping and moving around until he was behind her. She snarled, spun to face him, struck again. One obsidian claw caught his bare shoulder and once more, the scent of his own blood filled his nostrils.

It was enough to piss him off, but he still couldn't move past the bitter regret and guilt choking him. "Phoebe, this isn't you. The full moon's too close," he said, although he didn't entirely believe it. "You're letting it cloud things for you."

Her lips peeled back from her teeth, revealing a long, jagged line of teeth that bore no resemblance to anything human. "How would you know? You only want to be with me long enough to fuck me."

If he'd still been human, he would have blushed. As it was, several eyes slanted his way and he could feel it, it was enough to have his skin crawling with embarrassment. "I never made you think there could be anything more than that," he said, shaking his head.

Phoebe growled. Slowly, she sank to the floor and crouched there but it was in no way a good sign. He could see it, the slow, smooth coiling of her muscles. He braced himself.

When she lunged this time, he didn't move out of the way. He reached out, caught her by the throat and lifted her until her feet left the ground. Her furred body arched, contorted. She spat and snarled, clawed at his hands.

Something inside him unfurled. That dreaded, hated part of him. It wasn't strong yet and Kel hated to think what it would be like when it *was* strong. It was fear—but not his own. A nasty little magic trick, as far as he was concerned, something that let him use fear to cow those around him and he despised it. It rolled out of him and his peripheral vision revealed the effect as many of those gathered around them automatically fell back a few feet.

Not all of them. But enough.

It hit Phoebe full force and she whimpered, cried. As her rage dissolved into fear, her body started to shift. Kel's self-disgust escalated and he lowered her to her feet, letting go.

By the time her shift was complete, he was a good five feet away. He focused, dragged his shields back up, forcing the dangerous, deadly weapon of fear back into submission. "We're not doing this," he said quietly.

It didn't matter. Every damn person in the joint had the

96

same super-sensitive hearing that he and Phoebe did.

Phoebe stood there, her arms wrapped around her naked, trembling body. Sighing, Kel searched the floor for his shirt and then moved to grab it. The people standing near it fell back away from him. He paused, swore under his breath and then grabbed the shirt, carried it over to Phoebe. She stared at him with wide, dark eyes set in a face still pale with fear. Gently, he draped it over her shoulders and eased her arms into the sleeves, buttoning enough of the buttons so that it would stay closed.

"Go upstairs. Lay down," he suggested, dipping his head so he could whisper the words into her ear. "You don't love me, Phoebe. You don't really even need me...you just want to think you do."

She sobbed and tore away, glaring at him. "You can't tell me what I *feel*, Hunter. You can make me scared, but you can't make me not love you."

Darting into the crowd, she lost herself amongst the throng.

Closing his eyes, Kel muttered, "Shit."

The silence in the club was deafening and when he opened his eyes, he found every soul in the joint was still staring at him. He saw a range of emotions, running the gamut from derision to pity...and fear. He still saw the fear. It wasn't as prevalent as it had been before he sucked it back inside, but some of them were still feeling the effects.

Swearing, he turned on his heel, heading for the back of the club, and the exit that opened up onto an alley. The people behind him flinched as one and that didn't help his state of mind any. Ugly words boiled up his throat, but he kept them locked behind his teeth.

He'd made enough of an ass of himself tonight already.

"Hey, kid."

That low, raspy voice was the last one he wanted to hear and he would have just kept right on walking if Toronto hadn't been between him and the door. The shape-shifter was an enigmatic bastard, with pale, pale blue eyes, so pale they appeared colorless, and white-blond hair that a lot of people would pay money for. It fell past his shoulders when it was loose. Tonight he had it pulled back from his face, revealing a face that probably made women sigh. A series of platinum hoops and studs pierced his left ear and they caught the light as he cocked his head and studied Kel's face.

The sympathy in the shifter's gaze made something inside Kel go hot with fury. Toronto had gotten this weird idea in his head that he needed to look out for Kel—even when Kel started to slide out of his downward spiral, Toronto kept sticking his pretty face in where it didn't need to be.

"Get out of my way," he rasped. He was edgy, jumpy. The hunger he'd slaked earlier was back, like he hadn't fed in days, weeks. All brought on by vampiric instincts that Kel wished he didn't possess.

"You didn't do anything wrong, Kel," Toronto said quietly. "Not a damn thing." He slid his colorless gaze over the people in the bar who pretended not to watch them, pretended not to notice they were still there.

Fear colored almost every single one of them. The only ones who didn't seemed affected were a couple of the bartenders, the bouncer at the front door and a few random patrons.

Kel knew from experience the rest of the people there would carry the fading remnants of that fear for hours. Even after he was gone, they'd feel it.

"Maybe not, but I sure as hell haven't done anything right, either."

Toronto lifted a brow. "You sure? She attacked you. You would have been in your rights to fight back. The rules of the human world don't apply here."

Kel shook his head. "Just leave me the hell alone, Toronto. Okay?" Shoving past the shifter, he left the bar, escaping into the relative silence of the backstreet alley. Cool air kissed his chilled flesh and he glanced down, stared at the long furrows still marking his chest. They were mostly healed already and the blood on his skin had dried.

His feet were bare, he had blood on his chest and the woman he'd been sleeping with for the past year had attacked him.

"Shit. What a life."

Although it had been a late night, Angel found herself wide awake before it was even three a.m. She came awake on a harsh breath, a tearing pain across her chest, tears stinging her eyes...and the faintest sense of self-disgust rolling through her.

Groaning, she rolled to the side of the bed and covered her face with her hands. She had a nasty, cloying taste in the back of her mouth—the bitter tang of guilt.

Over what, she had no clue.

She felt like she'd...done something.

Hurt somebody.

Damn it, it felt sometimes like she was living some alternate life she was totally unaware of. A life that some part of her subconscious remembered...a life her subconscious wanted to punish her for.

Scrambling out of the bed, she stumbled over to the window and shoved it up. The cool, scented air of a spring night came drifting through. She could hear the call of birds and insects and beyond that, it was quiet.

After she'd finally graduated from college, a year late thanks to her walk on the less-than-sane side of life, she'd bought this tract of land and the farmhouse just because it was secluded, and because it was relatively close to town and she could get to Jake's place in under twenty minutes.

That last reason didn't matter so much anymore.

Jake was dead.

Quietly, one evening, just a month earlier, he'd passed away from a massive heart attack. One of his former parishioners had been visiting—had gotten up to use the restroom and when she came out, Jake was gone. Suddenly. Too suddenly.

Angel's last solid connection to the world was gone.

Now, without anything to get her out of bed in the morning, she spent far too much time sleeping, not enough time trying to live.

All she wanted was to stay here in her isolated, run-down

house and forget. Lose herself in the silence and forget.

But she couldn't lose herself in the silence right now.

There was an echo of music pulsating through the air. The sound of a deep, angry voice. Then another voice, just as deep, but lacking the anger.

No words, though. She couldn't make out any words.

"Since when do dreams make any sense?" she mumbled, dragging a hand through her hair. It felt startlingly short. Three days ago, she'd been in town for a meeting the lawyers had insisted on, and after that little fiasco, she'd ended up wandering the streets until she came to a halt in front of the barber where Jake used to get his hair cut.

Where Kel had come for his irregular appointments. Out of the blue, she'd decided she wanted her hair cut. The man hadn't been too thrilled—he'd looked at her like she was asking for something in Greek. Finally, he had rubbed his jaw and replied, "This ain't the beauty parlor, Miz Angel. If you want a new hairstyle, maybe you should go see..."

It had taken her five minutes to get him to stop worrying and just cut. Her hair, once down to her waist, was short, short enough to barely brush her shoulders. It felt weird and when she looked at herself in the mirror, she didn't quite recognize herself.

But she barely recognized herself anyway anymore. What did a physical change matter?

Pushing the shortened strands out of her face, she leaned forward. With her brow resting against the window pane, she sighed. Cool air drifted in through the opened lower half of the window, dancing along flesh left bare by the tank top and panties she wore in lieu of pajamas.

She shivered but didn't close the window. She needed the cool, early-spring air to clear the fog in her brain, a fog brought on by far too many nights like this.

You look exhausted, Angel. Maybe you should see about getting something to help you sleep.

Jake had been telling her that for years. But until recently, she hadn't bothered. She hadn't cared enough if she slept or not. The past year, things had leveled out a little. Those violent, gory dreams that faded even before she woke enough to fully remember them weren't as vivid as they had once been.

The edgy mood that so often plagued her, the anger at nothing, it had gotten better, as well.

But as those got better, the depression riding her got worse. Jake's sudden, unexpected death made *everything* worse and she'd finally given in and gone to the doctor. She'd left with two prescriptions and a gentle reminder to consider getting help.

Help. Like that would do any good.

She missed Kel more now than ever. How that was possible she didn't know. But every morning, it seemed a bit harder to get up and every night took a little longer to fall asleep. It was like her body's need for sleep was decreasing regularly.

Sometimes she wondered if she'd sleep at all in another five or ten years.

Her body might not need the sleep, but Angel sure as hell did. Her brain might not want to shut down to rest, but she *needed* it.

So she'd given in and talked to her doctor, gotten some sleeping pills.

Supposedly, the pills were less likely to cause dependence. Definitely a good thing, because the last damn thing Angel needed in her fucked-up head was an addiction to sleeping pills. But so far, she hadn't taken one.

The bottle was sitting on her dresser, along with samples of the antidepressant she knew she wouldn't take. Dr. C. Jane Miller had listened politely while Angel explained she didn't need medicine for depression—then she'd handed Angel a pamphlet and a bag of sample medications, along with the prescription for the sleeping pills.

Angel had no desire to take the antidepressant. Not because she didn't think she was depressed. She was. She knew it. But the cause of her depression was a loss she'd never recover from—taking something that increased this chemical or decreased that one, wasn't going to do a damn thing to help her get over Kel.

But she was going to take the sleeping pills. It was Saturday morning, she had no sweet old man waiting for her to come and keep the loneliness at bay, no sexy young man who'd be waiting for her when she woke up.

Nothing. And nobody.

Maybe, just maybe, she could pop a pill, collapse on her bed and get some sleep.

Preferably a deep, dreamless sleep.

Chapter Five

Kel awoke feeling it.

Two days after things with Phoebe went straight to hell, Kel woke to feel something pulling at him. Strong, demanding and determined to be obeyed.

He dressed hurriedly. Most of the Hunters had adopted a uniform of sorts, sturdy cargo pants done in basic black, close-fitting black shirt—long sleeved to keep as much skin concealed as possible—and sturdy, thick-soled boots. The shoulder holster went on over his shirt and then he put a jacket over that to conceal his weapon.

Tucking extra ammo clips into one of the pockets on his pants, he grabbed his gun, checked it and then slid the modified Beretta into the holster.

A couple of knives, one in his boot and another sheathed at his waist. After snagging a pair of reinforced cuffs, he was ready.

Slipping out of the room, he left the basement and headed to the main floor. A quick glance around told him that none of the other Hunters had felt it.

But he did. That low-level burn deep in his gut, one that would get stronger and stronger until he obeyed. Until he listened. Until he Hunted.

He was tired. His daytime slumber had been restless. Although he couldn't fight the urge to sleep yet, he didn't always sleep well. Normally, it wasn't so bad. Dreams of Angel, which really sucked, but at the same time, they soothed him. Made him feel a little closer.

But this time? Instead of falling into that deep, mostly

restful sleep, he'd kept feeling something pull at him. Like he wasn't supposed to *be* asleep.

That totally fucking pissed him off. If it was the only time he could be close to her, watching her without her knowing, drifting through her subconscious mind while he slept, then damn it, he wanted those dreams.

Odd—he'd spent twelve years waiting for something to reduce the in-living-color intensity of those dreams and the one day something did intrude? He woke resentful, tired and pissed.

Usually once the sun was nearing the western horizon, his body forced him into wakefulness, tearing him from the dreams long before he was ready. The vampire instincts took control, though, and sleeping once the sun had set was all but impossible. His body wouldn't let him.

Tonight, different story. If he could shut down a deep, basic instinct and just stay in the bed, he knew he would have slept. His body needed it, craved it.

But that low-level burn was there. That primal urge that no Hunter could ignore, pulling—like something had wrapped an unseen rope around his gut and was jerking on him.

Ignoring it wouldn't do much but bring him pain and stretch his control.

So he didn't ignore it.

He slid out of the house without speaking to anybody, although he knew both Rafe and Toronto watched him leave. He took the bike. Usually that was one thing that would ease the restlessness in him. Tonight, the powerful rumble of the bike didn't do a damn thing to help.

The restlessness wasn't just restlessness—it had grown into a full-out frenzy and if he didn't find it...

No.

Not it.

Her.

He could feel that much now. Hear a woman's scream as though he was right next to her. He kept going and going, following that internal summons all the way through town, heading for the Mississippi state line. There were no formal lines to Rafe's territory—Rafe and his Hunters followed urges into other states plenty and Kel was evidence of that. The calling a Hunter heard wasn't anything clear and defined and Kel wouldn't know where it was going to lead him until he was there.

In this case, it led him into Mississippi and along Highway 78 towards Tupelo. He left the bike in the parking lot of a crowded bar and continued on foot, following that summons. It led him to an industrial area that had definitely seen better days.

It was clearer now, that summons, coming from a big, sprawling warehouse that looked abandoned. But that was deceptive.

Kel felt something moving in there. Something living and hungry...

His skin crawled.

Foreboding choked him.

The scent of blood and pain colored the air around him in vivid, dark shades. The scent of blood didn't call to him at all, the stink of fear and pain drowning out what might have once been appealing.

Under the sour, bitter stench of violence, there was something disturbingly, distressingly familiar. It tickled his memory until Kel had no choice but to work past the abhorrence and make himself focus, make himself drag in a deep breath of the fear-tainted blood.

He went cold and for just the briefest of moments, he couldn't move. Denial wrapped itself around him, followed by some futile hope he wouldn't even allow himself to cling to. Hope was such a bitter, ugly disappointment.

Instinct took over, instinct that hadn't existed until twelve years ago. It wasn't just the instincts of a vampire—the fear coming from that place was enough to have the typical civilian vamp backing away damn quick. Definitely not vamp instinct—it was the instinct of a Hunter and while he'd do damn near anything *not* to have it, ignoring it hadn't ever been an option.

It pushed him into action. Without consciously realizing it, he slid into the shadows and cloaked himself within them. He pulled the darkness around him and used its cover as he made his way inside the warehouse.

He heard a broken, tortured moan.

It was a pitiful, faint sound and as it faded into the air, there was a laugh—icy and amused, so damn evil it made Kel's skin crawl. The part of his brain that wasn't controlled by instinct was screaming to get the hell away. That kind of evil wasn't anything he wanted to look at, anything he wanted to face, anything he wanted to fight.

A fucking failure, that was Kel. Hunter instincts, Hunter drive, and he still didn't want this fight. But he didn't turn around. He didn't leave.

There was no way he could, even when he heard her heartbeat falter, heard the rattle of her breath. It was the sound of death edging closer and Kel could even feel the chill of it looming near.

A man's voice broke into the silence, underlined by a dry edge of humor. "I told you that it was pointless to fight, darling girl. And yet...still you fight. Why is that? Unless it's to amuse me."

Kel's lips peeled back from his teeth as he heard a familiar sound, a wet *thwack* as a fist struck flesh. The only sound she made was a distant, almost non-existent moan.

He emerged from the shadows just as the feral bent down and fisted a hand in her hair.

"Let her go," he said in a flat voice. As he spoke, he also released his control on the shadows, an illusory talent some vampires had. It was all a trick of the mind, but it came in handy—muffled his presence, could cause an aversive effect where people avoided something without even realizing why.

And apparently, it worked on this one, because when his brown eyes cut towards Kel's, there was surprise in his gaze. His eyes widened and the faint, bored smile on his lips widened. Dropping his victim to the ground, he stepped over her...like she was so much garbage.

Something about the feral's features, the way he moved, was disturbingly familiar but Kel didn't know where he had seen this guy before. Hunters didn't let ferals live—if this was one Kel had fought and not killed, then Rafe would have sent another Hunter to do the job.

But he'd seen him before—

No time to worry about the past though, because the present was bearing down on him, hard and fast. Kel wasn't about to go hand-to-hand with a vampire that probably had a good century on him. Shit, if he'd known he was going to be dealing with a feral this strong, he would have enlisted help.

For vampires, strength came with age and in relative terms, Kel was just a baby compared to this fuck.

As the feral circled around him, something about the man's moves, something about that ugly sneer on his face, kept tickling at Kel's memory.

"A bit young to be out here trying to tangle with me, aren't you, boy?"

He slid a hand inside his shirt and closed it around the Beretta. Drawing it, he leveled it at the feral's brow and smiled. "I'll manage."

The feral paused, cocked his head as he peered at Kel. Something flashed in those brown eyes, curiosity. "Hmmmm... You're a cocky one, aren't you, boy?"

"Yeah, I keep hearing that."

"The Council really should be more careful."

Something cold slivered through the air. The temperature seemed to drop twenty degrees. But it didn't affect Kel. The fear that might have had some sway over him was one Kel had been trained to resist. As the temperature dropped and fear rolled through the room like a river, all Kel did was tighten his finger on the trigger.

The feral lunged to the side. Kel moved with him and when the vamp tried to circle around behind him, Kel echoed his moves.

Deja vu...

I've done this before, he thought. The feral across from him stilled, narrowed his eyes as he peered at Kel. Measuring...

They both figured it out at the same time.

Kel snarled and his finger tensed on the trigger as he stared at the feral that had forced the Change on him.

And the sick fuck laughed. That icy, cold laugh that Kel heard in his nightmares.

"You made it through the night." Abruptly, he stopped

circling around Kel and tucked his hands into his pockets, rocking back on his heels. "That damn Hunter—should have guessed he'd find you and feed you. Should have just killed you, you pathetic waste. Of course, you did slow the Hunter down a bit."

"Shut up."

The feral laughed. This time, instead of icy cold fear, the laugh seemed to emanate hot, ripe fury, stabbing into Kel's ears like little knives.

"Oh, so angry. Boy, you should *thank* me. Don't you get what you are now?"

Shoot the bastard, his common sense screamed. But he didn't want to shoot this one.

He wanted to gut him. Peel the skin from the bastard's body and then rip out his tongue.

"Put the gun away, *boy.*" The command came flying through the air, hitting Kel with leaden force.

But Kel had been able to resist twelve years ago as a human. Now? There was no way the bastard's mind tricks would work. Still...feigning dumb, dazed obedience, he holstered the gun. The feral laughed again and this time, it was warm and soft, like silk.

"That's a boy. You didn't really want to use that on me, did you?"

Honestly, Kel replied, "No."

The feral gestured to the woman lying a few feet away. Her face was awash with blood, her entire body bruised and battered. There were ugly, telltale bruises on her thighs and bite marks all over her body.

"There's not much left, but do you want a bite?"

The weight of it hit Kel a little stronger this time, a little harder. It was almost like a hand coming up between his shoulder blades and shoving him while a low, internal voice urged... *Go ahead, do it... You need it, you know that.*

He moved towards her and the rage that rolled through him almost made him snap. But he didn't turn and pounce the way he wanted—the way he *needed.* He edged forward a bit more, eying her face, the way her chest rose and fell in erratic stops and starts. The pallor. Her neck looked like she'd been chewed on by a pack of hungry, angry rats and her face was so battered, she couldn't even open her eyes.

But he recognized her...even under the bruises and the blood, he knew her. He'd know her anywhere.

"Go on..."

The voice wasn't internal this time. It was right over Kel's shoulder, murmured directly into his ear. The feral's evil beat against his skin like a cold, angry wind. He took a moment to look at her face once more, storing the memory of it in his head.

He'd need that memory to fuel him in a minute, he knew it.

He slid a hand into the belt at his waist and drew the knife, slowly, so slowly the silver-forged blade didn't even whisper against the leather. The feral's hand came up, wrapped around Kel's neck, fingers digging into flesh with cruel intent.

"Come on, boy..."

Wrapping his fist around the hilt, Kel jerked away from the restraining hand and slid in close. As he shoved the knife deep into the feral's side, for one moment, their eyes met. They stood so close, Kel could smell her blood on the feral's breath, see the tiny little striations of black in the hazel eyes.

"I stopped being a boy the night you attacked me, bastard." Jerking his knife free, he used his other hand to deliver a swift upper cut to the feral's jaw.

The feral's feet left the floor and he went sailing back but the moment he hit the ground, he was back on his feet, moving with smooth, sinuous grace. "That was a foolish move, Hunter whelp," the feral snarled, his lips peeling back from his teeth and revealing the sharp glint of fang.

"Pretty sure you said that to me once before." Kel's voice was flat, emotionless. Memories from that night, the ones he'd tried too hard to forget, surged through him. The feral moved and Kel remembered the eerie, inhuman grace from twelve years earlier.

It was still there, but Kel was no longer a nineteen-year-old boy trying to protect his girlfriend with nothing but a sterling silver letter opener. The silver knife he carried now was modeled after a K-bar, wicked sharp, and made especially for the Hunters. The metal alloy wasn't pure silver, but it didn't need to be. A wound from a silver blade wasn't going to kill unless it destroyed the heart—and a non-silver weapon would do the same.

But a silver-wrought wound hurt a hell of a lot more than the typical blade and it healed almost as slowly as a normal wound would. The feral's gaze slid from Kel's face to the blade in his hand and then back. "You don't really think you can kill me with that toy, do you?"

With a mean grin, Kel shrugged. "I wouldn't write the idea off. I did you a decent amount of damage with nothing but a letter opener, if I remember right. And a twig—hey, how's that eye feeling? Damn, I have to admit, I'm impressed. I wouldn't think an eyeball could regenerate quite so well."

A muscle in the feral's cheek twitched and his left lid flickered, almost like he was remembering the pain. "I'm going to rip your heart out of your chest and smash it. You will die this time."

Something sad, almost wistful moved through Kel and he smiled faintly. "Promise?"

There was little warning, but Kel hadn't spent the entire twelve years doing nothing but brooding. The lessons, the drills, the training, he'd taken it all in. He sensed the attack before it came and his body had him sidestepping before his brain recognized it. He slashed out, but missed.

Another lunge and this time when Kel slashed with his knife, it caught flesh. The scent of burned flesh filled the air and when Kel faced the feral once more, he saw a long, ugly slice that went downward, from brow to chin. Even the eye didn't escape unmarked—already blood was flowing.

The feral howled.

Hot, savage satisfaction flooded Kel and he smirked. "Better be careful or that eye of yours is going to end up getting ripped out."

Blood painted gory streaks across the feral's face. He wiped it out of his eyes and looked down at his hand. It was dripping with dark red blood. Hellfire glinted in his eyes as he looked up at Kel and roared.

He moved, quicker than a snake, quiet as death—but not for Kel. Kel spun around and ran to her, but it was too late. The feral straightened and flung the bloody wet mess in his hand at Kel's feet. That savage fury obliterated everything for Kel, even the desire for revenge. All he wanted was that fucking monster dead. Without blinking, he dropped his knife, drew the Beretta once more and sighted, so quick it seemed like one smooth move.

The scent of gun smoke stung his nostrils and the feral's screech was loud enough to shatter glass—but he didn't fall. Kel swore, squeezed the trigger. But the vamp slid away. He didn't disappear into the shadows the way Kel had, he simply took off, running at a speed that should have been impossible considering Kel had just plugged the bastard's chest with silver and lead.

"Missed the heart," Kel whispered.

The instinctive rage screamed at him to follow.

He couldn't though.

Her breathing had stopped.

Sinking to his knees beside her, Kel stared at that still face. Her throat was one raw, gaping wound. The silence seemed to echo, viciously loud.

No heartbeat.

No breathing.

"Phoebe, I'm so sorry," he whispered.

Angel awoke in tears.

They ran down her face, soaked her hair and her pillow. Her throat ached from the sobs trapped inside.

The vague, fleeting memory of a dream slid away even as she tried to reach out and catch it. Nothing there...nothing but a crushing weight of guilt and grief.

Useless.

Worthless.

The words seemed to whisper themselves in her ear and vaguely, so vaguely, she had some distant understanding that she'd failed. Failed somebody.

Kel... Yes, she'd failed him. But that was twelve years ago and although she hadn't moved past her grief or guilt over it, that wasn't what this was about.

This pain, it felt too fresh. Too new. Rolling onto her belly, she buried her face in her pillow and let the storm of pain take her.

There was no sense to it, no reason...and it seemed, no end. Without knowing why, without having any control over it, she lay there in her bed and sobbed. She sobbed until her throat was raw and sore, until she had no tears left to shed, and still the grief wouldn't release her.

The sun was rising when the storm finally eased. It didn't disappear. It was a weight in her chest that pressed down on her as she fought her way free from tangled sheets and blankets, a weight that made it seem impossible to stand.

When she finally did make it to her feet, she swayed. Darkness pushed in on her. As hard as it was to get moving in the morning, she'd always managed.

But today...? She couldn't even make herself take a step or two forward. Her brain didn't want to function and her limbs felt heavy and weighted. The knot in her throat was made so much worse by the hours of sobbing and when she swallowed, it felt like somebody had stabbed her with a knife.

Groaning, she tried once more to make her body move. But then she fell back on the bed and reached for the blankets, drawing them around her. Huddled under them, she lay shivering and shaking. Sleep pulled at her.

She was almost asleep...almost there—then music blared from the nightstand and hit her ears like an ice pick. She swung out with her hand, but when she hit the iPod, nothing happened.

It wasn't her alarm, she realized.

But the phone. Ringing...and ringing...and ringing... A niggling sense of responsibility made her grab it as she snuggled deeper into her nest of blankets. Shit. The yard sale.

Ronda Pickard, Jake's neighbor, was helping her with the yard sale to get rid of the stuff from Jake's house that Angel didn't want to keep or donate to the church.

With clumsy fingers, she grabbed the phone and croaked

into the handset.

"Angel, sweetie, is that you?"

"Yeah."

"Girl, you sound like hell."

"Sick," she lied. She dodged a few questions, croaked out a refusal for some lunch delivered.

"You sound terrible. Can I bring you anything?"

Angel convinced Ronda that she just needed some sleep and as she tossed the phone into the general direction of the nightstand, she muttered, "Yeah. Bring me a knife. Something to get rid of this ache. Anything..."

That was her last coherent thought before she escaped into oblivion.

But it was little escape, because even there, the pain waited.

He heard the soft knock at the door, but Kel didn't answer. For the past three hours, he'd lain on his bed, recalling the events from last night...everything from waking to feel that call, to burning Phoebe's battered, broken body.

Science made it necessary. There were physiological differences in a werewolf and too many curious souls had ended up with a dead non-mortal before them. Too many questions had already been asked.

Once, Kel was told they had buried their dead just like humans preferred. But as science evolved and both mortal and non-mortal alike began to research, it became clear to the non-mortal population that they had to protect their presence from mortals.

If there was no safe, certain way to transport their dead, then they had to burn the body. Kel knew there wasn't any way he could get Phoebe's body back to Memphis, not on a motorcycle. Instead of tracking the feral, Kel had seen to Phoebe's remains, standing beside the flames until little but ashes remained. He would have liked to burn the whole damn warehouse down, but there were too many other buildings close by, too big a risk.

With a terse call to Rafe, he told the Master what had happened and where. Rafe would get somebody out there for cleanup, and damn was there cleanup needed.

Kel had walked out of the warehouse a dazed, bloodied mess. Some of the blood was his, but most of it had come from Phoebe as he sat on the floor and held her lifeless body.

There was another knock and then the door opened. Closing his eyes, he averted his head. Sheila's footsteps were silent on the floor but he knew she was in here. The bed dipped beneath her weight as she sat on the edge and reached out, laid a hand on his arm.

"Wanna talk?" she offered, her voice soft and sad.

"No."

She sighed. "I don't imagine you do. But maybe you need to."

Laughing bitterly, he turned his head and glared at her. "Why? What the fuck will that do? It won't help me find him. It won't help her. It won't undo what that monster did..." Vivid images flashed through his mind, images he'd seen in his dreams through the long daylight hours.

"I didn't love her."

Abruptly, Kel couldn't be still any more. Jackknifing out of the bed, he stalked towards the dresser and grabbed a pair of jeans, dragged them on over naked hips before he turned and faced Sheila. "I spent the past year with her, fucking her whenever the hunger got too bad. I didn't love her—I knew I never would. But I cared about her and I was too damn blind to see that she was feeling something for me I couldn't return. And then he got ahold of her."

Sheila smoothed a lock of hair back from her face and licked her lips. Rising from the bed, she moved across the floor until she stood just a few feet away. "Rafe sent Toronto out to investigate, see if he could figure out what happened to Phoebe. She didn't show up at work the night after the fight. Told a friend she was taking off. Her stuff is gone. There's a civilian shifter, works as a cop in Tupelo and he sent word to Rafe about a car that was found outside a bar early this morning. It

was Phoebe's. The shifter recognized a werewolf's scent..."
Sheila's voice faded away and she turned her head.

"Tell me."

After taking a deep breath, she looked back at him, her
blue eyes soft with compassion. Kel didn't want compassion—
he didn't deserve it. But damn it, he needed answers.

"There was blood in the car. A lot of it. He also thought he
scented a vamp. Since Rafe's the closest Master, he sent word.
Toronto headed down there after we got that information and
he's been there since. There've been some weird deaths, looks
like the feral had himself a little playground down there."

"And Phoebe walked right into it."

Because of me.

"Kel."

He looked back at Sheila. "I didn't love her," he repeated
quietly. "Not at all. But she must have thought I did—or that I
could. When I made it clear she was wrong, she ran. From me.
From Memphis...where it was safe. And because of that, she's
dead."

"You can't blame yourself for not loving somebody, Kel."
She turned away from him and started to pace the floor.
"Look... Phoebe filled a need you have. It's a biological thing, it's
part of what we are. She *knew* vampires, Kel. She knew that sex
for a vampire is practically a need. How many vamps do you
think go to the club on a regular basis just to get laid? Not
because we necessarily *want* it, but our bodies push us to it.
Just like—"

Abruptly, she cut herself off, clamping her lips shut as
though she'd almost said something she shouldn't. The look on
her face was one of discomfort and there was a weird light in
her eyes.

"Just like what?"

"Shit." Sheila crossed her arms over her chest and hunched
her shoulders. "Look, Kel...I didn't know Phoebe, not personally.
But Rafe and I make it a habit to know what goes on here. Rafe
has to—and what affects him affects me. Phoebe had a
reputation for..."

Now Kel had a good idea what she was getting at. If he
wasn't so hollowed out inside, if he wasn't so cold and sick with

guilt and grief, he might have been a little embarrassed.

But he just didn't care.

"Reputation for liking mean, rough sex?" he offered, his voice flat and emotionless.

Frowning, Sheila said, "I wouldn't call it that. And it's not what I was getting at—at least, not exactly."

Kel shrugged. "Don't know why not. What else do you call it when two people get off on seeing who can make the other bleed more?"

Her voice gentle, she replied, "I call it dealing with a pain in the only way you know how. Kel, most of us don't come to this life that easy but we adjust. You've never been able to do that." She crossed back to him, reached up to lay a hand on his cheek.

Unwilling to accept her touch, unwilling to accept any kind of comfort, Kel jerked away. Sheila's blue gaze followed him as he slid away, moved around her.

"You feel dead inside," Sheila said. "There's not a one of us that can't see that. But Phoebe helped. You were a couple of broken souls and life got a bit easier when you two met. But that doesn't mean that you should feel guilty because you didn't love her. You *couldn't* love her, Kel. You gave your heart away a long time ago and there's nothing you can do for that."

Finally, *finally*, that gentle compassion in her voice pierced the ice shroud wrapped around his heart. "That doesn't make hurting Phoebe okay. That doesn't make chasing her away okay."

"You didn't chase her away, Kel. She ran." Sheila reached up and rubbed her hands up and down her face. When she lowered them, he saw signs of exhaustion, like sleep hadn't come easy to her. And traces of anger.

Anger permeated the entire enclave. That a vicious, brutal feral with a taste for rape and murder was so close—or at least *had* been so close, and they hadn't realized it until now, it weighed on the lot of them.

But it was crushing him. Destroying what little soul he had left. "She ran because of me."

"She ran because of her," Sheila countered. "I know you, Kel. You wouldn't have led her to believe in any way that you might love her. Women..." She shrugged, a bitter smile on her lips. "We can usually tell when somebody loves us or not. Too often, even when we suspect the answer is *not,* we don't want to accept that. You can't fault yourself for not loving her, any more than you can fault her for falling in love with you...or at least fooling herself into it. Phoebe was a big girl, Kel. She'd made it in this world before Rafe set up territory here. She knew there were risks and predators—and she made the choice to leave. Nobody forced it on her."

Neither of them heard the footsteps. Until Rafe's voice cut through the tension in the air, they hadn't even realized he was there. But as they turned to look at the Master, both of them felt something change...a subtle shift in the air.

Subtle—but it came with something icy and ugly. Something that filled Kel with dread.

"Don't tell me he's killed again," he rasped. Disgusted and furious, his hands closed into fists and the refrain started to circle through his mind once more.

Helpless. Useless. Worthless.

The feral's words whispered through his mind as he stared at Rafe's impassive face.

"I'm going to rip your heart out of your chest and smash it. You will die this time."

Kel's own response... *"Promise?"*

Better off if the feral *had* killed him. Kel could be replaced. Rafe could get somebody besides Kel's sorry ass in here, somebody who actually understood the purpose, somebody who cared.

"No, Kel. He hasn't killed anybody yet that we know about." Rafe glanced at his wife.

The look that passed between them didn't do a damn thing to make Kel feel better.

Neither did the appearance of Dominic and Toronto emerging from the hallway to flank Rafe. Toronto wouldn't have finished checking things out in Tupelo already—which meant he was back because Rafe had sent for him.

Dominic's brown eyes weren't quite as blank as Toronto's or Rafe's. Dominic wasn't that much older than Kel, in both human and vampire terms, and he hadn't yet learned the fine art of hiding every single emotion.

The look in Dom's eyes was one of worry, one of caution—and it had to do with Kel. He could feel it.

In a hoarse voice, Kel asked, "What's going on, Rafe?"

Rafe, his voice impassive, said, "It has to do with what you left behind."

Startled, Kel blinked. "What I left..." Understanding came fast and hard.

Home.

Angel...

She was the only one he'd left behind that could still matter.

"What exactly are you talking about?" he demanded through clenched teeth.

"There's a witch living a few miles away from Greenburg—moved there on my request." A muscle jerked in his jaw and for just a second, Rafe's emotionless eyes weren't quite so emotionless.

"Why?" Kel demanded.

"Because of Angel."

Kel didn't even remember moving. One second, he was ten feet away from Rafe and then he was in Rafe's face, his hands fisted in the smooth, buttery soft leather of Rafe's coat. Jerking Rafe forward, he rasped, "*Why?*"

"Because she was bitten too." Rafe glanced down at Kel's hands and reached up, closing his fingers around Kel's wrists. "Bitten...and fed."

"She's not..." Dear sweet heaven...*no...* The strength drained out of him and now, if he hadn't been holding onto Rafe's jacket, and if Rafe didn't have a hold of Kel's wrists, he suspected he would have gone to his knees.

"Kel."

Blood roared in his ears, blinding him, deafening him. Something soft, cool, stroked his cheek and without realizing it, he let go of Rafe and turned towards Sheila. Lost, shocked, he stared into her eyes. Her hands came up, cupped his face.

Her lips moved, but he couldn't hear the words. Not at first.

When they finally did pierce the fog in his head, they didn't even make sense.

But when they did, Kel *did* go to the ground, sinking to his knees and covering his face with his hands. Tears burned his eyes and the relief that washed through him was a sweet, sweet respite.

"Damn it, Kel...she's *not* a vampire." It was the third time she'd said it.

"I heard you." Lifting his gaze, he stared at Sheila and nodded. "I heard you."

"But..." He turned his head and stared at Rafe. "If she's not one of us, why is she being watched?"

"For her safety." Rafe sighed and turned away, pacing the room with a restless, caged energy. The two men at his shoulders fell back in unison but they didn't move far. They kept a close eye on Kel and once more, the tension in the room began to climb.

Higher. Higher.

"Rafe, if you don't tell me what the fuck is going on..." Kel swore and shoved himself to his feet. He planted himself in Rafe's path and waited.

"You remember when you were going through your training?" Rafe said.

A weird light glittered in Rafe's eyes and Kel's skin went tight as a dark, ugly premonition began to whisper in his ear. *Angel had been bitten*—he remembered that, had nightmares about it.

There had been blood on her lips.

"We don't generally want vamps feeding from one human in particular. Having a human as a regular feeding companion just isn't the best idea."

Kel's lip curled in a snarl. "I know that. I don't need a fucking ethics course or a refresher in postmodern Hunter psycho-shit."

"Would you shut the fuck up?" Rafe demanded in a harsh voice. "I'm trying to make this a little bit easier on you."

"I don't want *easy*—I want to know why Angel's being watched, and why in the hell you're telling me *now*."

"Because she's vampire bait, damn it!" Rafe shouted.

His voice echoed through the room, bounced over the walls...and inside Kel's head, growing louder and louder until it had the same deafening boom of a shuttle launch.

Vampire bait.

Vampire bait.

Vampire bait.

Kel hadn't ever been faced with a human whose blood had been altered after a blood exchange. It wasn't a common occurrence and the inherent risks had most vamps, Hunter and civilian alike, exercising caution to keep it from happening.

But he didn't need the experience of meeting such a person to understand that this was *bad, bad, bad...* Vampire bait— what else could that be but bad news? From the horror stories he'd heard, the altered mortals basically became some kind of forbidden fruit—and Kel's dad was a preacher. He knew what forbidden fruit led to.

That allure wasn't something easily ignored, it wasn't something the mortal could control, and it wasn't something that all vampires could resist. The stories he'd heard, the allure was actually pretty damn hard to resist.

There had been one story... Kel's gut started to churn as he remembered it. He hadn't thought about it in more than ten years, probably longer than that. Whether or not it was an urban legend the teachers at Excelsior had concocted to basically terrify the young vamps, he didn't know. The young ones had next to no control and even if they were decent enough on the inside, their hungers were too seductive and the urge to give in to temptation was strong.

It sounded like something a bunch of kids would tell each other at a campout, something to freak the others out. But the gorier details were the kind of things Kel hoped no child ever had to know about. A young couple, recently married, back in the seventeen or eighteen hundreds, was attacked—the man was bitten and fed, not enough to induce the Change, but enough that his blood was altered. The woman, though, she *had* been Changed.

That far back, Excelsior hadn't really been established and from what the instructors at the school claimed, the tragedy was one of the events that spurred things on.

The Hunter who found the couple ended up taking the woman with him—not to hurt her, but to protect the husband, because he recognized the Change in the man. But the wife didn't understand.

She went back to her husband—and ended up killing him. Then, driven mad by grief, she'd gone on a rampage that killed eleven other people. Her killing spree stopped after she set herself on fire—one damn painful way to commit suicide.

Kel didn't buy into fairy tales that seemed told specifically to scare people, but something about this one had stuck with him, and now, he couldn't get it to stop replaying in his head. Covering his face with his hands, he ground the heels of his palms against his eyes and swore. "Not happening," he muttered. "This shit is *not* happening."

An odd silence fell, broken only by Sheila's quiet voice. "I have a feeling we haven't heard the worst, Kel."

Kel dropped his hands, looked from the three men to Sheila and then back. Ignoring the other two, he narrowed his eyes on Rafe's face.

Shit. Something—something there. Kel couldn't quite put his finger on it. Rafe wasn't just a hard-ass bastard, he was an inscrutable hard-ass bastard. Unless he was with Sheila, he showed about as much emotion as a coat rack. Zilch.

But for a second, there was something in those eyes that looked like worry.

"Out with it," Kel said, forcing the words through a throat gone tight.

Rafe blew out a breath. Slid the other two men a glance and as one, the two men came up to flank Kel.

Kel didn't even spare them a glance.

"The witch near Greenburg called. There's a feral moving towards her. He isn't there yet—"

Kel didn't hear anything else.

He rushed for the door, but four hard hands caught him and restrained him—or tried to. Blindly, he turned his head, snapping at the body closest to him. He caught skin, bit. Somebody swore. Another arm came around his neck, immobilizing him. Rafe's voice came at Kel as if over some great distance, faint, indistinct. Even the command inherent in those words had little effect on Kel—some part of him recognized the command, but it didn't matter.

It didn't register.

Nothing registered.

Not even the fact that he'd managed to dislodge Dominic and knock him back. Not even the fact that when Dom came rushing back, Kel delivered a swift sidekick to the vamp's gut that sent Dom flying through the air to crash into a wall.

Around his neck, Rafe's arm tightened and it was a powerful enough hold that if Kel had been mortal, he would have long since passed out.

Rafe continued to talk to him, faster now, but it was like the Master was speaking some foreign language. None of it made sense. Nothing made sense. He reared back with his head, once, twice. Hearing bone crush, he kept at it and then abruptly, Rafe's arm was gone and all he had to deal with was the shifter still attached to his side.

He reached for Toronto—and instead of touching man, touched wolf. No, make that big, brawny wolf-man that towered over Kel by nearly two feet. Kel didn't even hesitate. He struck towards the wolf's throat—vampires didn't need to breathe.

But shape-shifters did.

Toronto jerked away just in time and the blow ended up glancing off the side of a thickly furred neck. A huge, clawed hand, the size of a dinner plate came up and caught Kel's arm. "Calm *down*," Toronto said, his deep, growling voice about as welcome as a fly buzzing in Kel's ear—and just as annoying.

Kel jerked away, but Toronto didn't let go.

Snarling, Kel automatically reached up, touching a hand to his waist, but he hadn't grabbed any of his weapons. All he touched was bare skin—shit. Weapons. Yeah, needed weapons because when he found the feral this time, he wasn't taking any chances.

A couple of knives, a Beretta? Not enough. Kel was thinking along the lines of rocket launcher. Explosives, maybe. A little flashier than the Hunters used, but hey, no such thing as overkill in this case.

"Toronto. Let him go."

Kel was released so abruptly, he stumbled into a wall. Shoving away from it, he headed into the hall. There was a weapons room. That was Dom's domain and the man did like his toys. Kel would just...

Sheila appeared in front of him.

It took a few seconds to register the fact that she was blocking him. He started to go around her and she moved with him. "Kel—"

She held out a hand and Kel cocked his head, staring at it, puzzled. Slowly, he lifted his gaze and focused on her face. She gave him a shaky smile. "Come on. Let's just slow down..."

"No." He reached out, picked her up and bodily removed her from his path—and then he kept going. Shoes. Needed some shoes. A shirt. And weapons—lots of them. Quick, though. Not too much time.

This time when the three men formed a barricade in front of him, Kel simply halted in his tracks and then turned, heading for the stairs. Clothes and shoes, how much did they matter? Weapons—some gas and a few matches would work. Anything.

Behind him, Dominic muttered, "Hell. This is going well."

Rafe swore soundly.

Off to the side, Toronto stood watching the whole tableau with a smirk on his face. "Any suggestions?"

"Yeah. Some elephant tranquilizers." Rafe scrubbed a hand over his face and then headed for the stairs. Kel hadn't slipped out of the house yet. He'd stopped in the front hallway and was dragging on a leather jacket over his bare chest. The shoes on his feet belonged to Toronto. The butt of a gun peeked out of the waistband of his jeans and unless Rafe was mistaken, it was *his* gun.

The look on Kel's face was blank. Disturbingly so. For the past ten minutes, it had been like trying to talk rationally to a shark caught in a feeding frenzy and Rafe was under no illusions that another attempt was going to be any more successful.

"Kel. You can't go to Greenburg." He kept his calm, hoped he had his emotions lashed down tight enough. Any sign of worry, fear or rage just might be what snapped Kel's tenuous grasp on control.

Kel had already proven that when he was in a rage, it was going to take more than a couple of them to keep him contained. From the corner of his eye, he saw Dominic holding something over the ugly wound in his shoulder. The scent of blood was strong in the air and he sent a silent command to his lieutenant for him to leave.

Dom stilled, his eyes narrowed.

Through their silent communication, Rafe shifted his gaze to the sluggishly bleeding wound and then to Kel. Dom hesitated for a moment and then nodded, withdrawing from the room in silence. "Kel, before you go off half-cocked, you need to listen to me," Rafe said. He focused on Kel's mind, focused on the blood oath Kel had given him ten years earlier—focused *hard*.

Kel's lids flickered. Then he blinked and when his eyes opened, he looked at Rafe with some measure of comprehension. "You can't stop me from going," he said, his voice harsh and low.

"I don't have a choice, Kel. You *can't* be around her. Ever. Your control is..."

"My control..." Kel laughed bitterly. "Fuck my control. I don't need control to find him and kill him before he hurts Angel."

"And how are you going to find him, Kel?" Rafe demanded. "If you did find him before he got to her, are you willing to risk *her* life you'll be able to stop him?"

The look that flashed through Kel's eyes then was enough to have Rafe spinning away, shame punching through him. But it had to be said...right? Kel was strong, but he was young. It was entirely possible he may even become a Master. But...he wasn't there yet.

Rafe had a responsibility to that girl, as well as to Kel. He turned back to Kel. "You need to stop and think for a minute."

"I'm thinking just fine. I *will* stop him," Kel said, the pain and horror Rafe had seen in his eyes gone, replaced by a careful, closed emptiness. He pushed past Toronto and headed for the door.

"Can you stop yourself?" Rafe shoved his hands in his pockets.

Kel stopped in his tracks. Without turning back to Rafe, he asked, "What's that supposed to mean?"

"Rafe..." Sheila's voice was soft, but he heard the censure in it loud and clear. He glanced at her and shook his head. He was doing what he had to.

"Just that," he said in answer to Kel's question. "Can you stop yourself? You haven't ever been face-to-face with one of the altered humans, Kel. Coming face-to-face with that, it's like coming face-to-face with an addiction you never knew you had, and one you can't fight. You got the control to walk away from her?"

Kel's shoulders slumped.

Finally—

Rafe edged a little closer, keeping his voice calm, level as he said, "I know you still love her, Kel. I'll take care of her. I—"

Something inside Kel snapped. The tension in the wide, open hallway seemed to explode and Kel spun around and lunged for Rafe. The two vampires crashed into the wall.

Kel's lips peeled back, revealing fangs that were dropped and ready. And that wasn't all. He had a blade in his hand. Somewhere between the basement and the front door, he'd managed to pick up a knife. All of a sudden, Rafe wished he'd listened to Sheila when she harped about how she hated weapons being left all over the house.

Kel snarled, pressing the tip of the blade into Rafe's throat. Flesh sizzled and smoke drifted up as the silver pressed into his skin.

Voice dripping with derision, Kel repeated, "You know I *love* her? What the fuck is that...love? Love doesn't touch it. She was my fucking life—the *only* thing that made the past twelve years bearable was knowing that what happened to me *didn't* happen to her and I will be damned if I risk it happening now."

Alerted by either the noise or the obvious change in the air caused by Kel's rage, every Hunter in the house came rushing in. Toronto went to block two of the younger vampires who went to grab Kel. Dom, his wound no longer bleeding, emerged from the gathered bodies and managed to block a shifter and another

125

vamp. But there were six vamps and four shifters in the enclave, not including Rafe, his lieutenants or Kel.

Four of them went for Kel even as Rafe barked out an order to stand down. All the years of them worrying that Kel's control would snap had them reacting out of pure instinct and they took Kel to the ground. Rafe grabbed one by the neck and dragged him off, went to grab another.

The air went tight, like it did right before a vicious storm. Tight and heavy, pressing down on them, but Rafe was so ticked off, he barely noticed it. "That's *enough*," Rafe snarled. He didn't bother trying to control his own temper and as the innate power rolled out of him, two of the younger vamps pulled out of the fray—most likely without even realizing why.

But the other two were older—Josiah was older than Rafe and Charlie just a few years younger. And—shit.

Kel had managed to use the K-bar on Josiah and the older vamp was beyond pissed. The wound, although not lethal, was going to bleed like a bitch and hurt like hell. It went from the right upper part of Josiah's chest and slashed down diagonal across his torso.

Dominic and Toronto managed to get Charlie away, leaving Rafe to deal with Josiah who was busy smashing Kel's knife hand into the floor with a force that would shatter mortal bone.

Rafe didn't quite believe his eyes when it happened.

One second he was reaching for Josiah, mad enough to throw both Kel and Josiah through a wall—repeatedly. There was little warning—that weird tension mounted in the air and then his skin broke out in goose bumps. His hand closed around the back of Josiah's shirt.

His eyes *saw* what was happening, but his brain didn't process what he was seeing until it was already done, until Josiah dropped downward, crashing into the floor.

Crashing into the floor—because Kel was gone.

Josiah swore and scrambled backward, a look of dumb amazement on his haggard face. His graying beard was kept cropped close and his long hair was always pulled back away from his face. He rubbed his hands over his face, unintentionally leaving smears of his own blood on his cheek.

In his mortal life, Josiah had been a bounty hunter and it

wasn't a stretch to picture the man in the Old West, chasing after wanted men and dragging them back to the hands of the law. He was rough, he was often too short tempered, as quick to laugh as he was to fight and it wasn't easy to catch him off-guard.

Rafe was pretty sure he hadn't ever seen that look of utter surprise on his face.

"Fuck me... Tell me I didn't just see that!" Josiah muttered, shaking his head.

Charlie sent a scathing look at Josiah but it seemed more of a habit than anything. Before he'd been Changed, Charlie had been a Baptist minister in South Carolina—a bit of an oddity altogether, not just because he'd accepted his new life with a grace most people wouldn't expect coming from a man of God. A bit of a pacifist, most of the Hunters had expected the man to be dead within a year—a Hunter that advocates peace seemed like he'd be easy prey for those who didn't much buy the peace bit. Except Charlie had an intolerance for those who inflicted suffering on others—and it showed in his work.

Josiah ignored Charlie, focusing instead on Rafe, his eyes disbelieving. "I didn't just see that, did I?"

Abruptly, Sheila laughed and Rafe sent her a narrow look.

"This isn't funny, Belle. This is bad. Hell-in-a-fucking-handbasket bad."

"Oh, I don't know." Her laugh faded, but the smile on her face didn't. "Rafe, sweetie, a baby vamp just dematerialized right in front of us. He's only been a vamp for what...twelve years? I've been doing this three times as long as he has and I can't dematerialize. *You* have been a vampire for more than a hundred years, and *you* can't do it. And then poor Kel—everybody feels sorry for him, none of you trust him any farther than you can throw him..." She broke off, winced. "Okay, you can throw farther than you can trust. Kel, a vamp twelve years—and he dematerialized. He's not a Master, he can't do that very cool mist thing and he doesn't feed enough to keep an anorexic teen alive—and *he just dematerialized.*"

Through gritted teeth, Rafe said, "I *know* what he just did, Sheila. I also know this is beyond bad news."

A sad smile curled her lips. "I don't think you're giving Kel much credit at all. I don't see him hurting her."

"As a decent guy, I give him plenty of credit. But his control? It sucks," Rafe said, his voice flat.

Sheila lifted her gaze and glanced at the mass of bodies crowding the hall. She said nothing, but as one, they all withdrew until only Rafe, Sheila and his lieutenants remained. She ignored Dominic and Toronto, coming forward until she was close enough to reach out and cup Rafe's face. "Rafe...what if it was me?"

A muscle jerked in his jaw and the immediate blast of instinctive, protective rage had him reaching for her, dragging her soft body against his. "You think I haven't thought of it that way? You think I don't realize this is killing him? But he's got too little control for this, Belle. You *know* that."

"Actually, no, I don't." She slipped her arms around his waist, lifting her face to his. "What I know is that he's pissed off, he's hurt—I know it's because of her. I know he hasn't allowed himself to go back there even just to see her one last time, because he doesn't trust himself. But that's caution, Rafe. That *is* control. More, it's love. He won't hurt her."

"Is it control or the only way a weak man can resist temptation?" Sighing, he dropped his head down and pressed his brow to hers. "Belle, I know he loves her. But..."

Reaching up, she pressed a finger to his lips. "No. There's no *but* in this, not for me. He won't hurt her, he'll die to keep her safe, and you *know* that. You'd do the same for me. Besides, if he doesn't go, and something does happen to her..." Her voice faded away, but the look in her eyes spoke volumes.

"If that happens, he'll break," Rafe finished, closing his eyes. Shit, he was such a screw up. This was happening under *his* watch. He was supposed to protect the men and women who chose to serve under him.

Not let them go off half-cocked. Not let a feral slip so close to his territory and kill a woman who was sleeping with one of the men.

"Rafe."

Lifting his head, he met Dom's eyes across the hallway.

"What do you want us to do?"

He lingered in the warm comfort of Sheila's embrace for

another heartbeat, and then he eased back. "We have to go after him."

Sheila shook her head. "Bad idea, slick. You're so worried about Kel's control, but you want to put two dominant vamps in close proximity to his woman. What do you think *that* will do to his control?"

"I'm aware of that," Rafe snapped, his voice harsher than he'd intended. "Damn it. I'm sorry."

He turned away and pinched the bridge of his nose. Vampires weren't immune to headaches any more than they were immune to heartbreak and the pounding within his skull had grown to massive proportions. "I'm sorry. But Sheila, I don't see much choice. If we don't go after him, and he gets hurt—killed, Angel is going to need protection. If he does somehow manage to kill the feral, then she will still need protection."

He turned in time to see her mouth firm into a flat line. She shook her head but before she could speak, Rafe said, "I want to believe he could control himself, too, Belle. But if he can't, an innocent woman gets hurt—I can't take that risk just because I want to trust one of my men."

And there was another *if.* None of the scenarios had much appeal but this one was the worst. "Sheila, I also have to think about what will happen if he can't save her. We both know what will happen. He *will* break. He'll shatter. I can't have a walking time bomb out there among a bunch of innocent, unsuspecting mortals."

"I'll go."

Sheila, Dom and Rafe all turned as one to look at Toronto, watching as he shoved off the wall. Vamps, shifters, they all had ways of measuring each other's power and Toronto was a damned powerful shifter, but he was also the sort that usually thought, *If it doesn't affect me or the job...* He rarely made an action or offer he didn't absolutely have to.

"One of us might not be enough," Rafe said.

A faint smile curled Toronto's lips. "Depends on which of *us* is the one." He went quiet for a minute and then, almost like he'd made an internal decision, he nodded. "Kel's the main reason I'm here, Rafe."

Rafe blinked. Squinted his eyes and studied Toronto's pretty-boy face, trying to deduct the meaning of *that* statement, but he couldn't. "What exactly are you talking about, Toronto?"

Toronto reached up and pulled out the leather thong restraining his hair, toyed with it in an absent, unconscious way as he started to pace. His hair, that long, silvery blond hair, hung loose around his shoulders, falling halfway down his back. It shielded his face from Rafe until the shifter lifted his head and faced the Master. "I was sent here. Told I might be needed."

"Sent." Rafe's voice was flat and disgusted. He didn't have to ask *who* had sent him.

There was only one answer.

The Council.

"You want to tell me why?" he asked, an edge of anger making its way into his voice. "Why in the fuck the Council sent somebody into *my* territory?"

If Rafe's anger bothered Toronto in the least, it didn't show. His pale blue eyes reflected nothing of what he was feeling or thinking. His voice, when he spoke, was calm, almost bored. "Because the Council was informed it might be necessary. Don't get bent out of shape over this. It has nothing to do with you."

His brows dropped low over his eyes and he stalked forward, putting his face in the shifter's and snarled, "Since it has to do with one of *my* Hunters..."

Sheila pushed between them, literally had to wedge her body between them. Toronto fell back with a smirk, hooked his thumbs in his front pockets and rocked back on his heels.

"*Your* Hunters—yeah, but theirs, too. This is your pond, Rafe, but you don't control all of them. You aren't in charge of all Hunters. When the Council learns there may be something that can have destructive consequences to some or all of us, they do what needs doing."

"How can a pissed-off vampire with a broken heart have destructive consequences that could affect all of us?" Rafe demanded. His hair tumbled into his eyes and he shoved it back before folding his arms across his chest. It was that, or punch the shape-shifter in his pretty-boy nose. "And exactly what are *you* supposed to do about it?"

"Considering what Kel's heading into, I'm surprised you have to wonder what the consequences would be." Toronto shrugged restlessly. "There's a chance this woman could get hurt—could die. I'm going to make sure that doesn't happen. I don't doubt Kel's ability to handle the feral, not this time, not on this. Not when she's involved. But the possibility is there that she could die. And we know what that would do to *him*. He's been on the knife's edge of sanity since he was Changed. He doesn't need that push over the edge. If it happens, do you really need to ask why that could have destructive consequences?"

"You're thinking he'd go rogue," Sheila said with a scowl.

It was a possibility. It was one Rafe had been aware of for a long time, and it was why he watched Kel so closely. "And if he slips, what do you plan to do?"

The look on Toronto's face said everything.

"Just like that." Disgusted, Rafe turned away. "Just like *that*? He's one of us—damn it, he never asked for this."

"No. He didn't." Finally, some sign of emotion worked its way onto Toronto's face. "You think this is *easy*, Rafe? You think I want to think about putting a bullet in his chest? I like him. I feel bad for the shit he's gone through and I hate that none of us were there to save him. I respect the hell out of him for joining us even when it's clear he doesn't want to be here. But if he goes rogue, other innocent people will suffer...and my responsibility is to them. Before anything else, before *everything* else, my responsibility is to them."

"You've been here all this time, waiting to see if you'll have to act as a Hunter's executioner." Dom finally spoke up, staring at Toronto with scathing contempt.

"It's what I do."

"Who appointed you judge and jury?" Dom demanded.

"The Council." Sheila answered when it was clear that Toronto wouldn't. "You're one of them, aren't you?"

"Hell, I don't even have to ask." Rafe shook his head, swearing under his breath. "You trained with the Select, didn't you? As a fucking assassin."

Toronto's lids flickered. But if Rafe expected to see some sign of remorse or regret, he knew he'd be waiting a damn long time. The Select, a hand-chosen unit of Hunters, weren't chosen for their people skills. Or some lingering trace of humanity. They were chosen for their ability to do what needed to be done—things that most Hunters would hesitate over.

"Right now the only thing I'm here for is to watch him."

He slipped past them then, walking away on silent feet, moving with the eerie, sinuous grace of a shifter. He disappeared from view and Rafe cursed.

"Did things just get better or worse?" Dominic muttered. "What in the hell is the Select?"

"Our version of Internal Affairs—a rat squad basically sent in on the jobs that are even ugly for us. Like when there's a Hunter perceived to be a threat," Sheila said.

Dominic hadn't spent years being trained at Excelsior. Rafe had taken over that responsibility. It happened sometimes, if there was an established Hunter willing to step in and oversee personal training for a new were or vamp. But some of the formal education, mostly boring academic crap Rafe hadn't messed with, was missing from Dominic's education.

"So I get that somebody has decided that Kel could be a threat. Hell, *we* think Kel is a potential threat. But if Toronto thinks it's necessary, he just kills him? Just like that?"

Disgusted, Rafe said, "That's the way it works." Unable to stand still, he turned away and stalked into the living room off to the side of the hall. By the windows was a bar made of gleaming mahogany. Generally, Rafe wasn't much for drinking but right now, he needed it.

Dominic followed him. "That's the way it works...and we just sit around and let it?"

"Dominic, we can't interfere," Sheila said, following them.

Rafe splashed some Jack Daniels into a glass and tossed it back, watching as Dominic wheeled around to stare at Sheila. "Why the hell not?"

"Because the Select act on the orders of the Council. They don't give these orders lightly but when they do, they are carried out. If we tried to get in the way..." Sheila's voice trailed away.

Rafe emptied his glass. As he refilled it, he finished her sentence. "The Select won't stop, Kel. Not until the job's done. If one of the assassins isn't enough, they'll send ten. Ten isn't enough? Fine, there will be a hundred of them pouring out of the woodwork."

Dominic's jaw dropped. Then he snapped it shut and shook his head. "This ain't right, Rafe. They don't *know* him. They can't make a judgment like that without even knowing who in the hell they're talking about."

"They do know who they are talking about."

Whether they were too caught up in the rather harsh discoveries of the night, or just too damned exhausted from them, they were caught off guard as Toronto emerged from the hall, a duffle bag hooked over his shoulder. He didn't come into the room, just stood in the doorway and looked from Dominic to Sheila to Rafe. "That's why I was sent. To watch him, get to know him. If they were just going to make a rash judgment, they would have taken care of him before he even finished training. It was made damn clear at Excelsior that Kel's hold on control left a lot to be desired.

"We don't like doing this." Toronto reached up and rubbed a hand over the back of his neck, sighed tiredly. "*I* don't like this. But I like the alternative even less."

He turned to go but then abruptly turned back to face Rafe. "I don't plan on letting anything happen that would force me to act. I know what I'm doing... I'm good at it. Trust that even if you can't trust me."

"What the..."

Kel's head was spinning. One second he was trying to free his hand, his head full of the scent of blood and his gut churning with the need to get to Angel—

And then he was flat on his ass in a field with silvery moonlight the only illumination. Off in the distance, he could hear the sounds of traffic and through the trees, he saw the headlights of cars and trucks.

Slowly, he sat up, stared around him and tried to figure out where in the hell he was. And *how* he'd gotten there. The busy interstate in front of him didn't offer any clues, not from where he was. Nothing around him looked familiar—hell, the air even smelled different then it did in Memphis.

So obviously he wasn't in Memphis.

Check.

The exact where, and the exact how…? Kel had absolutely no clue to those. He shoved to his feet and turned around. His head—fuck, his head was pounding like a bitch. Muffled and foggy, too, like somebody had slipped him a couple of sleeping pills without his knowledge.

It was cold. Might be spring, but it felt like snow was in the air. The cold, while it didn't bother him much, was enough to clear the rage from his thoughts even if it didn't totally dispel the clouds.

He smelled blood and it wasn't his own. Lowering his gaze, he stared at the K-bar in his hand, stared at the drying blood on it. Drying—not dry. The blood came from Josiah. He'd been fighting with the other Hunter, focused on nothing but getting away, getting to Angel.

The sight of that tacky blood made him aware of a hundred clues that made little sense.

There was blood on him.

He was wearing a jacket that wasn't his, a pair of boots that weren't his. The K-bar in his hand wasn't his and neither was the gun he pulled from his waistband.

Vaguely, he remembered grabbing the gun and knife from a narrow table in the main hallway as he headed for the front door. The shoes had been in the foyer and that was where he'd grabbed the jacket too.

Under the jacket, his upper body was naked.

He hadn't thought about grabbing a shirt, lacing up the boots, nothing. Angel was pretty much it as far as his thought process went.

But now, with the pain churning in his head, he was excruciatingly aware of some things. Like the fact that he'd used the knife in his hand on a fellow Hunter. Like the fact that he hadn't been able to stop the feral from hurting Phoebe—how in the hell could he protect Angel?

"Shit." Bile churned in the back of his throat and he swallowed it down. He slid the K-bar into the sheath at his waist, then pushed the Beretta into his waistband at the small of his back, making sure the jacket covered it. Not that it mattered. Any damn person saw him, they were going to call the cops. Even if the bruises from the scuffle back at the enclave healed before somebody saw him, cops would be called. Blood streaked his chest and face and Kel had no doubt he looked every bit as wild as he felt.

Covering his face with his hands, he took a deep breath and made himself think. It hurt—his fricking *brain* ached, the way muscles did after a hard, brutal workout. The answer was there, lost in his aching, clouded mind and once he started to focus, he found it with relative ease.

But it didn't make much sense. That seemed to be par for the course tonight, though.

He had dematerialized.

That was the only answer that made sense. He'd been thinking about Angel, nothing but her and getting to her, protecting her. Even the men struggling to immobilize him hadn't mattered beyond the fact that they were in his way.

But where had he dematerialized *to*—that was the next question. Probably somewhere between Memphis and Greenburg and that could be any number of sites in the 400-some-odd miles separating the two towns. Kel decided it was most likely a halfway point. He had no clue how he'd managed that little vamp trick and even if he could figure it out, it wouldn't help him much right now.

It was the reason for the fog in his brain, he knew it. The reason for the ache. And it probably wasn't a stunt he'd be able to pull off again anytime soon.

Didn't matter. He was that much closer to Angel—and he was away from the enclave and Rafe. None of them knew where in the hell to find him—right? They knew where he was going, but tracking him, hopefully, would take a little more work.

Crouching on the ground, he tied the boots and then glanced towards the highway. Walking alongside it would be an invitation for trouble, but he needed to figure out where he was and that was the best way to do it.

Mind made up, he headed towards the strip of trees, moving at a quick jog. The tree line edged right up to the road and once he got close to see through them, he started moving along a parallel path, keeping his eyes out for some sign of where he was.

It might have been a mile or two before he got one. The I-20 East. A little outside Birmingham if he remembered right. Okay...so about 200 miles from Greenburg. No way he could travel that far in one night—so he needed a ride.

His internal clock assured him there were hours left before sunrise but he needed to get someplace where he'd be safe from the sun and it needed to be a hell of a lot closer to Angel. He wouldn't have much time to act before the feral made his move.

Getting the ride was actually the easiest part. The brightly lit oasis cast light into the sky from a long way off. The scent of exhaust and the rumble of truck engines clued Kel into what it was even before he saw it through the trees. The truck stop was busy, even if it was edging close to midnight. Keeping outside the lights, he circled around until he found a lone man standing outside his truck as he stowed groceries.

Vampire compulsion was something Kel hated.

Forcing his will on somebody else was just wrong. But he didn't bat a lash as he slid out of the darkness and approached the man. The trucker glanced up, startled. Kel made himself smile as he focused.

"I need a ride to Georgia."

The man blinked. Looking confused, he glanced from the truck to Kel and said, "I'm heading towards Atlanta."

"Maybe you could offer me a ride."

His lids lowered and as their gazes were cut off, Kel felt the man's own mental blocks trying to reassert themselves. Kel pushed harder. A little too hard, the poor guy flinched and swore as he reached up and touched his temple. Easing back, Kel repeated, "Maybe you could offer me a ride."

"Why don't you climb on up in the cab?"

The feral's name was Martin.

He'd been a vampire since 1804, the most important year in the history of the world as far as Martin was concerned. It was the day he'd truly begun to live.

Before that, he'd been a private instructor for the daughter of a disgustingly rich earl in England. Hours upon hours trying to educate women who were more concerned with bonnets, dresses and soirees than learning. A useless existence and Martin had been quite happy to be done with it.

In all the years since he'd been Changed, he never once regretted it.

In all the years since he'd been Changed, he had never once come up against the Hunters, although the woman who had Changed him had made him very aware of their presence. Martin, being an intelligent man, was careful to avoid any one place that had a large non-mortal population. It was only wise. Too many vampires or shape-shifters in one place was going to have the attention of the self-important Council and their fool Hunters. By avoiding such places, he wouldn't attract much notice.

He was also careful in selecting his victims, taking those who society was unlikely to miss—the indigent population was a particular treat. So many young runaways—and Martin did like youth. It had been that affliction that had caused his few brushes with the Hunters but he had managed to elude them with little difficulty and it had lulled him into complacency.

Which was the root of his current situation.

He was careful never to feed from any of the non-mortals, civilian or Hunter. It was merely common sense. The non-mortal population had its share of loners, its share of those who were unlikely to be missed—but it wasn't as prevalent. If too many of them disappeared, somebody would take notice.

But the pretty little brunette had been too sweet to walk away from. Fury, grief, jealousy, pain, the emotions had colored the very air around her and that misery had drawn him like a moth to flame.

She'd been outside a bar, leaning against her car and crying. Like so many of the desperately lonely, she'd been all too willing to accept an offered shoulder and hadn't once tried to look beyond that. By the time something inside her had whispered an alarm, it had been too late.

Martin selected his playgrounds with care. That near miss with the young blonde a few years back had taught him a valuable lesson and he believed in taking lessons to heart. His hunger had gotten the better of him. He'd been watching that girl for weeks. He might never have learned of her if it hadn't been for the mother. A whorish bitch, but a very fuckable one, had come on to him and taken him home and that was where he'd seen the girl.

He spent close to a week watching the pretty young woman, waiting for the best time to move on, the best time to toy with her before he took what he wanted. Several times, he'd almost lost interest, but in the end, that power simmering inside her had been too hard to resist.

Banked power, but it had called to Martin like a siren's song. That power had caused him to make one of the most foolish mistakes of his life—he'd wanted her, he'd gone after her, and he had ended up alerting a Hunter to his presence.

Martin considered himself a practical man. Knowing that the girl would likely have Hunters checking on her from time to time after his thwarted attack, he'd made the wise decision to cut his losses.

But he'd made a tactical error in judgment. The boy... Shite, he hadn't thought of that little fool in years. He'd recovered from the wounds the boy inflicted on him within a few days. Even his injured eye had fully healed and Martin had been concerned about that. As his injuries faded, Martin forgot about the boy. The Change from mortal to vampire was brutal and easily half died. A boy, weakened from the beating Martin had given him, wasn't likely to survive. And he'd been left in a place where the early morning sun would quickly find his body. Even if the Change did start, the sun would kill him.

Martin hadn't counted on somebody helping him.

That was the only logical explanation. It hadn't been the Hunter trailing after Martin, that much he knew. That bastard had spent most of the night on Martin's arse, so there must have been another.

The boy had survived—and not only had he survived, he'd become one of the fucking Hunters.

Martin's lapse in judgment had landed him in hot water twice, the pretty blonde mortal in Georgia, and the sleek little werewolf in Mississippi. Now there was a Hunter who knew his face and that just wasn't to be tolerated.

The plan itself took only a bit of time to develop. He had to kill the Hunter whelp. That boy had gone too far, and considering that he'd become a Hunter, he was a risk to Martin. The whelp had seen Martin's face. Tracking him down would be a bit harder, because there were no active Hunters in Tupelo, Martin had made sure of that.

He had come from elsewhere, but Martin wasn't sure where. However, that bit of information wasn't needed.

He knew how to get the boy's attention.

Through the girl.

Chapter Six

Sleeping pills weren't going to help. By the time the sun set, Angel knew that much. There was no way she'd sleep tonight, even though after last night, she desperately needed some rest.

She might as well be hyped up on speed, her entire body flooded with tension. The past twenty-four hours had been an emotional roller coaster, swinging from a sense of purpose devoted towards some unknown goal, to anger, to rage, to grief.

It had hit a plateau around sunrise and she'd catnapped for a while, the grief dulling to a muted roar. After a short nap, she'd spent the day at Jake's house, cleaning it, getting it ready for some prospective buyers. Getting through the day had taken every last bit of will she possessed and if she hadn't been so desperately ready to be done with the chore of selling Jake's house, she wouldn't have bothered.

Come dinnertime, she'd finally finished. All day long, she'd been desperate to escape. Once she had the chance, she realized she couldn't go home.

It would be worse there. It was going to be bad, no matter what. But trapped inside the house, certain she was losing her mind, it would be worse.

So instead of going home, she did the one thing she thought might help. She went to Kel—or rather to his grave, hoping she could find some measure of peace there.

For whatever reason, as the sun set and night came on, the emotional roller coaster started and the grief that had choked her all day bloomed into guilt and self-disgust before morphing into fury. A blind fury that had no target.

The empty coffin buried below the dirt seemed an odd place

to seek comfort. But Angel had spent many, many evenings sitting at the graveside and talking to a man who had been dead for years.

Tonight, though, even that bit of comfort was denied her. She stood by the grave, staring at the headstone with her hands shoved into her pockets and had to fight the urge to scream.

Scream at what?

At fate? At God? She'd done both of those in the past but neither fate nor God seemed to be her target. Angel couldn't even put her finger on it. She was a mess of worry, fear and anger and trying to make sense of that tangle was impossible.

She was slipping, she realized.

Once more slipping into a deep, dark place where nothing made sense and nothing seemed real.

The relative tedium of the past year was gone. Once more Angel felt like she was fighting something from the outside, something that didn't belong in her head but was there nonetheless.

It wasn't as bad as it had been after Kel had first died. She could think, still focus, still maintain a fairly normal facade that kept people from intruding with well-meaning worry.

"But for how much longer?" she muttered. Pulling a hand from her pocket, she tucked a loose strand of hair behind her ear and then cupped her hand over the back of her neck, rotating her head in an attempt to ease the tension knotted there.

Slowly, she tugged the prescription bottle from her pocket that she had grabbed before she left the house. It was the antidepressant the doctor had prescribed for her. Would medicine for depression help her recognize reality? Help her figure out what *she* felt instead of focusing on all the alien emotions that threatened to swamp her?

Disgusted, she tucked the bottle back into her pocket and then crouched by Kel's grave. With a shaky sigh, she smoothed a hand down the carpet of grass. "I'm a mess, Kel, you know that? I've been like this ever since you left, but it's getting bad again. I don't even know who I am right now."

Sighing, she settled on the grass, drawing her knees to her chest and looping her arms around them. Resting her chin there, she whispered, "I miss you. That's one thing I do know. But it seems like the only thing. I ought to be able to make a bit more sense of my life than that."

A cool wind whispered through the cemetery. The thick fleece sweatshirt she wore might as well have been made from paper because she felt frozen to the bone. But she was used to being cold.

"Twelve years, baby." Closing her eyes, she tried to think about what life might have been like if that night hadn't happened.

They'd be married. That was one thing she didn't doubt at all. Would they have had kids? Stayed in Georgia or gone somewhere else? Would Kel's mom be alive? Jake?

Bitterness swamped her and she had to blink back the tears suddenly burning her eyes. "This isn't *fair*." Angel wasn't much for railing against the unfairness of life, but this was tearing her apart, killing her inside, bleeding her bit by bit.

She'd been slowly hemorrhaging for the past twelve years.

"I'm so tired of it." Exhausted, knowing she'd never sleep, she lay back on the grass, ignoring the chill of the ground as she rolled onto her side and rested her hand on the grave. She tucked her other arm under her head to use as a pillow. Closing her eyes, she mumbled, "I'm so tired, Kel."

How fricking classic—a vampire sleeping the day away in a cemetery.

If he'd had much choice, he would have tried to find someplace else, but choices were limited. The trucker had left him just outside Greenburg a little before dawn and with the clock ticking, Kel went for the first secure place that he came across.

Instinct drove him to get closer to Angel, but he hadn't known where to look. As dawn crept closer, he had to focus on finding someplace dark and solitary. The private mausoleums in the old Greenburg Cemetery definitely fit that description.

He'd banked on being able to get into one of the older ones

that didn't get visits often and he'd been right. The one he'd selected had none of the stained glass windows and a recessed doorway.

Inside, with the door closed, it had been as dark as a tomb, just the thinnest sliver of pre-dawn light visible under the door itself.

As sweet, safe darkness wrapped around him, it took everything he had just to stumble away from the door and get one of the freestanding vaults inside the crypt between him and the door as an extra precaution.

Kel didn't even remember getting horizontal. As enraged and scared and worried as he was, he'd thought sleep would elude him but it didn't, hitting him hard and fast.

Normally Kel only needed four or five hours of sleep, but by the time he came awake a little before dusk, he'd been out for probably twelve hours.

The setting sun had kept him prisoner within the small crypt for a while longer. He shrugged out of his jacket long enough to pull on a T-shirt that he'd "borrowed" from the trucker earlier. Killed a bit of time pacing endlessly up and down the stone floor.

Finally the sun set. His body recognized the moment it was safe. He slipped out of the musty, confining crypt with the sure and certain knowledge that he was glad his body wasn't going to end up in some quiet, private resting place for all eternity. When he did die, he'd be burned and that suited him just fine.

Outside in the cool night air, he lifted his head and breathed in, letting the air wash over and through him, sweeping away the stink of decay.

The sound of a truck moving over the road had him retreating and swearing. It wasn't that late yet, probably only around seven, and he sure as hell didn't need anybody seeing him here. Greenburg was a small town and Kel knew for a fact his face hadn't changed a bit since he'd lived here.

He slipped into the tree line, his mind focused on finding Angel. But something, he couldn't even explain what, stopped him. Physically stopped him. He couldn't take another step away and everything inside him urged him to turn around. Unable to deny it, he turned and his eyes sought out the truck creeping along one of the cemetery paths.

It was a beat-up old Ford and even with his eyesight, he couldn't quite see through the windows. But he knew.

Somewhere inside him, without even seeing her, he knew. He slipped forward, just where the trees gave way to grass and there he crouched, one hand resting on the trunk of the tree, the other clutching the ring at his neck.

Hiding in the shadows, he watched, spellbound, as the truck came to a stop and the door opened. There was a fist wrapped around his throat, around his heart, and it wasn't going to ease up anytime soon.

It was her.

Angel.

Tears stung his eyes but he couldn't move to wipe them away so they just fell down his cheeks unchecked. Angel...

She slid out of the truck and moved through the maze of headstones and aboveground crypts. She came to a halt in front of one... Close, so close. He could smell her now. The cool breeze brought the scent of her to him and he closed his eyes, lost himself inside it.

Her hair was shorter than he'd ever seen it, the ends just barely brushing her shoulders. The silky blonde curls gleamed silver in the moonlight, blowing in the breeze. A stray strand blew into her eyes and she reached up to brush it back.

Even though she was a good thirty feet away, when she spoke, he heard the words as clearly as if she murmured them into his ear. "But for how much longer?" Her voice was soft, sad...despondent. Oblivious to his presence, she reached inside her pocket and pulled something out.

His ears heard a faint rattle, but he couldn't see what she held. Whatever it was, it caused a look of bitter anger to cross her features. She tucked it back into her pocket and then crouched by the grave.

His heart didn't beat often, but it did still beat. But when he heard her next words, he thought it might just stop altogether—stop, crack and then wither up and blow away just like so much dust.

"I'm a mess, Kel, you know that? I've been like this ever since you left, but it's getting bad again. I don't even know who

144

I am right now."

*Kel...*shit. Yeah, he knew logically his parents would have had some sort of funeral, however it was done without a body. Logically, he knew he probably had a headstone or something out there somewhere with his name on it.

But logically knowing that couldn't have prepared him for the sight of his woman kneeling by the side of his grave. She shifted and sat down, pulled her legs to her chest. The grief on her face made a knot form in his throat.

"I miss you. That's one thing I do know. But it seems like the only thing. I ought to be able to make a bit more sense of my life than that."

He clenched his jaw shut to keep from speaking out loud, but he couldn't keep himself from answering her silently. *Dear God, baby. I miss you too.*

The wind picked up and he watched, helpless, as she started to shiver. He wanted to go to her, wrap his arms around her and offer her some warmth. But how could a vampire offer her warmth? He had to steal it when he wanted it for himself, through blood or sex.

"Twelve years, baby."

Twelve miserable years.

What would have happened if that night hadn't ever come to pass? He would have married her, he could have spent the past twelve years sleeping next to her at night, rising to make love to her before they left the house to go out and do whatever in the hell normal people did...in the daylight.

Her voice, harsh and broken, came again. "This isn't *fair.*"

The sound of the tears thickening her voice had his hand tightening and he didn't realize he'd torn the bark from the tree.

Shit, this was killing him. He'd been bleeding and dying inside bit by bit over the past twelve years. Now, face-to-face with her, he saw that she was suffering just as he was.

"I'm so tired of it."

As she started to lay back onto the grass, Kel shoved to his feet. Fuck, he couldn't sit there and watch as she lay down to cry over an empty grave. Couldn't—

A hard hand closed over the back of his neck. "That's not a

good idea, kid." Toronto's voice, deep and gruff, was sympathetic.

Caught in the spell of seeing her again, Kel hadn't realized he wasn't alone until Toronto grabbed him and physically kept him from approaching Angel.

Rational thought encroached on the need to go to her and he swore. "Let me go," Kel said woodenly.

He was prepared to listen to more rants and rambles on control, much like what Rafe had doled out last night. But Toronto let him go and said nothing, just moved to stand by Kel's side and watch as Angel rolled onto her side and smoothed her hand down the grass covering the empty grave.

"I'm so tired, Kel."

Kel closed his eyes as her voice, weary and sad, drifted to him over the distance. "Where's the rest of the cavalry?" he asked sourly, glancing at Toronto from the corner of his eye.

"I'm it."

"It?" Startled, Kel turned to the shifter. "You're *it*?"

Toronto laughed softly. Keeping his voice pitched low, he murmured, "You make it sound like you don't think I can do much on my own."

Kel shrugged. "It ain't that. I just don't see Rafe letting it go that easily."

Smirking, Toronto replied, "He wouldn't have, but you sort of took the matter out of his control. Last thing we need is a couple of vamps, already on edge because of a feral, sniffing around some pretty mortal who just happens to be vampire bait."

Without thinking, Kel reached out, grabbed the front of Toronto's shirt and hauled him close. "Watch how you talk about her," he snarled, flashing his fangs.

Toronto's hands came up, slowly prying Kel's fingers off his shirt. He shot a narrow look in Angel's direction and muttered, "Keep your voice down, damn it." He moved back a few feet, keeping his hands lifted, palms out, like he was trying to calm a wild animal. "Chill out, Kel. I wasn't insulting your sweetheart. Just stating a point."

Kel turned away and shoved a hand through his hair. He

tugged sharply, trying to clear his head, but it didn't do any good. He couldn't think, couldn't focus. Getting a few feet between himself and Toronto, he leaned against a huge oak and looked back at Angel.

"So nobody else is coming?"

Toronto shook his head. "Not a good idea." He slanted Kel a look and added, "Stick another vamp around her, it's going to be just asking for trouble. Especially if you can't keep that temper of yours under control."

Control...

Rafe's words came back to him, a ghostly whisper, *You can't be around her. Ever.*

"What if he's right?"

Toronto didn't need to ask. "I don't think he is. You're a walking time bomb but I don't see you hurting her."

"Shit." He stared at her face, watched as she reached up to wipe her cheeks. She was crying. Lying on his grave and crying. It wasn't ever going to end, Kel knew. The pain inside him wouldn't stop, wouldn't ease. "You can't see it, can you? I'm already hurting her. She's laying on a pile of dirt and grass and crying over my sorry ass."

"Kel, she's crying over the guy she should have been able to grow old with. You aren't responsible for that."

"Aren't I?" All those dreams...the ones where Angel would lie in his arms, her weight warm and soft against him. *This feels so real...* She'd said that to him so often over the past years, he'd lost count. And he'd never let himself think about how those dreams might be affecting her. If it was the only time he could be with her, he'd selfishly wanted it.

And the feral—shit, Kel had no doubt it was *him* coming here. Possibly already here, searching for her. "If I could have made myself let her go, maybe she could have had some kind of life." He flicked Toronto a glance. "We dream together. I'll dream of her and for a little while, she's there with me. Even if she's asleep and I'm not, or I'm asleep and she's awake, our dreams merge. I can feel her thoughts and if I don't work to keep my shields up, I know she would feel mine...and she thinks I'm dead. How can she let go of me with all that going on inside her?"

Blowing out a breath, he added, "And not to mention the fact that I couldn't kill that monster."

Toronto took his time to answer, like he wanted to think through each and every word before he spoke. "You're talking about killing a vamp that's been around for a lot longer than you. That's not an easy task and you, as well as anybody, should know that's not a reflection on you." He gestured towards Angel and this time, when he spoke, his voice was soft, gentle. "And seriously, Kel, what I see out there is more or less the same thing I see when I look at you. Somebody who loves so completely, letting go would probably be about as easy as willing your heart to stop. That love, it's a part of you, both of you."

He sighed and leaned back against a tree, resting his blond head against the trunk and staring up at the sky. "If things were different, it would be a blessing for you both. As it stands, it's become a curse." Toronto looked at Kel. "That's not on you, Kel. That's on the mean bitch of fate."

"I don't believe in fate," Kel said. No. This wasn't some pre-destined twist—it was payment. Penance for something Kel had done wrong. He was paying for something, he had no clue what, but he knew it just the same. Maybe it was for failing to get to Angel in time that night.

And speaking of payment, that mean bitch of fate was sending one wickedly mean bill collector after him. He could feel it.

It was faint.

A cold whisper in a cool night. A darker shadow lost in a world of them.

Kel straightened away from the tree, distantly aware that Toronto had done the same, moving closer. As one, they looked at Angel. She continued to lie by the grave, stroking her hand up and down the grass like she was petting a cat.

"Fuck," Kel muttered under his breath.

"Double-fuck." His lips compressed down in a narrow line, Toronto slid Kel a sidelong glance. "Heard a rumor or two this lady is gifted."

Unsure of what Toronto was getting at, Kel said, "Yeah. Psychic. Why?"

"She strong enough to resist vampire compulsion?"

Eyes narrowed, Kel said, "If you think I'm going to..."

The shifter reached out, grabbed the front of Kel's shirt and hauled him forward. Face to face, Toronto growled, "Damn it, stop thinking like a protective, lovesick kid and think like a damn Hunter. Can she resist compulsion?"

Fury started to surface, that ugly, consuming rage. Thinking like a *protective, lovesick* anything pretty much defined him when it came to Angel. But thinking like a Hunter would do her more good than anything else. "If she's gotten stronger over the years, then she probably can resist the typical vamp. Master level? I doubt it."

With a short, decisive nod, Toronto muttered, "Good. I don't want to do this here. Let's get her home."

Kel snorted. "And we do that...*how*?"

Cracking a smile, Toronto replied, "Have a little faith, Kel. Give me your hand."

Kel blinked. Looked at the outstretched hand, and then back at the shifter.

"Come on, kid. We don't have all day." Toronto reached out and grabbed Kel's hand—a second later, the storm hit. It was like nothing Kel had ever felt, an ugly, gut-clenching storm of fear that rolled out of Toronto—towards Angel.

Kel couldn't see it, but he felt it. Snarling, he jerked away from Toronto but the shifter wouldn't let go. "What the *fuck* are you doing?"

"Getting her to leave. We want her home, remember?" Toronto replied impassively. Even as the words left his lips, Angel was sitting up, then shoving to her feet, glancing all around. There was naked fear on her face and confusion in her eyes as she started back towards the truck.

"You vamps aren't the only ones who can pull the fear trick," Toronto said, glancing at Kel. "Fear's emotional, not mental. If she stopped to think about *why* she was afraid, might be different. If I made some attempt to *compel* her to leave, it wouldn't have worked so well. But people get the spooks all the time and it's instinctive to get away from whatever's freaking them out. You would have felt the brunt of it too if you hadn't been touching me. Fear's not overly selective."

They watched as she climbed into the truck. Toronto reached into a pocket and tossed a set of keys towards Kel. Moonlight filtered through the trees, highlighting his face as he started to strip. The clothes came flying towards Kel and in under thirty seconds, Toronto was bare-ass naked. "Car's on the road just outside the cemetery."

Kel didn't bother asking what he was supposed to do with the clothes or the car. Toronto shifted and in seconds, he was racing across the cemetery in full wolf form.

Faster than a speeding wolf, Kel thought inanely. Clothes tucked under one arm, he ran through the cemetery, the cool wind a rush against his face and the moonlight illuminating the darkness under the trees.

Toronto's car, a classic Mustang, was almost always in a state of rehab, but the engine ran as smooth as silk. It purred like a big cat when Kel started it up. Following Toronto's elusive scent, he hit the road.

Chapter Seven

Halfway home, Angel's mind started trying to think past the fear suffocating her. She had no idea what had happened—one second, she'd been lying by Kel's grave, drifting closer and closer to sleep. It wasn't the first time she'd drifted off at Kel's grave. Even knowing that he wasn't *in* there, something about the cemetery comforted her.

Then, abruptly, that comfort had vanished and Angel was jerked into a cold, hard awareness. Unsure why, she'd been filled with a sense of fear that had jump-started her instincts Single woman, at night, alone in a cemetery—shit, it sounded like some kind of B horror movie.

The more she tried to think past the fear, the easier it got and by the time she was five miles away, she wondered what in the hell she was doing. She'd been half-asleep—had somebody driven by? Had there been somebody else at the cemetery?

She didn't know.

But she wasn't going back there tonight, that was certain. She glanced in her rearview mirror and although it was nothing more than her mind pulling tricks on her, it seemed as though darkness chased her.

Darkness... That was all it took. That one thought passing through her mind, and the fear was back. Seriously back and trying to think past the fear wasn't helping this time because the more she thought about it, the more afraid she got.

"Then don't think about it. Your imagination is going to be the death of you," she muttered. Five minutes later, she turned onto the rutted, winding road that led to her house. When she pulled in front of her house, the motion-activated floodlight came on and she breathed out a sigh of relief as it managed to dispel some of the gloom.

For some reason, the sight of the light, of her little house badly in need of repair, made her feel better. Beyond the front door there was safety.

She grabbed her purse and keys, striding up to the door. The skin along her shoulder blades went tight. She almost paused long enough to look back—somebody was watching her. She felt it.

Her body was screaming a warning at her. That vague sense of fear was back, magnified, and now it had a focus. She didn't just feel fear.

She sensed malice, something evil. Something ugly.

Human nature—it could make a person hide under the covers to avoid seeing the monsters or it could make them turn around when to do so was death. Never made sense.

But Angel would be damned if she played into that B-movie mindset by slowing down to look instead of getting someplace safe. No—not someplace. In her house, across the threshold with the door shut behind her.

Angel got the door unlocked in record time and slid inside, shutting it with a bang. She turned the locks, the one in the doorknob, the deadbolt and the chain.

Something brushed her leg and Angel yelped, tearing away, only to realize it was Rufus. The big ugly mutt stared at her, his head cocked. He went to nuzzle her leg but then he froze, his hackles rising and his lips pulling back from his teeth in a snarl.

That elusive fear was pushing in on her again, choking her.

She checked each of the locks.

Wasn't enough. A scared, high-pitched voice kept whispering through her mind. *Not enough, not enough, not enough.* Rufus came to brace his warm body by her leg and she reached down, buried a hand in his fur.

The calmer, rational part of her mind told her to chill out. She was inside the house. Inside the house was safe. Inside the house was a big, mean dog that would rip any burglar to shreds and he'd also sound a warning if somebody was trying to break into the house...right?

This ain't no home intrusion, she said silently.

And Rufus wasn't exactly throwing out the welcome mat, either. Not with the way he began to pace stiff-legged back and forth in front of the door.

Angel had no idea which voice to listen to. Bad things happened to people in their own houses all the time—she knew *that* from experience. Closing her eyes, she pressed her brow to the door, pressed her shaking hands flat to it and just breathed. In. Out. In. Out. Concentrating on the feel of the air moving in and out of her lungs, the way her chest expanded.

After five seconds, the shaking in her hands subsided. After ten, the cloud of terror wrapping around her mind cleared. Rufus paused in his guard-dog duty long enough to nose her leg and whine softly. Angel reached down, scratched him behind the ears. "It's okay, boy."

Once more able to think on her own, she straightened away from the door and edged over to the window. She looked through the gap in the curtains, staring down the drive.

Darkness.

Just darkness.

"You're not afraid of the dark, Angel," she told herself. As little sense as it made after the attack, she was more at home in the dark than in the light. Whatever was going on, whether her mind was playing tricks on her or whether it was trying to warn her of some impending threat, she wasn't going to cower in the dark.

Deep breath in...deep breath out...deep breath...

Shit!

The deep breath lodged in her throat like a lump of ice. She reached up, rubbed her eyes and squinted, focused on the drive. Something had moved.

Something *big*. The faint, indistinct shadow made her think *dog*, but it was too damn big to be a dog. Way too big. Unless the dog was the size of a pony.

And once more, Rufus started to growl. Softly, almost like he was trying to ask her what in the hell was going on?

"Shit..."

In the shadows, something stirred. When the yellowish

gleam first appeared, Angel didn't notice. But then it—*no—they* moved. Disappeared for a second, reappeared—blinking. And closer.

Eyes. Shit. Blinking yellow eyes in the front yard, something that looked like a big-ass dog. The very air around her felt heavy and cold, weighing down on her. Swallowing the huge knot in her throat, she slowly eased her mental shields down. Like rolling down a car window, she let them lower bit by bit.

Tensed.

Waiting.

There. She felt it—no. Him. Those thoughts had a decidedly male tone. Her first instinct was to jerk away, close her mental shields up tight and grab the phone. But human nature intervened again and instead of pulling back, Angel lowered her shields a little more, enough to not just *sense* the thoughts but *make* sense of them.

There was nothing of evil to them.

And she had the most fucked-up feeling whoever—or *whatever*—was aware of her psychic probe. It came in images and emotions, not words, but there was no denying what she was picking up.

Just like there was no denying the blackness that suddenly emerged from the night, rushing at her.

Racing towards her.

Rufus' growls were no longer soft. He backed away from her, just a bit, and stood with his head low to the ground, hackles up and body stiff. The deep, angry growl sounding from him had gone from protective and worried to downright pissed.

Mouth gone dry with fear, Angel retreated, one step at a time, until she stood by the phone. From the corner of her eye, she saw the illuminated keypad of her phone and she started to reach for it.

But then, before she could touch it, she curled her fingers into a fist and let it drop to her side. Without understanding how, she knew that the cops couldn't do a damn thing.

Fear could be so many things. It could be insidious and creeping—like what she'd sensed that night years before when somebody had broken into her mom's house and attacked her, killed Kel.

It could be a fast, unending slide into madness—the slide she'd taken after Kel's death had been riddled with fear, self-doubt and guilt.

It could be a foggy, indistinct cloud like what she'd sensed as she raced towards home only moments ago.

And it could be a storm. The storm coming at her now was hurricane force and there was nothing to shelter her from it. The silence in the air was deafening and that only made everything that much more terrifying. It was quiet, save for the sounds of her ragged panting and Rufus' snarling growls. He inched forward even as she tried to close her fingers around the thick ruff of his fur. He kept moving, ignoring her silent commands, and placed his body between her and the door.

A low...nasty...*cruel* chuckle.

Far, far off. Moving closer. Closer. Closer until she knew now that if she looked out the window, she'd see him. There was no shadow outside the window, but she didn't care. *He* was out there now.

Out there with whatever or whoever else she'd sensed.

The hair on the back of her neck stood up and blood roared in her ears. That laugh.

She'd heard it before. In her dreams, a lingering taunt of the night that had cost her the one person in the world that she loved.

"God, not again," she whispered, her voice ragged and harsh. "I can't do this again."

Something sounded just outside the door. A footstep—deliberately loud, he wanted her to hear him. To know he was near.

With her shields still down, she could feel him and the cloying, cold chill of his thoughts was as terrifying now as it had been that night. Memories once so dim, hidden by her subconscious, rose like a tidal wave, capsizing any and all attempts to think rationally. In a vain attempt to stem that flow of memories, she jerked her shields back up.

"Where are you..."

His voice was loud—too loud. Like he'd spoken through a

microphone, echoing through her house, across her land. But he wasn't speaking to her.

He was aware of her—as aware of her as she was of him, she knew it. But his question wasn't directed at her.

The other—that presence. Was he looking...?

"You have no lack of protectors, sweet baby," his voice crooned and this time she knew he was talking to her. She heard his words clear as a bell even though he was still outside.

Protectors—?

She glanced down at Rufus and then towards the window where she'd stood when she saw those eyes out in the darkness.

"Hmmmm... What do we have here?"

Angel jumped when she heard another speak.

Another voice. Deep. Gruff. Completely unfamiliar. "You know you shouldn't have done this. We're talking a mistake of epic proportions."

The *thing* laughed. He was no man—she could sense nothing of humanity within him. Nothing but a pure, malicious intent. Angel had long believed that sometimes monsters walked in human form—what else could describe serial rapists, child molesters and cold-blooded killers?

Now she knew without a doubt that she was right. The monster on her porch—if he'd ever been human, it was a long, long time ago.

"You don't really think you can stop me, do you? Nobody has yet."

"That's because you were smart enough to stay below the radar. But you're in it now," the other one said, his voice a deep, bass rumble.

The thing laughed again—that laugh seemed to be a favored taunt, managing to pack derision, amusement, malice and challenge all into one single sound, no words needed. "Tell me, Hunter, where's the boy? Why isn't he here to save his lady love?"

"What makes you think he isn't?"

Another voice. It came from off to the side, faint but

growing louder. Another sound, and then a shadow passed in front of the window closest to Angel. The shadowy shape paused just in front of the window and Angel stopped breathing as his head turned.

She had the weirdest feeling he knew she was there—knew exactly where, and neither the curtains nor the darkness within the house was any kind of barrier.

That voice—she licked her lips. Familiar. Tears burned her eyes. *Too* familiar. Slowly, she took a step forward. Then another. Another. But before she could get to the window and jerk open the curtain, he moved away.

"Ahhh... There's the white knight. I see you brought reinforcements this time. What is it, boy? Aren't you man enough to protect your woman on your own? Aren't you up to a fair fight?"

Your woman—

That voice—

A whimper escaped her lips and she reached up, pressed her fingers to her lips to stifle the sound.

"Yeah, I saw just how you like to fight fair, bastard. Silver handcuffs, a weaker creature—big on equality, aren't you?"

The words didn't make sense to her. But they didn't have to. She focused on the voice and when he stopped speaking, she wanted to scream. She went to the door, pressed her hands against it and rested her cheek against the smooth, painted surface. *Say something!*

But there were no more words. Just a huge crash. Angel jumped, fell back from the door and ended up on her butt. Scrambling backward, she stared wide-eyed and terrified.

Under the fear, though, there was something inside she hadn't felt in years. Twelve long empty years. It wasn't *hope*—hope was all too often fragile and elusive.

This wasn't hope. It was belief, strong and certain, and it wouldn't let her stay where she was any more. Shoving to her feet, she rushed for the door but she never made it.

Hands came up from behind, grabbing her. She screamed or tried to—but one of those hands came up, covered her mouth. From the corner of her eye, she saw Rufus, but the dog lay on the floor and as she watched, he rolled onto his back in an outright display of submission.

"Calm down, cupcake." The voice, that deep, grumbling growl, was soft and gentle but she was too damn terrified to be reassured.

She brought up a foot to smash down on his, but he moved too quick, evading her with ease. She tried striking back with her head, trying to smash his nose but he moved, evaded with that same seamless grace.

"Calm down," he repeated. "Listen, I'll take my hand away but do me a favor...don't scream. I fucking hate screams."

He lowered his hand. Without batting a lash, Angel opened her mouth and screamed as loud as she could.

"Damn it!" he swore, clamped a hand back over her open mouth—and got bit.

Angel closed her mouth as hard as she could, biting until she tasted blood and she still didn't let go. He hissed and let her go. Angel stumbled away, crashing into the couch and instinctively, she jumped over it, putting it between them before she turned to face him.

She flinched as he reached out and turned on a lamp, squinting against the brightness. Rufus continued to lie on his back by the front door, his eyes rapt on the face of the man before her. A man she hadn't ever seen in her life. He probably wasn't even an inch taller than her and he had hair that would have done a Hollywood starlet proud, long, razor-straight and the palest blond, almost white. His eyes were equally pale, ice-blue, surrounded by a rim of deep navy.

The look on his face was one of exasperation. Scowling, he looked at his hand. "Damn it, you're a little she-cat, aren't you?"

Angel didn't answer. Instead, she backed away.

The man sighed and reached up with his uninjured hand, pushing his hair back from his face. "Look, you can stay as far away from me as you want but if you try to leave the house, I'm going to stop you. You won't like that. Let's just avoid it."

There was another crash outside, strong enough to shake the house down to the foundation. Low, ugly curses, an animalistic snarl. The nasty, slimy voice promising—*no. You didn't hear that. You didn't hear that.*

The words broke off mid-sentence—or they were cut off, probably by a fist. She could hear it, the ugly thwack of flesh on flesh. Her mind shied away from what was happening on the porch—even from *who* was on the porch, because she couldn't think about that and the man in front of her, the man she had to get past if she was going to get out of here.

"What do you want?" she asked. The words came out through a throat gone tight with fear and had as much substance as cotton candy, but he heard her well enough.

A small, gentle smile curled his lips and he said, "Just to help. That's all."

He cocked his head and when he looked at her, Angel suspected he saw far deeper than most.

Her suspicions were confirmed when he said, "You can tell if I'm lying or not, if you'll let yourself."

She swallowed and jerked her gaze away from him. There was no way she was lowering her shields right now, not with...with...whatever that was outside her front door. She couldn't take having that evil taint inside her thoughts again.

Sidling along, she edged a little farther away from Blond, Strange and Scary. He stood where he was. His chest was bare, revealing sleek, coiled muscles. Save for the slow rhythm of his breathing, he hadn't moved at all and he looked content to just stand there watching her.

"What's going on?" she asked.

He glanced towards the window and then back at her face. "That's a story that would take a very long time." He frowned and moved forward. "You need to step away from the window."

Angel slid her gaze to the window and then back to him. With a sneer, she asked, "Why? You actually think I'm going to try to climb through it?"

"No. I think—" The look on his face abruptly changed and although some part of her mind realized he'd moved, her eyes couldn't track him. Before she could figure that bit out, he had already grabbed her and spun her away from the window.

Just as something crashed into it. Or someone. Whoever it was didn't come flying in but shards of glass did. Angel felt a few graze her left hand, but the rest of her body was shielded.

Shielded by his very bare upper body.

"That's why." He lifted her up with one arm and carried her around the couch, depositing her onto the thick cushions. Eyes narrowed on her face, he crouched down in front of her, "Stay away from the windows, if you please."

Then he stood and as he turned away, she saw the blood on his back. Long, thin rivulets of red running down his back— the glass. Somehow, he'd known the window was going to break and he'd kept it from cutting her. Swallowing, she decided she might just stay right where she was. For now.

A soft whimpering sound caught her attention and she turned her head to look at Rufus. He was still on the ground, but he wasn't lying prostrate any more. He had rolled onto his belly and lay with his head on the floor as he crept forward, eying the blond stranger.

"What did you do to my dog?"

He turned away from the open window to look at Rufus. Shoulders rose and fell in a deep sigh and then he moved away to kneel down in front of the dog. "I didn't do anything to him, ma'am. He just..." A faint smile cracked his somber face, a smile that made him look all too human, all too friendly. "He knows who the bigger dog is, that's all. Come on, boy." That deep, bass rumble dropped a bit more and he held a hand out to Rufus. Rufus whimpered, whined and crawled forward until he could lick the man's hand. "That's it. I ain't gonna hurt you, but you already know that, don't you?"

He slid Angel a look and then added, "Maybe you should tell your mistress that." He gave Rufus one final stroke and then gestured to Angel. "Go on, boy."

Rufus, as pleased as a puppy, bounded over to Angel, leaped onto the couch and sat with his big body braced against her side. Hooking an arm around his neck, Angel leaned into him. As the sounds of fighting continued outside, she pressed her face into his fur and tried to tell herself she was dreaming.

Dreaming.

Yeah. She could be.

It was possible, right?

Then the man's voice, low and furious, jerked her out of that mindset, jerked her straight back into reality. Jolting, she shoved herself to her feet and watched as the blond paced back and forth between the two windows.

When the low, ugly laugh started, dread rolled through her.

"You didn't really think *you* could stop me, boy, did you?"

"Fuck...*you*." A roar.

Angel caught the flash of movement from the corner of her eye and unable to remain where she was, she headed for the window. Blondie intercepted her.

"Stay back. If you please." He said the words this time through clenched teeth and there was a look in his eyes that she didn't like at all.

Worry.

Somebody outside the house screamed. It washed over her like a cold flood and unable to silence it, she cried out. A pain flared in her side and she moaned. Her legs gave out and she stumbled, swayed and hit the floor.

Dimly, she saw the blond man moving. Heard him swear.

Then he was gone, leaping through the empty window frame.

That laugh. Then a howling sound and the laugh ended abruptly, followed by something that made her belly turn just to hear it—wet, gurgling, like something out there was drowning. Drowning in what? *Stupid, stupid mind*—always trying to puzzle something out, even just little personal thoughts—and now her mind was hard at work to fill in the *what*.

Blood. Choking on it.

It was the only *what* that came to mind and she looped her arms around her knees and hid her face against her legs. Common sense dictated she stay just where she was. It was nice and safe there... Nice and dark and if she could just block out the noises coming from outside, maybe, just maybe she could manage to convince herself this was nothing but a bad dream and she'd wake up...

Not if it's not a dream.

Slowly, she lifted her head and looked at the windows. She could hear Blondie out there talking, his words not making much sense, but at least she could hear him. She'd take hearing that harsh voice over the *other* one any day.

But no matter how hard she listened, she couldn't pick up

161

on that third voice...the one that sounded so heartbreakingly familiar. And it was the need to find out who'd been talking that brought her to her feet. Had her creeping to the window, peering out.

The moonlight shining down wasn't bright enough to illuminate much—and her floodlight was no longer working. She had no idea why. It came on if a rabbit hopped across the yard and this was definitely more than a floppy-eared bunny. Blondie was easy to see, the moonlight reflecting off that pale hair of his. He stood out in the yard, looking down. She scanned the yard and the porch, searching for something else. Squinting hard, she could just barely make out someone lying on the ground at his feet—he was looking down and talking to whoever it was on the ground.

Instinctively, she tore her gaze from them. They weren't who she was looking for. Not who she needed to see. Where... Something moved—close. On the porch. She could just barely see it.

A hand.

It twitched. Fingers curled inward. Just the hand...that's all she could see. But the sight of that hand hit her as hard as hearing that familiar voice had just a few minutes ago. She swayed and ended up locking her knees just to remain upright. Leaning against the wall, letting it support her weight, she moved towards the front door.

Stupid, stupid girl...don't go out there! Finally, the two voices in her head had merged into one and both of them were screeching at her.

But she couldn't listen.

Not to save her life.

She had to go outside.

Had to look.

Had to see what was making her heart race like this—race like she'd just taken a freefall and knew without a doubt she'd land safely. Exhilarating. Intoxicating. Addictive.

No reason to feel like that when some freaky blond breaks into her house while a couple of unseen men battle it out like some live-action version of *Mortal Kombat.* In her front yard, no less. No, no reason to feel more alive now than she had in twelve years. She ought to be too scared to think, not burning with anticipation.

But she was. Slowly, she reached for the door and unlocked each lock with careful, steady deliberation. With that same careful, steady deliberation, she eased the door open and looked through the narrow crack down the porch.

She could see his arm now, could see that he was trying to sit up.

But she couldn't see *him*. And she desperately needed to. She took one small sidestep through the door, followed by another. A third. His upper body was fully visible now, including his averted head. The shirt he wore was in tatters and she could just barely make out the glint of a gold chain through the smears of blood all over his chest.

A lot of blood, but she didn't see any wounds.

Then he sat up—and she saw.

A huge, gaping wound in his left shoulder, gushing blood. It was huge. Fricking huge, like a-kid-could-put-his-fist-inside-it huge. And he was moving. Not just breathing and hanging on, but moving.

Moving...moving...he swung his head towards her and the sight of his face totally drained her strength. The full moon overhead cast silvery light down on him, revealing a face that haunted her dreams.

Angel sagged to her knees, staring at him in dumb, stunned amazement.

"Kel...?"

His lids drooped low. His voice, broken and ragged, drifted to her as he rasped, "Get in the house, Angel. *Now.*"

But she couldn't have moved if her life depended on it.

And it did.

From the yard, she heard Blondie's unmistakable voice as he swore. "Son of a bitch! Damn it, girl, get in the—" Abruptly, his words ended and a weird, muffled-sounding *pop* echoed through the air.

Kel lurched to his feet, moving with a speed that shouldn't have been possible, considering he had a gaping hole—no. No, it wasn't gaping...but it had been...right? He came towards her, reached down and grabbed her arm and without slowing, hauled her upright and shoved her towards the door. "*Inside,*" he rasped.

None of it made sense.

Not seeing him.

Not the way he pushed her towards the house.

Reaching up, she touched her fingers to his face and whispered his name. A tortured look passed across his face and he murmured, "God, Angel..."

For the briefest second, she thought he was going to... She wasn't sure. But all he did was shove her. *Hard.* So that she stumbled into the house. His lids drooped and then he looked at her. In the depths of his sea-green eyes, she saw a screaming, endless hell. Then he blinked and it was gone. "If you ever loved me, you'll stay in that house until dawn. You hear me? Don't—"

"Oh, how my poet's heart leaps at such an ardent plea."

From where she sat on her ass in the doorway, she shifted her gaze and focused on the face of the man who had destroyed her life. Destroyed Kel's life—or so she'd thought for twelve years. But the man turning away from her wasn't dead like she'd believed for so many years.

In a voice that sounded too old for his years, Kel said, "Let's finish this."

"Hmmm. Indeed. Just you and me." The other man—the thing—moved with a silken, boneless grace as he circled around Kel. "Finish it so I can get to dealing with her. I've already wasted much of the night."

He slid her a glance and that alone made Angel feel so dirty, she wanted a bath. "If I'd known you were going to bring friends, I would have brought more of my little presents. You fool Hunters. I must give you credit; you have the most amazing knack for crafting weapons. Like silver nitrate. Even now it's poisoning that stupid wolf. I'd planned to use it on you. A pity."

His stringy black hair fell into his face, half-obscuring his pale features, but not enough to hide his gaze, that hideous dark gaze that somehow managed to gleam red in the night. There were dark splotches all over his clothes that made Angel think of blood, but she saw no obvious signs of injury. Even the bloodied marks on the man's neck—was it even blood? If his throat was bleeding that much, wouldn't he be unable to move?

Kel's bleeding like that—and he's moving.

Because of her. He was there because of her...somehow, through some bizarre quirk of fate or some divine miracle, he was here, again, to keep a monster away from her. The blinders that had hidden that night from her conscious memory shattered under that knowledge. Some of the night, she'd never remember—she'd passed out from blood loss, but for a few seconds, she'd come out of that black haze, long enough to see Kel struggling with a man.

That was all she remembered, but she knew that Kel had stopped this man from hurting her in the past. And he was determined to do it again—even when blood pumped from the wound in his chest.

Kel lunged. The two went rolling across the yard, fists flying, harsh curses drifting through the air. A laughing, mocking voice. "You've lost all your toys, Hunter brat. You can't hope to beat me..."

Angel tuned out the voice. Tuned out everything but getting to her feet. The gray fog of shock was pressing in on her, but she made herself think through it, past it. Rufus appeared at her side, pressing his big body against her leg in support. Sinking her fingers into his furred neck, she stepped back over the threshold.

Rufus whined—something about the sound caught her attention and she glanced down at him. He was looking towards Blondie with soulful, dark eyes. Angel looked back towards Kel but when she did something else snagged her attention.

Something matte black.

Hurt him.

That was all Kel could focus on. If he hurt the bastard bad enough, he'd have to run away. Kel had done it before. He could do it again.

Angel was in the house and so long as she stayed over the

threshold, she was safe.

Toronto wasn't dead. Kel could hear his heart beating and his breath wheezing in and out of his lungs. Whatever kind of poison the feral had shoved into the shifter hadn't killed him yet, so that was a sign it wouldn't kill him. Toronto was strong. Strong enough to battle the effects of silver, provided he was given the time and not injured further.

All Kel had to do was hurt the feral enough that he ran away—give Toronto that time and then Toronto would take care of Angel. It didn't matter if the feral managed to kill Kel doing it.

Didn't matter—hell, probably better that way.

The feral struck Kel in the healing wound high on the left side of his chest, his fingers digging into tissues, sinew, muscle and bone. He grabbed, ripped, twisted. Raw pain shuddered through Kel and he just barely managed to hold his scream behind his teeth.

He let go of the feral, just for a second—it was a risk, but one he had to take. He had to... The world swam sickeningly before his eyes as the feral continued to tear into Kel's chest wound. But Kel didn't stop, didn't slow, didn't falter, as he reached for the final weapon he had.

A silver knife.

Not a K-bar this time, but a sliver-thin stiletto. He grabbed it and struck out, burying it in the feral's neck. Hissing, the feral tore away and clawed at the blade until he knocked it free.

"Enough of this," he spat at Kel.

Kel wasn't the only one who'd come into this armed, he realized. The gun in the feral's hand was a different make than the Hunter preferred. A Glock—and Kel had no illusions about what sort of ammo the gun carried.

"Enough." A faint, eerie smile curled the feral's lips and he flicked his glance towards the house.

Unable to keep from doing the same, Kel followed the feral's gaze. But he didn't just glance. He looked. And because he looked, he saw Angel rising from a crouch on the porch.

And in her hand, she held Kel's Beretta.

His very-much-loaded Beretta.

"Yes." Kel's lips curled in a smile as she lifted the gun. He dropped the shields that had held them apart for twelve years and felt her calm, certain resolve as she squeezed the trigger. "Enough."

He looked back at the feral just in time to see the feral turn his head towards Angel, just in time to see the very messy results as a specially made bullet, a hollow, silver-tipped little sucker, the head filled with silver nitrate, tore through flesh and bone.

The feral's head exploded and brain matter, blood and bone littered the night.

"Enough," Kel whispered.

And then, his head fell back onto the ground and his lids drooped.

Blackness wrapped around him in a comforting cocoon, thick, impenetrable. Warm. He hadn't been warm since he'd lost her, but it made sense that now, he was warm one last time.

Death, he decided, wasn't going to be that bad.

She was safe…and she'd be free of him. She could start to get over him. That was what mattered.

It was his last conscious thought as he slid into oblivion, the wound in his shoulder spilling blood onto the ground.

Chapter Eight

The clock's ticking was abnormally loud. Or at least it seemed that way to Angel as she shifted on the floor and rolled her head to stare at Kel.

Her entire body ached from the chore of dragging him into the house. Even as she'd done it, she wondered why she bothered.

He was dead.

This time, well and truly. She'd never have answers for where he'd been, what had happened...why he'd left her. The ugly injury in his chest had long since stopped bleeding and when she'd touched her fingers to his neck, desperately seeking a pulse, there hadn't been one.

After trying to feel one for a few seconds, she'd bent over him, listened desperately for the sound of his breathing. Anything. But his chest didn't rise, his heart didn't beat and even though it had only taken her seconds to get to him after she'd shot...the other...his body had already started to cool. Getting him in the house—had she wasted precious time? She didn't know much about first aid, but if she'd stopped the blood flow sooner would it have helped?

Logically, her brain said no. There was so much blood. It didn't seem possible somebody could survive losing that much blood.

He was dead.

So she sat there on the floor beside him, staring at his face through a veil of tears. Occasionally, she reached out and combed her fingers through his silken gold-touched hair, or traced the line of his jaw. If she'd had any doubt, the coolness of his skin, his absolute stillness would have destroyed it.

He was as cold as a corpse and he hadn't once tried to breathe since she'd dragged him into the house nearly an hour earlier.

The tears continued to roll down her cheeks. She'd long since stopped wiping them away, long since stopped trying to come up with answers. There were none. No answers. No justice. No explanation for why she'd lost him, why he'd returned after twelve years only to die, truly die this time, right in front of her.

"Girl."

She should have been afraid. After the hell she'd witnessed through the night, the sound of somebody speaking to her should have terrified her. Especially when she turned her head and saw that it was the blond stranger, swaying in the open door, naked as a jaybird and staring at Kel with wide, worried eyes.

There was an ugly, and she did mean ugly, wound in the guy's belly. It was almost like something had tried to claw its way in—or out, perhaps. It was seeping red, wet blood, blood streaking down over his right hip, over his thigh. It wasn't the only injury, either. There were bruises that looked days old, yet he hadn't had them before he left the house, had he? He'd had the cuts from flying glass on his back, but he hadn't looked like he'd gone a round or two with Rocky Balboa.

He did now, though. His body was liberally littered with injuries. Scratches, bruises, bleeding cuts.

"Sunrise."

That was all he said, but it didn't make much sense to her. She slid her gaze past his shoulder to stare at the eastern horizon at his back. The sun was rising and in a few minutes, she'd be able to see the results from last night in bright, vivid detail.

Instead of answering, she just turned her head and stared at Kel. At his still face. He still looked so damned perfect. Under the blood and the scrapes and bruises, she suspected he'd still look pretty much like he had then.

"Damn it. *Sunrise.*"

The man's voice was imperative this time and it hit her

shields with enough force to make her flinch. Turning her head, she said in a clear, level voice, "What the fuck do I care if the sun is rising?"

His eyes narrowed. He lurched inside, blood dripping from his side to plop onto the floor. He stumbled to his knees beside Kel, but when he reached out to touch him, Angel came off the floor and leaped for him. "Leave him *alone!*" she snarled, swinging out and clipping him on the chin.

He caught her wrists in a brutal, merciless grasp. "He can't be here..." His voice broke off and he panted for air. "When the sun rises...it will kill him."

Something about those words should have bothered her. If she had cared about anything. But she didn't. In a dull voice, she replied, "He's already dead."

"Fuck." He shoved her off to the side. Weak as he appeared, he had the strength to send her stumbling back onto her ass. He grabbed Kel's body and slung him over a wide, blood-streaked shoulder in a fireman's hold, like Kel didn't even weigh fifty pounds.

"Leave him *alone!*" Angel demanded again, shoving upright and reaching out.

This time, he caught her wrist and jerked her against him. He bent down low and put his face in hers. "I didn't live through this to watch him die now."

"He's already dead!" she screamed. So loud, so ragged—it hurt her throat, but she didn't know how much of that came from saying the words or from her screaming.

But he wasn't affected at all. He just pulled away, stumbled out of the living room, leaving behind him a dripping trail of blood.

"Not happening this way," Toronto muttered, keeping one hand braced against the wall in an effort to keep from falling forward on his face. "Not going to happen."

The silver lingering in his system pretty much sapped what little strength he had, but sheer determination had gotten him to his feet, just like it had gotten him into the house, just like it had gotten him to pick up Kel—and it would get him into the kitchen because there was a door there that led downstairs. He'd seen it when he came in through the back door, and being the good little soldier he was, Toronto had taken two seconds to check it out. It led to a basement. Someplace dark where Kel could sleep safely, away from the daylight.

She was following along behind him and Toronto wished he had the strength to reassure her. To say something. But it was getting harder and harder with every step just to stay upright. By the time he'd stumbled into the kitchen, his legs were shaking and by the time he made it to the basement door, his vision was graying out. One step at a time. One step...

On the fourth to last step, his strength gave out and his abused, toxin-filled body went down. Kel, limp as a rag doll, hit the ground. Casting a quick look around the basement, Toronto reached out, grabbed Kel's wrist and began to crawl. Crawl until the two of them were in the far northeast corner of the house, out of sight of the few windows and hopefully...away from the sun.

Stunned dismay was the only thing to describe what she felt as she followed the blond down the steps, watched as he fell. Kel's body went flying and Angel stifled a scream. Her heart, already barely beating, died just a little more.

But the man wasn't done.

No, it wasn't enough that he'd grabbed Kel away from her and used his physical strength to keep Angel from getting to him. On his knees and one hand, the other hand holding Kel's wrist, he dragged both himself and Kel into the shadows. She stood at the bottom of the steps now, staring as he settled in a corner and pulled Kel closer, kind of the same way a girl might hold a rag doll, with him tucked up against his side.

"Sunset."

Angel blinked and tried to focus on the man's face better, but all she could see was his eyes. Those pale blue eyes—blue...but in the darkness, they gleamed yellow. His lids drooped, shielding his gaze.

He muttered it again. "Sunset. You'll see. It's okay. 'Sall okay."

Then his head slumped to the side and he passed out.

"Sunset." The word slipped out through numb lips. Angel shuffled forward, her limbs stiff. She knew from experience how very physical the pain from a broken heart could be—it was a pain that no medicine could ease, no doctor could fix.

Nothing could fix it. Even time... Time may dim the pain a bit, but nothing took it away.

But this guy seemed to think sunset was going to do...what, exactly? She swallowed the lump in her throat and crouched down by the two men. Blondie's chest was moving up and down in a slow, steady rhythm, but Kel—he was still now as he'd been upstairs.

She wanted to cry, but her eyes were painfully dry as she reached out and trailed her fingers along his jawline. How could it be possible that he looked exactly the same? No signs that he'd aged, no physical signs of change at all.

So cold.

So cold.

The cold of his flesh seemed to seep into hers and she shivered, pulling away. The ugly, pitted wound in his chest caught her eye just before she stood and she frowned, leaned in a little. It...no. A trick of the light? Had to be. Something made that wound seem a little smaller.

"You can't just stay here like this. You need to do something," she mumbled. She needed to do something. Call the police. An ambulance for the crazy blond.

Slowly, she straightened, bracing her weight against the wall. If she hadn't had something to lean on, she never would have made it upright. Once she was, she leaned against the wall and closed her eyes.

She felt painfully, achingly ancient—as though she'd aged decades in the span of one night. Each step took far too much energy and by the time she reached the basement stairs, her legs were shaking with exhaustion. Still, she forced herself to climb and she didn't once look back.

It wouldn't help.

He was dead. All these years, Jake had been right to hope that somehow, Kel had survived whatever happened to him that night. He'd survived that night only to die now.

Man. Fate was such an ugly bitch.

The phone caught her gaze but instead of going to it, she shambled into the living room and stared at the gaping window frame. The glass was shattered, laying all over the floor. A few distant thoughts circled through her mind that she should clean up the glass—she didn't want Rufus cutting his feet.

But the distant thoughts never quite spurred any action. All she did was shuffle around the perimeter of the room until she could get to the door. She hadn't even closed it after she'd dragged Kel inside her house and now the interior of the house was cool. Shivering, she reached for the door and started to shut it—

But the sunlight creeping over the horizon caught her eye. *Don't look don't look don't look*—but she looked. Smears and splatters of blood all over the porch. A couple of busted floorboards and the banister on the western side of the porch was trashed.

She could also see why the floodlight hadn't been working earlier. It had been mounted on a wooden pole next to the driveway, and now that wooden pole was split into two pieces, one laying off to the side and the bottom half jutting up from the earth.

One foot in front of the other, one step at a time, she moved out of the house, onto the porch and down the porch steps. The farther she went, the worse it got. As she neared the place where Kel had lain as he died, there was grass still wet with blood.

Sunlight fell across the grass at her feet—and the body laying just off to her right. Angel felt oddly disconnected as she shifted her gaze from the blood-stained grass to the corpse.

That weird disconnected feeling persisted as she stood there. In some part of her head she heard a weird, crackling hiss and in that same part of her head, she realized she smelled smoke. But she didn't attribute the sounds or the scents to the body at her feet until the flames broke out.

It was sudden—one moment, nothing. Then next—*whoosh*. Flames exploded, greedily consuming the flesh and reaching out to lick at hers. Half in shock, Angel didn't acknowledge the danger until the fiery pain scorched her flesh through her pants and she stumbled back, landing on her ass a few feet away as fire ate the body.

Even the bones burned and Angel was pretty certain that wasn't normal. Bones didn't burn like that...right?

The moments dragged on as she watched the fire consume the dead man's body and those moments seemed to last forever, but in all reality, Angel knew it had only taken minutes. As the flames died down and faded away, completely on their own, the sun was still slowly rising in the east so it couldn't have taken that much time.

A vise wrapped around her throat as she shoved to her feet, staring at the smoldering pile of ash. She fell back a step and as she did, something under her foot hissed. It felt like slow motion as she lowered her gaze, looking down...down...down...until she was staring at the blood-splattered grass.

The grass was steaming. Little wisps of steam rising up as the sunlight shed its light across the land. Steaming, the way water did when splashed on a hot skillet. But that wasn't the only thing that happened.

As the grass steamed, the blood disappeared—no, burned. The sun's rays touched the blades of grass and steam rose upward, there was a hissing sound and then the grass was true and green once more. No sign of blood.

The blood—the sun was burning away the blood.

She jerked her head and stared at the pile of ash. A breeze kicked up and the pile of ash went flying. Angel hissed out a breath and backed away as a gray cloud filled the air. The wind died down and when it did, little of the ash remained.

And where the body had lain, the grass underneath was untouched. Not one blade of grass was burned.

Angel prided herself on being fairly rational. Aside from the few months she spent in a pit of despair after Kel... After that night, she tried to act with reason and not with emotion.

But no amount of reasoning would explain this away.

She retreated backwards towards the house, never dragging her eyes away from the spot where she'd watched the body burn. Save for a dusty bit of remnant ash, there was no sign that just a few minutes ago, a body had been burning in the front yard.

Once inside the house, she closed the door, taking extreme care to turn each lock. The care seemed a bit foolish since just off to the side, the gaping window frame would pretty much give anything or anybody a very easy entry.

"Maybe you've finally lost your mind."

The more she thought about it, the more she realized that maybe there *was* a rational explanation. She'd gone crazy. It was a lot more rational to think she might be hallucinating than to consider the possibility that the sun had made that body burn.

This was real life.

Not fiction.

In real life, bodies didn't burn on their own and they didn't burn under sunlight either.

That only happened in movies or TV shows.

Her mind jerked away before she let herself finish that thought. Her thoughts shut down on her, jerked away, retreated back inside her and hiding, much like she was doing as she settled on the couch and pulled her knees to her chest, closing her eyes.

It hadn't happened.

She didn't know what was going on, didn't know if something had happened to push her over the edge, but that was where she was.

It was the only thing that made sense.

Angel just might have spent the rest of the morning, maybe even the entire day, working to convince herself of just that. But a little after eleven, there was a knock on the door. Angel stayed where she was, her face pressed against her knees, her arms wrapped around her drawn-up legs. There was no reason to get up. No reason to answer the door. Something, maybe guilt, stirred in her chest and she thought of the injured man down in the basement—and...no.

No. Don't think about him right now. Not yet.

But she should think about the guy who'd been hurt. Without understanding what had happened, she knew he had been hurt trying to watch out for her.

She should at least care about that as somebody continued to bang away at her door.

But before she could convince herself she needed to get up, answer the door before somebody panicked and called the cops, the knocking stopped. It occurred to her that maybe the cops had already been called.

Even without the corpse in her front yard, it was probably pretty obvious that something seriously weird had happened here. Her busted window. The destruction on the porch and the floodlight, its pole split apart like a toothpick. The glass littering the floor.

The glass—

If the glass hadn't crunched, she might not have realized somebody was now in the room with her. But the glass did crunch out a quiet warning and Angel opened her eyes and leaped over the couch, placing it between her and the...

Girl?

Or at least, she looked like a girl. A high school senior, complete with a loose French braid, a fuchsia hoodie and skintight blue jeans that ended at a pair of slender ankles. Her small feet were clad in a pair of black ballet flats that had big yellow smiley faces all over. The expression on her face should have made her look like a petulant teenager, brows drawn low over her eyes, her pink-slicked mouth compressed into a tight frown.

But Angel's gut told her it wasn't a teenager she was facing.

"Who are you and what the hell are you doing in my house?" Angel demanded.

The girl sighed, reached up to tuck a strand of hair behind an ear that was boasting some serious metal—a good ten silver hoops, studs or strands. She didn't answer Angel's question though. She planted her hands on her hips and asked a question of her own. "Where are they?"

That crisp, clear British accent seemed very much at odds with the girl's appearance—or at least, Angel thought so. A little startled by both the voice and the question, she blinked and then squinted. "Who?"

Rolling her eyes, the girl said, "Santa Claus and his elf, sweeting. You know who I'm looking for—I see it in your eyes."

Too much, Angel decided. It was just too fucking much. After the night she'd had, this was too much. The man she loved had come back from the dead, only he very much was dead now. Some seriously weird naked guy was down in her basement with her dead lover's corpse—*oh, God...*

The monster from forgotten nightmares emerging from the night and even though he was dead now, he'd taken Kel with him and then she'd watched in utter shock as the thing's body lit up like some magic act's pyrotechnic display, burning away to ash.

And now some short, stuck-up kid was standing in her house...

Angel snarled and pointed to the door. "Get the hell *out.*" She just barely managed to keep from stomping her foot.

The girl narrowed her eyes. They were heavily made up, but for some reason, it suited her—just like the hoops, studs and fishhook earrings suited her. And just like that look of icy disdain suited her.

"I didn't come all this way to have some silly psychic chit try to throw me out before I can do what I came to do."

Psychic—

Angel went cold. Not because of the word—she knew what she was.

But because nobody *else* knew. Kel had, but he was gone. Nobody else. She hadn't even told her dad. Through stiff lips, she asked, "What did you say?"

"Bloody hell, what am I doing this for?" The girl turned away and heaved out a sigh, her shoulders slumping. She covered her face with her hands and muttered under her breath.

Although Angel couldn't hear the words, she didn't need to. If she hadn't been so completely shaken, she would have had a few of her own.

The girl took a deep breath as she turned back to Angel. The look on her young face didn't seem to fit, not now, not as the girl's eyes softened on Angel's face. "You've had a time, haven't you? I'm sorry. I don't want to be here, but that's hardly your fault, now is it?"

Angel tried to reach for her anger again. It was a lot easier to deal with than the icy fear snaking through her. But she couldn't quite manage to find the anger—hell, she barely managed to find her voice as she said again, "Get out."

177

The woman shook her head. "I can't do that, love." She tipped her head back, her lids drooping low over her eyes. She sighed and the sound whispered, echoed through the house.

When she looked back at Angel, her eyes were glowing.

Then she blinked, and whatever it was, disappeared. Her face was blank, devoid of weariness, devoid of disgust, devoid of any sort of emotion. But there was a world of it in her voice as she murmured, "I always get stuck cleaning up the messes."

With that rather cryptic comment, she made her way through the mess of broken glass towards the kitchen. Angel went after her and reached out, grabbed the girl's shoulder. "Damn it, you're in *my* house."

"Yes...and your house somehow ended up in the middle of our mess. I can't just leave it like this, now can I?"

Angel had one of two options... Well, maybe three, but she wasn't so sure that calling the cops was wise. Of course, she didn't have much choice...not with—no. *Damn it, no. Don't think about that yet.*

But Angel didn't know how much longer she could *not* think about it.

Calling the cops didn't seem to be the best choice, but she didn't have the strength, or even the will, to drag some pissed-off, possibly insane coed out of her house kicking and screaming. So she went with the third choice. She followed along mutely and when the girl saw the two men and reacted like she'd found exactly what she'd expected, Angel realized she wasn't all that surprised.

"Shite, Toronto. I'd have expected better of you." She spoke in a level, calm tone, but she might as well have shouted it.

The words cracked through the basement and echoed back around them. The man on the floor hadn't moved an inch since he'd lost consciousness earlier and Angel suspected the girl was wasting her time. Normally, Angel didn't mess with pointing out the obvious, but hey, if it got the girl out of here quicker. "He can't hear you."

But to Angel's surprise, the man's lips curled up in a faint, sardonic smile. His eyes didn't open and his voice was slurred, heavy with exhaustion. "Yeah. Me, too. Bastard had silver nitrate..." He sighed, licked his lips.

"Enough, boy. Tell me about it later."

Boy... The naked man on the floor looked like he was fifteen to twenty years older than this chick. Yet he nodded, mumbled out, "Yeah. I'll do that. Glad you're here, Ness."

Within another second or two, he was out again.

"Ness?"

The blonde flicked Angel a glance. "Aye. That's me." She sighed and there was a world of weariness in it. Reaching out, she laid a palm on the still-bleeding injury in the man's side.

Although she didn't know the guy from Adam, something inside Angel that still cared didn't want to see him injured further. "He needs a doctor, not some kid poking at him."

"Needs his head examined, that's what he needs," the girl muttered. Her voice was thick with disgust and she shot Angel a dark look from under her lashes.

Her eyes—those soft, misty blue eyes—shit, were they *glowing*? But then she blinked and looked away. So focused on the woman's weird eyes, though, Angel completely missed something else glowing—the woman's hand as it lay on the blond man's injury. She rose after just a few seconds and shook her head. "Truly, Toronto, how the mighty have fallen."

Angel might have wondered about that curious, cryptic statement, but the girl turned to Kel. She crouched down by him but when she reached out to touch him, Angel's futile grief exploded into white-hot anger. She leaped forward and grabbed her hand. "Damn it, leave him alone."

Ness—whatever kind of weird name that was, jerked her hand away and gave Angel a hard look. "I can't very well help him if I don't look him over, now can I?"

"He's *dead*," Angel shrieked.

And just like that, it hit her. The knowledge she'd shied around accepting came crashing down on her and she broke under the weight of it. A scream of harsh, raw denial tore from her throat and she sagged to her knees.

Sobs wracked her body, tears blinded her and she cried so hard, her throat and chest ached with the force of her grief.

Angel was unaware of the look that crossed over the girl's face, unaware of anything and everything. Even when the girl sighed and came to her, knelt down and wrapped a slender arm around Angel's shoulders, Angel was unaware.

Nothing could penetrate the heavy, choking shroud of grief.

She cried until there were no tears left. She cried until her voice gave out on her and her cries were little more than harsh pants. She cried until her entire body ached with it. And even when the storm started to ease, the pain lurked inside her heart, all too real, all too consuming.

A hand stroked down her back.

It took a few seconds for her head to process that she wasn't alone—she'd forgotten about her unusual, unexpected guest until the girl spoke. "You haven't a clue what's going on, do you, sweet?"

Angel struggled free from the comforting embrace, crawling away. Her head ached, her throat was raw and when she swallowed, it sent a fresh lance of pain screaming through her system. The crying jag hadn't alleviated the pain at all. She got a few feet between herself and the girl before she sat down and drew her legs up. She pressed her face to her knees and had to work just to breathe.

Ness sighed. "What an absolute fucking mess," she said.

When she spoke again, her voice was demanding, commanding and firm—a voice not to be ignored. "Look at me, girl. Listen up." Without understanding why, Angel looked.

Ness went to kneel down by Kel, touch her hand to his face and then looked at Angel. An odd, rather eerie smile curled her lips and she said, "With that gift of yours, you should understand well enough that there are many, many things in this world that cannot be rationally explained. That things aren't always as they appear."

She cocked her head, her attention completely focused on Angel. "Do you believe that?"

Angel's voice was a broken, raspy whisper, but the girl seemed to hear it well enough. "I know that a dead body is just that...*dead*."

"Hmmm. But his body isn't dead." She held out a hand and said, "Come."

Angel didn't want to. She didn't want to do anything but sit there and try to will her heart to stop beating. So why was she standing...walking...placing her hand in the girl's uplifted one?

Ness tugged until Angel knelt beside her and then she guided Angel's hand to Kel's neck. Angel tensed and jerked away. She didn't—couldn't—the feel of his lifeless body, the sight of it, they were forever burned on her memory and she didn't want to add to it.

But the girl either did some serious weight lifting or she was a cyborg under that fluffy fleece hoodie. She kept her hold on Angel's wrist and forced Angel to lay her hand on Kel's neck. "Wait..." she murmured. "Just wait."

"Wait for *what*?" Angel snarled and tried to jerk back.

But then...she felt it.

It wasn't a pulse. Not really. It was too vague. Too insubstantial to be a pulse. A flutter, maybe. Like the brush of a butterfly's wing. Her breath lodged in her lungs, her fingers tensed, spread. Angel swore and went still, waiting.

Five seconds passed. Ten. And nothing... Swearing, Angel tried to free her hand again. She was going to go upstairs, get the phone and call the cops. So what if she couldn't explain...

Another flutter.

Five seconds later, another.

A soundless sob escaped her lips. "What in the hell is going on?" she demanded—or tried to. Her words came out in a gruff, rasping croak that barely made sense to her.

But Ness seemed to understand well enough. A sad smile curled her lips and she shook her head. "Now that's an explanation that isn't mine to make."

"Then damn it, who will make it?"

"I'd say he better."

"How is he supposed..."

Ness smiled. "Don't you get it, sweet? He isn't dead...and he isn't going to die. At least not from this." She let go of Angel's hand, and in an abrupt shift, the sharp, clear focus of her gaze went cloudy and a frown appeared on her face as she focused on Kel. "Damn ugly mess on your chest, lad. Did he try to open you with his own hands?"

She let go of Angel's wrist and Angel, thrown off balance, ended up on her butt on the cold, hard concrete. But she didn't notice, her head was too busy spinning, too busy trying to make sense of whatever she was being told.

Dead was dead.

"Fuck me..." It was a soft, disgusted mutter and something about it made Angel look from Kel's still face to the girl's. While the *sound* of Ness's voice hadn't changed, the tone of it, the rhythm of it had. Her accent was a bit more slurred, not so clear and crisp. "Lad, 'e done worked you up good. 'Ealing up, though, aren't you?"

She pulled away Kel's tattered, bloodied shirt and instinctively, Angel went to knock her hands away. But then she *looked*—

And what she saw was something her mind was totally unprepared for. This was no trick of light. There was no way she could have mistaken the seriousness of the injury. What it was, she couldn't say, other than the plain, undeniable fact that the gaping, ugly hole in Kel's upper chest had been grotesque and large, larger than a child's fist and deep. A wound like that should be fatal. It hadn't struck the heart but it had to have gotten the lung. The loss of blood alone would have probably been fatal.

But now? There was reddened tissue, almost like scar tissue, surrounding the open part of the wound and with every passing second, that scar tissue paled out, smoothed out. The wound was shrinking, easily half the size it had been a few hours ago.

Like the floor under her had suddenly grown scorching hot, Angel surged to her feet. She swallowed the knot in her throat as she stared at Kel's chest. "What's going on?"

She might as well have addressed her question to the wall, because the girl had this spaced-out expression on her face and didn't blink when Angel shouted a repeat of her question in her broken, frog croak of a voice.

All Ness did was systematically work shreds of Kel's shirt out of the wound and once she'd done that, she eased the torn shirt away from the wound, leaving it tangled around his torso.

Angel made herself look at him, really look. There had been other injuries on Kel, ragged gashes that made her think of something clawing at his flesh. Bruises, scrapes and abrasions.

Now, save for the ever-shrinking wound in his chest, his body was perfect. Unmarred.

Part of her wanted to hope.

Part of her wanted to believe.

With that gift of yours, you should understand well enough that there are many, many things in this world that cannot be rationally explained, that things aren't always as they appear.

But hope, belief wouldn't soften the blow when she finally accepted the cold and ugly reality. Angel's reality was already desolate enough. She didn't need the added burden of shattered hope.

The logical part of her mind demanded she get out of the basement and away from the girl with the split-personality thing going on. Demanded she call the cops. Demanded she call the doctor and get a psych referral. Because none of what she was seeing was possible, because she couldn't be trapped in the basement with a dead body and two crazy people and because she'd questioned her sanity a lot of times in her life, but never so much as now.

She did none of that.

What Angel did was settle on the foot of the stairs and watch. When Ness stood up and left in silence, Angel watched. When the girl reappeared a few minutes later with Angel's big yellow popcorn bowl filled with water, Angel watched. As Ness cleaned the blood away, as she bodily hauled him a little away from the still-sleeping blond, Angel watched.

The woman worked in silence and once Kel was cleaned up, she knelt by the other man, washing away blood and dirt with a practiced ease. If Angel had let herself think, she might have been thrown by that calm, unaffected manner.

But she wouldn't let herself think—couldn't.

Even when Ness gathered up the bowl, the bloodied water, the torn bits of Kel's shirt and the scissors, all Angel did was sit and watch.

Time passed, the day crawled on by and Angel knew she was alone in the house again. Or almost alone.

Although she didn't sleep, her mind went into a state of semi-shut down, cluttered with vague, surreal thoughts. Caught in a state of dim awareness, she wasn't prepared when somebody brushed past her. Instinct, driven by the night of sheer hell, guided her and Angel swung out, caught the person by the back of the legs and sent her flying.

Only a natural eerie grace and speed kept Ness from plunging face first into the concrete. She caught herself with her hands, tucked her head and rolled with the momentum, coming back onto her feet with a cat's grace. She rose and turned, glaring at Angel. "What the..."

But her words faded when she saw Angel's face. "You didn't hear me come in."

Mute, all Angel could do was stare.

Ness sighed and reached up, rubbed the back of her neck. "Maybe I should wear a bell?" Then she shook her head. "No. No need for that. Not staying. I've brought some clothes for them. I'm not really needed now."

That was when Angel noticed Ness's black duffle. The woman dropped it to the floor and then headed back towards the steps, keeping a careful distance between herself and Angel.

"Where are you going?" Angel rasped. It hurt so much to force the words from her abused throat, it almost brought tears to her eyes.

Ness paused on the step just above Angel. "You cried yourself raw," she murmured. She reached out a hand.

Angel would have jerked away, but there was something on the girl's face that was completely enthralling. Utterly compelling. This time, no mistake about it, her blue eyes *did* glow.

Her hand touched Angel's throat and there was warmth— warmth that quickly became heat and heat became fiery pain— but then the pain flared, exploded...and slowly faded.

"Better?"

Angel jerked back as the woman's hand fell to her side. "Is *what* better... Oh. Oh, *shit!*" She brought up her hand, touching the heated, tingling skin along her throat. Her very much free-from-pain throat. Hell, even the vicious headache brewing behind her eyes had disappeared. "What did you do?"

A grin flirted with the corners of Ness's mouth and she replied, "Nothing much...just a little friendly magick, sweet."

184

Without another word, she jogged up the stairs. Angel sent a glance towards Kel's still body but then she tore up the stairs, determined to get some answers.

But the house, even the yard, was empty and when Angel lowered her shields to search physically, she found nothing. She leaned back against the wall, smacking her head into it and groaning. That she was able to do it without pain only added to her frustration.

She couldn't go from crying herself raw to just *fine* in two blinks of an eye.

But it had happened. Confused, and still so achingly tired, she flopped down onto the couch. Rufus appeared and jumped up to lay half between, half on her legs, his big head resting on her hip.

Absently, she reached down and scratched him behind the ears and closed her eyes. If this really was happening, then she needed to try and make sense out of it. If it wasn't happening, then maybe she could just lie here, be still, and this hallucination or whatever would just *end.*

But her chaotic mind had no desire to let her make sense out of anything. Her thoughts leaped from one memory to the next, from one bit of impossible information and then onto another. She probably spent a good hour lying there, trying to make sense of it, but it wasn't going to happen unless somebody explained.

Angel gritted her teeth. "I want to know what in the *hell* is going on."

A low, grumbling voice came from off to the side. "I might be able to help a little."

Angel yelped and tried to roll off the couch. She ended up falling on her ass because Rufus wouldn't untangle his massive weight from her legs. Shoving to her feet, she immediately backed away before she recognized the voice. The blond. Of weirdness and speed and a body that healed far too quick. He stood before her naked—completely naked, and completely unaffected by it, and it allowed her to see without a doubt none of the injuries he'd acquired earlier were visible.

Not even the ugly-ass wound on his torso, the one that had been leaking blood all over him. The blood. Unable to help herself, she looked down at the floor and saw the blood trail he'd left behind earlier.

But there was no sign of an injury on his nude body. The only imperfection that she could see at all was a mark low on his belly, bright red. And shit—*fading,* disappearing like his body was absorbing even that faint imperfection.

She watched, unable to move for a full minute, and by the time she could tear her gaze away, it was gone.

Blood rushed to her cheeks as she looked up and found him staring at her, a faint smile on his mouth.

"If Kel saw you looking at me like that, he'd gut me." He grimaced and rubbed a hand over his flat belly, lingering where Angel had glimpsed that weird reddened area. "I've had that experience and then some. Don't want a repeat."

He frowned and glanced down. When he looked up, a crooked grin appeared on his face. "Don't suppose you have anything that might fit me, would you?"

"Ahhhh... Uh..." Angel blinked, remembered the black duffle. "There was a girl here. Ness. She brought a bag."

"Ness? You probably mean Nessa." He nodded and glanced around.

"Whatever. Some short, bossy, blonde little brat."

A grin curved his lips and abruptly, he started to laugh. "Yeah, that would be Nessa and damn, but I love hearing her described like that."

"So you know her." Crossing her arms over her chest, Angel scowled. "Then maybe you can tell me how in the hell she ended up here, what in the hell she wanted, or even who in the hell she is."

He shrugged. "Complicated answers. She's a friend of mine, an old friend and she was here because she knew we needed her." Glancing around, he asked, "You said she brought a bag? Where is it?"

She blinked, opened her mouth to answer. But couldn't. The words were locked in her throat. *Downstairs. Downstairs with Kel.*

Again, the girl's words... *Things aren't always as they appear.* Angel wanted to believe that.

Desperately.

Violently.

His eyes narrowed as he studied her thoughtfully. "Downstairs, right?" He glanced behind him towards the door in the kitchen and then he held out a hand. "Come on."

She jerked away, shaking her head furiously. She couldn't go down there—

Silent screams echoed in her mind. She wanted to shout her fury to the skies, the uncaring God that had done this to her...placed Kel back in her life only to have him die right in front of her. But she couldn't do anything but stare at the stranger in front of her and shake her head.

He sighed. A look crossed over his face and then he muttered, "Fuck it."

That was all the warning she had. He moved towards her, too fast, way too fast, and grabbed her. When she tried to pull away, he simply lifted her body and threw her over his shoulder. His grip over her thighs held her firmly in place and if he was at all bothered by her fighting, he never showed it. As he carried her down into the basement, she jerked at his hair, bit whatever body part she could reach and dug her nails into his flesh.

Down in the dark, cool confines, he lowered her to her feet and although his face was impassive when he looked at her, his eyes weren't. They glittered with some suppressed emotion. She'd like to think he was pissed, but her instinct, fueled by her gift, told her that he was laughing at her.

"You're a little cat, aren't you?"

Angel didn't bother answering. She whirled around, rushing for the stairs, all without once looking at Kel. She *couldn't* look at him. Not right now. Not yet. Not until her mind processed that it really was him, that he was dead, that whatever the girl had done to make her hope otherwise had been a trick.

She made it two steps before a hard, strong hand closed around her elbow. "You're not leaving just yet, sugar." He forced her to turn around and face him and she could tell by the look on his face that he didn't give a damn about anything else but keeping her down here, for whatever reason.

He guided her away from the door and then grabbed the bag. When he went to pull on a pair of jeans he found inside, Angel sent another look towards the steps. He stilled, caught her eye and shook his head. "I'll just chase you down, sugar. I'm good at it, believe me."

Clenching her teeth, she gritted out, "Damn it, what in the hell do you *want?*"

He glanced towards the window set high in the wall. Fading sunlight just barely filtered through and the horizon was painted with shades of gold and pink. Abruptly, Angel realized the day was gone. She'd passed the whole day mostly existing in a fog of denial.

Sunset. You'll see. It's okay. 'Sall okay.

Sunset—shit, what had he meant?

She looked back at his face and that weird, secretive smile appeared on his lips. He tugged on his jeans and then held out a hand. "Come on, sugar. Ask yourself this... How can things get any worse?"

Her eyes sought out Kel and she knew, without a doubt, nothing would be worse than seeing him lying dead at her feet. Not even the twelve years she'd spent thinking he was already dead. "What's the point of this?" she asked wearily as she reached out and laid her hand in his.

As though escorting her into a formal affair, he tucked her hand into the crook of his arm and guided her to Kel's side. "The point, sugar, is that not everything is as it seems." He knelt down, and because he still held her hand, she had to kneel with him.

They sat like that for a few seconds, him staring at her and Angel staring everywhere but at Kel or the man. "Toronto—the girl called you Toronto. Is that seriously your name?"

He shrugged. "Seriously, no. But it's the only one I've ever gone by."

From the corner of her eye, she saw his hand, saw him lifting it to touch her face. She braced herself, and still, when he touched her, she flinched. Even through her shields, she could feel the rush within his mind. Indistinct words, thoughts, emotions, all of it a blur. If she lowered her shields, she knew she'd likely pick up more, but she didn't want *more.*

Angel had taken in far too much over the past twenty-four hours and she felt like she was going to crack.

His hand cupped her cheek and guided her face around until their gazes met. "He never stopped thinking about you. Never once stopped loving you. When he realized there was a danger coming your way, he thought of nothing but protecting you."

Tears burned her eyes but she blinked them away. Crying now wasn't an option. Once she started, she knew it would take a long time to stop and she'd rather not fall apart around a stranger twice in one day. "Already figured that much out for myself, thanks," she said, her voice harsh, her tone purposely derisive.

Toronto crooked a grin at her and murmured, "Yeah, that doesn't surprise me. I am a little thrown that you aren't asking where he's been, why he stayed gone...?"

Damn it, the tears were trying to slip free anyway. "Does it really *matter?*"

His only response was a loose, restless shrug. "Maybe. Maybe not. One thing that does matter though He never stopped loving you. Nothing could change that. But what about you? You still love him? Anything gonna change that? Because the answer to that matters quite a bit."

In a voice gone tight with emotion, Angel rasped, "I *never* stopped loving him...not even thinking he was dead all this time could change that. Nothing ever could."

"Good." Then he let go of her arm, reached for something outside her line of sight.

She didn't see what it was at first. But then she saw it, the silver surface reflecting the dim light back at her. A knife. A wickedly mean, serious-looking knife.

Shit—so much for things not getting worse.

But he didn't bring that shiny silver blade within a foot of her. He wasn't looking at her at all. He slashed it along his wrist, then, as blood welled, laid it on the floor at his side. Sparing her a quick glance, he said, "'*Nothing ever could*,' you said."

He lifted Kel's upper body, braced him with one arm.

Angel's eyes went wide as Toronto lifted his wrist to Kel's

189

mouth. "Come on, kid. It's wake-up time."

Whatever Angel had been expecting, it hadn't been this.

Whatever Angel thought that freaky girl from earlier might have meant, it wasn't this.

Whatever weird thing could cause a body to so rapidly heal from injury, it wasn't this.

This was scientifically impossible.

But as she watched, Kel's lashes fluttered. He groaned, low in his throat and then, like a baby rooting for milk, he turned his head towards Toronto's bleeding wrist. His lips parted and she caught a glimpse of something white—then, he struck.

Feeding.

The silence in the room stretched out. Ten seconds passed. Twenty. Thirty. When his eyes abruptly opened, a startled hiss escaped Angel's lips. He didn't see her—something about the glassy, glittery look in those green depths made her think he *couldn't* see her.

It made it a bit easier, actually. Made it easier to focus on the fact that his pale skin was no longer that deathly white. Made it easier for her to shift around a bit until she could look at his upper chest and shoulder.

The sun had set, taking with it the soft golden light that had shone through the windows. Now the light came from three naked bulbs hanging from the beams in the ceiling and their bright light was harsh, unforgiving—and it allowed nothing to hide.

That bloodied, ugly hole was gone. All that remained was a wound that looked almost innocuous, something that might need a few stitches, but not something that could make a man bleed to death before help arrived. And with every passing heartbeat, that wound grew smaller and smaller, the flesh knitting together in a smooth, seamless fashion.

Chapter Nine

"My God." It was the first sound Angel had made in five minutes, since she'd gasped when he opened his eyes and stared off into the distance with a dazed, drugged gaze.

It was a soft, bare whisper but it had a hell of an effect on Kel. He simultaneously cut his gaze towards her and shoved away from the man kneeling beside him.

Toronto rose to his feet and walked over to the dryer, grabbing a rag from the basket on top. As he pressed it to his wound, he turned back to them. There was an expectant look on his face.

But Toronto no longer even existed for Angel. All she could see was Kel. If she was brave enough to lower her shields, she knew he would be all she could feel.

"Kel...?"

His lids flickered but he didn't say anything. He turned away from her. Wide shoulders rose and fell and he brought a hand up.

Edging around, she watched as he wiped the back of his wrist across his mouth. He shot her an unreadable glance and darted away. He bent and grabbed a shirt from the open duffle. He pulled it on as he circled around her and made his way towards the steps.

"Damn it, Kel, what in the hell are you doing?"

He stilled, braced one hand against the wall. He didn't look at her, but at least he finally said something. "Leaving, Angel. This, me, it's nothing you need in your life."

"Leaving...? Life?" She stalked across the cold, hard floor

and grabbed his arm. Under her hand, his skin still felt cool, but not cold like earlier. "What *life*? There's no life without you. Not for me. There hasn't been, from the time I met you."

He slanted a glance at her but just as quick as their gazes met, he looked away again. "You haven't let there be."

His hand came up and he folded his fingers around her wrist, gently, but inexorably tugging until she let go. He lifted her hand and pressed it to his face, rubbing his stubbled cheek against her palm. His lids drooped low over his eyes and a soft, shuddering sigh escaped him. He turned his face into her palm and pressed a kiss there. "Goodbye, Angel."

Oh, hell no. Not now, she told herself, reaching for him again.

But he was already gone, moving on swift silent feet, moving so quickly her brain couldn't catch up with what her eyes saw.

She tore up the stairs, determined to catch him. He couldn't get away from her that easily. He was miles from town, on foot and even if he did move fast, he couldn't...

But he had. She burst through the front door and came to an abrupt halt. Overhead, the sky was becoming ever darker, but it was still just barely light enough to see. Light enough to see that her front yard was empty, as was the long, pitted drive that led out to the road.

"Kel..."

Dazed, she dropped onto her ass in the grass, her arms hanging limp and her eyes focused on the drive as though it would somehow reveal Kel to her.

When a pair of big naked feet appeared in her line of sight, she didn't react. Even when Toronto knelt by her side, she didn't do more than blink and continue to stare down the drive. But she couldn't bite back the words. "This isn't happening," she whispered, shaking her head. "It isn't. It can't be."

He sighed. "Come inside. It's cool out here and you've had a bad few days."

"Few days...no. A bad few years. Bad life." Feeling so completely lost, she lifted her gaze to his face. The compassion she saw on his features was more than she could handle and the tears began to well in her eyes. "I don't understand. Not any of it."

"No. I don't imagine you do." He didn't wait for her to place her hand in his—instead, he lifted her into his arms, rising from the ground like he held a young child instead of a grown woman who stood inch for inch as tall as he.

His body felt ridiculously hot, almost scaldingly so. Burning her. She hated it and as soon as he lowered her to the couch, she scurried away. She ended up huddled against the arm of the couch, staring straight ahead.

Distantly, she heard him speak. But it was distant. When he sighed and reached out to stroke a hand down her hair, Angel barely noticed. He tucked a blanket around her shoulders, tried to push the edges into her hands, but she ignored him.

The blanket sagged and he swore gruffly. "Shit."

He left and she didn't even notice. In a soft, far-off voice, she murmured, "This isn't happening."

She started to rock back and forth, murmuring to herself. Each passing second, she retreated further and further inside herself—inside, where it was safe. Where it was quiet. Where nothing could rip her heart out so completely.

The wolf emerged from the trees along the roadside. Kel didn't see Toronto yet, but he could scent him. He ignored the big creature as it drew even with him and kept on walking. Had to keep walking, couldn't slow down, couldn't think. If he did, he'd never find the strength to keep walking away.

A ripple of energy rolled through the air and the shifter once more wore his human form. Stark naked, he fell into step next to Kel. In a friendly voice, Toronto said, "You know, it's been ten years since I met you. Ten years since the two of us ended up at Rafe's. All those years, I never once thought you were stupid. Reckless, yeah. Foolish, yeah. Careless. Absolutely. But stupid? Nope. At least not until tonight."

Kel flickered Toronto a look but didn't respond. *Keep walking, don't think. Keep walking, don't think.* He chanted it to himself in silence with every step. So far, it had taken him about three miles from Angel. The sun had just barely retreated behind the horizon when he left her house so he easily had a good eight hours or so before sunrise. He could cover plenty of distance—and if he didn't find a secure place by sunrise, what the fuck did it matter?

Dematerializing wouldn't work, he knew because he'd already tried. So he'd have to walk. And that's exactly what he'd do.

"Got nothing to say?"

In a harsh voice, Kel asked, "What is there to say? I can't be around her, Tor. I can't."

"You just were," Toronto pointed out.

"Yeah. For five minutes. Less."

Kel narrowed his eyes and came to a halt, turning to face the shifter. "You think this is all because she's altered."

"Not all. But some? Yeah. Your control isn't an issue, Kel. Not with her." He cocked his head, giving Kel a curious stare. "What did you feel when you saw her? What did your instincts say?"

Kel scowled and started walking again. But ignoring Toronto's question didn't keep his mind from forming the answers. *Whole. Complete.*

His instincts? They had screeched at him to grab onto her, hold her close. Never let go.

Some deeper urge had been there, something that recognized the subtle difference between Angel and other humans. It was sweet, exotic...tempting. His fangs had throbbed in their sheaths and his mouth had watered when he thought about brushing her hair aside, pressing his lips to her throat.

But the stronger urge had been to kiss her. To touch her. Not feed.

"You don't have to tell me, you know," Toronto said, walking along beside Kel once more. "I know when a vamp's got the bloodlust. You didn't."

"I'd just fed," Kel reminded him.

Toronto shrugged, unconcerned. "Not that much, and your

body could have used more. The hunger wasn't sated and you know it. After the beating you took, it's amazing you could stop when you did. But you did stop—easily, seems to me. And you didn't feel it move on you once with Angel."

"The hell I didn't." Kel clenched his jaw and reminded himself, *Walk... Walk. Don't think. Walk away.* But that mantra was harder now.

"So you're just gonna leave?"

"She deserves better than what I can give her, Toronto. She deserves a life. She deserves...everything."

A memory of her voice, soft and tortured, rose up to haunt him. Those memories would do it for a long, long time, too. *What life? There's no life without you. Not for me. There hasn't been, from the time I met you.*

And not for him, either. But there had to be something he could do, some way of convincing Angel she could find something better. He just had to rip this need out of him, his obsessive dreams—they'd forged something between them that had survived the past twelve years, and now, more strongly than ever, Kel realized that while Angel was no longer consciously aware of his thoughts unless he allowed it, he hadn't cut her off. Not completely. Not entirely. Some part of her was still open to him and that was what he had to block, what he had to cut off.

It was time to finish it. All there was to it.

Toronto's voice droned on in his ear and he shot the shifter a dark look. "What in the hell do you *want?*"

The shifter came to a stop and Kel turned to face him.

The small smile on Toronto's face was one Kel had seen before. It was the same look he had when he went on the hunt—both kinds of hunting. That lambent, sleepy look in Toronto's eyes set an alarm to shrieking in Kel's gut.

"Her, man. I don't trespass, but if you're sure..."

Growling, Kel took a step forward and demanded, "Sure about what?"

Toronto shrugged. "That you don't want her. If you're sure, tell me." A wolfish grin lit his face and he added, "Right now she's back there alone and confused. I can help with that. Maybe I can even get her to thinking about somebody but you."

195

He shrugged. "Dunno if I'll have much luck but I don't see what it can hurt, not if you aren't going to be around. One thing is certain and that's the lady definitely doesn't need to be alone right now."

Kel was too stupefied to answer. At least at first. But he stood there sputtering and steaming for too long, because Toronto turned away and called out a cheerful, "See ya back in Memphis in a few days, man...maybe."

Then he shifted, a smooth, seamless change and took off running back the way he'd come.

Her, man. I don't trespass...

Trespass.

Shit.

Kel's hands closed into fists and his pulse pounded in his temple, a hard, rhythmic tattoo. *Her, man.*

What life? There's no life without you. Not for me. There hasn't been, from the time I met you.

Life—Kel didn't feel he had any inside him.

Toronto, the bastard, all but radiated life. His was a warm power, one that warmed even the vampires around him. That warmth would be a sweet, sweet relief to a woman that had just gone through what Angel had.

Her, man.

"Over my dead body," he growled. He took off running, his feet pounding over the pavement with blurring speed. It occurred to him a minute later, he could have tried to dematerialize. But his temper wasn't at all steady and he couldn't think—couldn't focus, couldn't think, couldn't...

But in that moment, his mind started to function. Function in an all-too-fucked-up manner. As in Toronto doing some focusing of his own. On Angel.

Through the bond that he tried so hard not to acknowledge, he could feel her. Vulnerable. Battered. Empty. Lost.

By the time he reached the run-down little house where she lived, he was seeing red and that bloodlust Toronto had mentioned was up in full force.

But it wasn't Angel's neck he wanted, wasn't her blood. It was Toronto's. He wanted that bastard's blood...

The first thing that caught his eye was the window. Free from glass, the curtain fluttering in the breeze. He dove through it, landing on the balls of his feet inside the house. Toronto was already there—damn it, fucking wolves. Vamps were fast, but they were nothing compared to a shifter. Toronto, once more wearing his jeans in addition to a T-shirt, was settled on the couch next to Angel and she was so damn close, she was practically on his lap.

The blank look on her face didn't register.

Her empty gaze didn't register.

All that made sense to him was that he could see another man's arm wrapped around her shoulders, that Toronto was stroking her knee.

"Get up," Kel growled.

Angel's lids fluttered but there was no response other than that. But Toronto reacted, looking at Kel with a patently false expression of mock innocence. Kel took one slow step in their direction, snarling.

Toronto's innocent smile faded, replaced by an expression that Kel couldn't quite place. Later, he'd look back and think about how easily the shifter had manipulated him. But now all he could think about was getting the bastard away from Angel.

He eased Angel away, but it was like moving a mannequin. Angel didn't blink and she hadn't so much as looked in Kel's direction. The complete lack of expression on her face started to tug at his internal alarm, but he couldn't focus on it—on anything, not as long as Toronto stood so close.

"What's the problem, Kel?"

Reaching out, he grabbed a fistful of Toronto's shirt and jerked him close. "Don't. Touch. Her."

Arching his brows, the shifter asked softly, "Why not? You won't. She needs it from somebody." His grin took on a decidedly sly cast and he added, "Better me than some jackass out for a quick, easy fuck, right?"

Control splintering, Kel grabbed Toronto and whirled around, sending the shifter flying into the wall. He crashed into it with a force that cracked drywall. Toronto shoved to his feet, giving Kel an indignant glare. "What the fuck are you doing?"

"Don't. Touch. Her."

The look of mock indignation faded from Toronto's face, replaced by a sympathetic smile. "Is that just in regards to me, Kel? You can't completely block yourself off from her—I know that's what you're thinking, but it ain't going to happen. She's always inside you and with her gift, with yours, the connection you two have, she's always going to be inside you." He glanced at Angel and added, "And you'll always be inside her. Even if she does try to move on, get a life the way you seem to think she should, she won't get over you. But she'll get lonely. What happens when she reaches out, goes to bed with some guy? You going to show up and warn him off and then just disappear? You want her to have a life, but I can't even sit here and try to comfort her a little without you looking like you're ready to rip my throat out."

"What in the fuck do you want from me?" Kel snarled.

"To give yourself a chance. Give her a chance."

"A chance at what? Spending her life with a guy who's not much more than a parasite? I can't *live* without taking from others. I can't be with her the way she deserves."

"Screw that. That's nothing but bullshit," Toronto snapped. "But fine, I'll humor you for a minute. Say you're right, say she can find somebody else... Can you even let that happen? Let any other man be with her? Could she even let herself do it? All she wants is *you*."

"That's all she allowed herself to want," Kel muttered. Realizing this had been Toronto's goal from the get-go, Kel turned away, disgusted with himself.

"You're wrong." Toronto's voice was clear and the look on his face was pretty much the immovable expression he took on when he set his mind to something.

But he couldn't convince Kel to feel any different. Kel knew what he wanted for Angel. And it was something more than what he could give her.

"Look at her, Kel." Toronto looked over Kel's shoulder at Angel and there was pity in his eyes. He took a step closer to Kel, lowered his voice. "Look at her, man. *Look.* Does she look even remotely alive to you? She's been dead inside for twelve years, thinking you'd been killed. How much worse is it going to be now that she knows you're alive...and knowing that fact doesn't matter to you? That you won't come back to her?"

A huge, aching hole had completely overtaken Kel's chest and he hadn't thought he could hurt more. "She deserves more, Tor."

"Bullshit. What she deserves is a decent guy who loves her." Toronto reached out, wolf-quick, and hooked a finger under the gold chain around Kel's neck.

Snarling, Kel reached up and knocked Toronto's hand away, closing his fist protectively around the ring.

Toronto just shook his head. "You think you don't fit that bill, I get that. But *fuck* what you think she *deserves* from life. What about what she *wants*? What she *needs*?"

Hard hands came up and shoved Kel around, forcing him to stare at Angel. That blank, empty expression on her face managed to penetrate something in his head, in his heart this time and Toronto, damn the bastard, somehow sensed Kel's momentary weakness.

"Does she look alive to you right now? Yeah, she'll snap out of *this* on the outside, but what about in her heart? She won't get over you, not any more than you got over her. She's dead inside and if you walk away from her, you've pretty much destroyed any chance she has at whatever happy life you've dreamed up for her. That happy isn't going to happen without you."

Toronto let go of Kel and moved away. He circled around the couch and brushed his fingers down Angel's cheek. She didn't blink. Shit—that dazed, shocky look on her face seriously worried Kel, and he suspected it bothered Toronto quite a bit as well.

Toronto sent Kel one last, telling look and then he left in silence.

Kel edged closer while his common sense demanded he leave. He could call the cops, leave an anonymous tip about a break-in—and Angel's house certainly looked like something had happened. A break-in at the very, very least. The police would come, they'd get Angel to the hospital and if shock was settling in they'd treat her for it. Kel could even hang around until the cops got close, just to make sure she was okay.

But he couldn't do it.

Even if she needed medical treatment for the shock, he

couldn't walk away. He steeled himself. Now that his rage at Toronto had passed, something else was rising inside him, a hard, driving need that went deeper than hunger, deeper than sex, deeper than lust and love—a craving.

For her.

It had to do with Angel, not a damn thing to do with the slightly altered scent of her blood. Just slightly—it hit him with nowhere near the impact he'd been expecting, but that puzzle wasn't one he could focus on.

He heard a low, worried whine and glanced down to see a big, ugly dog with floppy ears and soulful eyes staring at Angel. The dog rested his muzzle on the couch next to her, nudged her thigh and wagged his short, stumpy tail. When she didn't respond, the dog sent Kel a look that very clearly said, *Do something.*

Closing his hands into fists, he muttered, "I can do this." Hell, all he'd wanted to do for twelve years was hold her again. No reason he couldn't manage it now, right? He settled down on the couch, sitting behind her. She was sitting sideways on it, with her legs drawn up to her chest, huddled in on herself. Nestling up behind her, he slid his arms around her waist and tucked her against him.

She was cold. Too cold. Nuzzling her neck, he whispered, "Come on, Angel. Snap out of it."

The rapid, irregular beat of her heart was clear to him as if he'd had a stethoscope pressed to her chest. Sliding one hand down her arm, he closed his fingers down on her wrist. The thready beat had him swearing. Scooping her into his arms, he strode through the house, searching for her bedroom. The dog followed along behind him and when Kel laid her down on the bed, the dog jumped up as well and stretched his length out against her side.

Kel let the dog be. As cool as Angel's body was, she needed heat from somewhere and she wouldn't get it from him. There was a fat quilt folded down at the end of the bed and he tossed it over Angel. As the dog wiggled up to poke his nose out from under the blanket, Kel lay down on the other side of her and wrapped his arms around her.

Snap out of it, he thought. If she didn't soon, he was going to have to get her to a hospital. Most of the Hunters received crash courses on emergency first aid and as far as he could tell, she was in shock. She hadn't been physically hurt—

No. You just pretty much ripped her heart out. Kel didn't mind feeling guilt. Sometimes it was the *only* thing he did feel. But the weight of this was too damn heavy, crushing him. Easing her over onto her side, he curled his body around hers and pushed up onto his elbow, staring at her profile.

"Do you remember that summer you broke your arm..."

He talked. Seemed like he talked for hours. He might have given it up after the first few minutes, but her body no longer felt so cool against his and her heart rate slowed down, taking on a more regular rhythm. By the time he got to their last summer, she had a faint blush of color to her cheeks and her gaze would flick his way for a minute, then just bounce away.

"That night you moved out of your mom's place...remember that?"

Her lids lowered over her eyes, shutting him out. Pressing on her shoulder, he guided her onto her back. A soft breath shuddered out of her, but other than that, she made no response. Kel took her hand and twined their fingers. His voice was harsh as he muttered, "I remember it."

Shit, did he remember. *You need to find something else to talk about, man. Fast.*

But before he could wrest his attention to something other than that first night they'd made love, her lids lifted, revealing heated, hungry eyes.

"I remember." She laid her hand on his cheek. "Are memories all I'm ever going to have of you, Kel?"

"Angel..."

She shook her head. "Never mind. That's answer enough." She started to wiggle away, but the dog's weight kept her from moving away too fast. He brushed a hand over her shoulder but she jerked away. "Move it, Rufus." At the sound of her curt voice, the dog shoved his mammoth weight upright and leaped off the bed.

Kel watched as she headed towards the door, the rational voice of common sense telling him to let her go. Disappear from her life. She'd be better for it.

He didn't remember leaving the bed. He didn't remember

crossing the room, or barring the doorway. He didn't even remember reaching for her, but he must have, because she was pressed up against him, his hands gripping her upper arms. She had her palms pressed against his chest, keeping him at bay. He held back but it took a measure of control he wasn't sure he had.

"Go ahead, Kel. Disappear. I know that's what you want." She stared at him, her blue gaze icy and cold. She tried to twist away from him but he wouldn't let go—couldn't seem to manage it.

"You think that's what I want?" he rasped, dipping his head and pressing a kiss to her neck, just below her ear. Her scent was strong there, warm, soft and female and he wanted to lose himself in it. The rapid beat of her heart was a siren's song and he could almost imagine how she'd taste, could imagine pressing his mouth to her neck, his teeth piercing her silken skin...

Instead of doing it, though, he lifted his head and stared down at her. "Can you really believe, even for a minute, that I wouldn't do anything to have you back in my life?"

His words had little effect—if anything, her gaze became more aloof. She flashed him a hard-edged smile. "Doesn't look that way from where I'm standing. Let me go, Kel. Despite what your nudist friend thinks, I'll be fine."

"Nudist... Toronto." Narrowing his eyes, he studied her face. "You heard him."

"Yeah, Kel. I heard him—sort of. I took a mental trip but that doesn't mean I've completely taken leave of my senses."

I only wish I had...maybe life would *be easier that way. Insanity sounds a lot easier. That or just plain dead.*

Angel never spoke the words aloud. But those words echoed between them. She paled and jerked against his hold as his eyes flew wide. He snarled and wrapped an arm around her waist, locking her against him as she struggled. "Damn it, Kel, let go of me."

"Not going to happen, babe," he growled. Reaching up, he fisted a hand in her hair and jerked her head back, forcing her to meet his eyes. "You don't think like that, Angel. You hear me?"

A sneer curled her lip. How such a derisive expression could be so damned appealing, Kel would never know.

"You can't tell me how to think, *babe.*" Her voice was deliberately scathing, deliberately insulting.

His control stretched tight, he tried to let her go. He needed to do just that—get some distance between them before need, love, lust and fear got the better of him.

But his body wasn't listening to his head's commands and instead of letting her go, he shifted, turned, pressed her back against the door. Leaning into her, he slid one hand up and rested it over her neck. His thumb lay in the hollow of her neck, feeling the silken softness of her skin, the warmth of life rushing just below.

"I said, *don't*," he muttered as he dipped his head and pressed his mouth to hers.

She gasped...and it was like she was breathing him in—absorbing him, their bodies melding into one. He slanted his mouth more firmly against hers, licking the seam of her lips. Angel moaned and opened for him, rising on her toes and hooking an arm around his neck, pulling him closer

In the back of his mind, a faint voice tried to warn him to stop now before it was too late. But Kel knew it had been too late from the moment he started down this path. Coming back into Angel's life could have only led to one place...right here. All the self-denial and rambling about self-control had been nothing but a waste of time.

Slowly, he pulled back, watching her. Angel's lids lifted, revealing turbulent blue eyes. But for the life of him, he couldn't pick up anything from her. She had her mental shields locked down so tight, she could have been silently ranting at him and he wouldn't know. He extended his thoughts, tried to touch hers, but she deflected the mental probe, throwing it back at him. A look of surprise crossed her face, but she said nothing.

He curled his hand over her neck and lowered his head, pressing his brow to hers. "Let me in, Angel," he whispered. He felt so broken without her.

Her body, so soft and pliant against his, stiffened and she turned her head aside. Panic erupted—she was going to pull away. Before she could, before she could say anything or do anything, he kissed her again and this time he didn't stop until she was moaning in his arms and rocking against him. Through the layers of her clothes, he could feel her heat and he wanted desperately to strip her naked, hold her against him and lose himself in the warmth of her.

When he lifted his head this time, she mewled low in her throat. That hungry, kittenish sound hit him with nuclear force. His blood, pumping hotter than it had in years, roared in his ears and his hands ached to tear her clothes away.

Instead, he eased back, held her gaze as he reached for the placket of buttons that held her simple red shirt closed. One button, another, another...and all the while he watched her, waited for some sign that she was going to pull away from him.

But she didn't. When he reached the last button, she was the one who pushed it off her shoulders, shrugging out of it. The plain red cotton fell to the floor, forgotten. She wore a bra, simple red cotton, and her pale white flesh seemed to glow against the rich, vibrant tone. She reached behind to free the hooks at her spine but Kel caught her hands, urged them down to her sides. Instead of stripping the bra away immediately, he turned her around until she stood with her back to him. Dipping his head, he pressed a kiss to her shoulder. She shuddered, arching her neck to the side—it was an instinctive, innocent movement, but it lit through him, burned through him.

Unable to resist, he lifted his head from her shoulder and stared, watched as he trailed his fingertips down the elegant curve. Entranced...it would be so easy...

Her soft moan broke through his daze. He almost pulled away—almost. But then she swayed back against him and once more, he was lost. *Control it, Kel,* he told himself. He could do that. He would do that.

His hands shook a little as he stripped her bra away. From behind, he cupped her breasts. From over her shoulder, Kel stared at the way his hands looked on her smooth, ripe curves. Her breasts were high, full and round, her nipples drawn tight and blushing the same shade of rose as her mouth.

She arched into his touch and at the same time, pressed her lower body back against him. A soft pleading whimper escaped her lips. Her soft curves cuddled up against him and he swore. Banding an arm around her, he lifted her and carried her back to the bed. Lowering her to her feet, he reached for the snap of her jeans, jerking it free, fumbling with the zipper. Stripping her out of the heavy denim seemed to take forever, but the minute he tossed them aside, he wished he hadn't been in such a damn rush.

He needed to take his time, move slow, make this moment last and last...but the sight of her long, slender body clad in nothing but a simple pair of black panties wasn't doing a damn thing to help him slow down and take his time. It also didn't help that she reached up and twined her arms around his neck, urging him closer. With her strong, sleek curves pressed against him, the beguiling arch of her neck now just inches away from his mouth, Kel felt his control crumbling under him like sand.

He had no firm place to stand on and he was left floundering, with nothing to hold onto...but her.

As though she sensed his torment, she turned in his arms and lifted her gaze to his. Lifting a finger, she traced the line of his lips. "You think too much, Kel. Stop thinking already." Then she pushed up onto her toes and pressed her mouth to his. She licked his lips and he opened for her, groaning as she took the kiss deeper.

Without thinking.

Without thinking about the fact that his hunger and his need had caused his body to react—that reaction was instinctive. His fangs had dropped and now she was tracing one of them with her tongue. He stiffened and jerked back and Angel reached up, fisted both hands in his hair, pulling his face back to hers. "Would you please...for five minutes...just stop thinking?"

She kissed him again, nibbled at his lower lip, traced to the outline of his lips, whispered his name. The naked longing he sensed inside her was reflected in her voice, in her eyes.

He was a weak bastard. He had to admit it to himself, and he could castigate himself later. But for now...he opened his mouth for her and when she once more started to kiss him, exploring his fangs with her tongue, he let her.

Angel tugged at his shirt and he pulled back long enough to strip it off and then he dipped his head, rubbing his lips against hers. If it would have been possible, he could have spent the rest of her natural life kissing her...*her* life...for a moment, he almost let his mind roam down a path he really didn't want to follow. Her life would be shorter than his. Unless he got killed on the Hunt, he'd be walking this earth long after she died.

But he couldn't think about that now.

He couldn't think about anything but her hands on him, her mouth against his. Soft but strong hands moved over his chest. Her fingers toyed with the chain at his neck, paused briefly as she touched the ring it held. When she pulled away, he tensed, braced for whatever questions, but she didn't ask any. All she did was lean and press a kiss to his neck before reaching for the snap of his jeans. He hissed as she dragged the zipper down, freeing his aching flesh. The kiss of air on his cock was almost painful.

Kel let her strip his jeans away but when she would have wrapped her fingers around his cock, he caught her wrists.

He needed more than just her hand on him.

He needed to lose himself inside her.

Guiding her to the bed, he urged her to lie down and then he sank down beside her, smoothing a hand up her thigh. Shifting, he settled on his knees between her legs, watched her face as he opened her. Their gazes locked, held as he lowered his mouth to her pussy and licked her.

She moaned, her lashes fluttering down. Her hands cupped his head, held him close but she didn't need to worry. Kel had no plans on doing anything but this until she was limp and barely lucid from the pleasure.

Her hips bucked and automatically, Kel shifted, moving with her so his fangs wouldn't graze that sweet, delicate flesh. He licked her clit, sucked on it and listened to her cry out his name. He smoothed a hand up her thigh, seeking out the wet heat of her sex. He touched her, hot and soft—and tight. Pushing two fingers into her sex, he lifted his head and watched her face.

So tight...

She keened out his name, arching her hips up in a sexy little plea. He lowered his mouth back to her sex and circled her clit with his tongue. Twisted his wrist as he started to pump his fingers in and out, screwing them deep into her pussy, watching from under his lashes as her body started to flush and gleam with a light sheen of sweat.

Heat. Life. It had been missing from him for far too long.

He growled, pulling his hand away and cupping her butt, lifting her more fully against him. He pressed his mouth against her sex in a full, open kiss, circled her entrance with his tongue, greedy for the taste of her. Stiffening his tongue, he fucked her with it, pushing and pushing until she went screaming over the edge.

His cock jerked demandingly and he lowered her hips back to the bed, crawled up over her. Staring at her flushed face, he waited until her lashes lifted and her eyes cleared before he spoke, before he moved. "Open for me," he whispered—but he wasn't talking about her body. Or at least not just that.

She brought up her knees, squeezing his hips. Her lashes drooped. He bent his mind to hers once more and this time, she opened for him. This time, she welcomed him.

Minds merging, he reached between them, grasped his cock. Watching her, he pushed inside. She gasped out his name and the dazed pleasure wasn't just in her voice...it was within *her*, he could feel it, feel need that was almost painful, feel the pleasure that wrapped around her, flowed through her.

It was an echo of what pulsed inside him. A driving need that went deeper than sex.

He slid a hand down her knee, along her thigh, holding her as tight as he could even as he withdrew. Their gazes locked, they stared at each other, silent save for her ragged, hungry moans and his harsh, desperate growls. Angel stroked her hands down his shoulders, hooked one behind his neck, tugging him closer. The other hand, she pressed to his heart— and it beat for her.

The cold, all but lifeless piece of flesh leaped up under her touch. It pounded, pulsed—not with the speed it would had he been human, but it beat, sending blood coursing through his system and bringing a sense of life that he hadn't felt—not once since he'd left her.

No Hunt could equal this. No hot, desperate or even hard and bloody sex could equal this—and even as his body became lost in the pleasure, guilt choked him. He'd tried finding it—

tried, failed, substituted. And nothing could compare. Shame darkened what should have been perfect and priceless. Kel went to lock her out, tried to jerk his shields up.

Angel lifted her hands and cupped his face. "No." And she shoved—not physically. Strength for physical strength, she couldn't match. But psychic strength, she damn well could. And she would—she felt his retreat, felt the ugly blackness of shame, but she'd be damned if she let him pull away.

She focused her mind, flooding him with all that she felt for him, telling him in images and emotions that no words could describe. She moved under him, clenching her muscles around the thick ridge of his cock, showing him with her body. "Don't pull away from me," she whispered. "Don't."

Curling upward, she pressed her mouth to his, caught his lower lip between her teeth, biting gently. He shuddered. One hard, calloused hand came up, curled around her neck. With his thumb, he angled her face up and he slanted his mouth over hers and kissed her. Their tongues twined, that awful mental retreat stopped and once more, they were lost in each other.

Lost.

What was broken became new and old hurts and miseries faded away as he moved within her. Her hands, smooth, gentle but so demanding, clutched at him, racing over his sides, down to his hips to pull him deeper—deeper. He couldn't take her any deeper—couldn't get any closer without their bodies simply merging into one.

Angel's nipples, tight, aching and hot, stabbed into his chest. His body felt blissfully cool against the heat of her own. Cupping one breast in his hand, Kel pulled his mouth from hers and kissed his way down her neck, lingered over her pulse and down until he could close his lips around the stiff peak. Careful...so careful...he touched her with such care.

She could feel the contained strength within him, felt the need raging inside him. His fangs grazed her flesh and sent an erotic thrill shooting through her. Lifting a hand, she cupped the back of his neck as he started to lift away, urging him closer. A look flashed in his eyes, something dark, deep, indefinable. But then it was gone and he lowered his head, licked her nipple, caught it between his teeth and tugged.

Angel moaned, greedy. He alternately licked, nipped and suckled, each one driving her so much closer to exploding. He pushed up onto his hands, hovering over her. Angel reached for him, tried to tug him closer. In response, he caught her hands and pinned them over her head. She groaned, closing her eyes and jerking on her hands.

Kel rasped, "Look at me, Angel. I need to see you."

Unable to resist the naked need in his voice, swirling through him, she lifted her lashes and stared at him. He rotated his hips against her, minutely changing the angle of his thrusts, and then he started to shaft her. Slow. A slow possession and retreat. The thick, ridged head of his cock rubbed against her in the sweetest way and each stroke felt like it would do it, be the one that sent her flying off into the stratosphere.

She went higher and higher, teetering on the edge and pleading with him. He shifted her wrists so that he could hold them in one hand, then trailed the fingers of his freed hand over the outer curve of her breast.

"Tell me you love me," he whispered.

"I love you."

His lids drooped. A shudder wracked his body. A look crossed his face, primal, terrifying...erotic. A sexy, sensual snarl darkened his features and Angel stared, mesmerized. His fangs...she could see them.

Her neck throbbed. Pulsed.

There was an ache there, almost like the ache clenching in her belly. Unconsciously, she arched her neck, bared it. His gaze rested on it. Groaning, he lowered his head, pressed his lips to her neck. Licked her.

Bit her softly.

He freed her hands, reaching up to brush her hair out of the way and then he raked his teeth along her skin and then lifted up, brushing his lips down her cheek. It was sweet—but not enough. Angel didn't even think about what it was she needed, what she was doing. She hooked her hand over the back of his head, guiding him to her.

There was a blind look in his eyes. That primal hunger, primed, ready...and blind.

Angel didn't care.

Even the voice of her common sense had fallen silent. Everything inside her *needed* this. She pressed his face against her neck, her lids fluttering down. He growled, a deep sexy rumble of sound that vibrated deep in his chest. His body tensed over hers and she thought, feared, worried he'd pull away.

But he didn't—what he did was slide a hand under her head, fisting it in her hair and jerked her neck to the side. He struck and as his fangs pierced her flesh, his cock jerked in her pussy. He started to draw on her flesh and at the same time, that slow, lazy rhythm became frenzied. Kel's hips pummeled hers, taking her with a force that should have hurt—instead it was so gloriously perfect, she screamed out his name and pressed her lips to his shoulder, sinking her teeth into his flesh, the same as he'd pressed his into hers.

She bit down, unaware of just how hard until the taste of blood filled her mouth. Blood...but it wasn't coppery. Wasn't metallic...it was sweet. So sweet.

As one, they started to climax, and it spun on and on...his mouth at her neck, hers pressed to his shoulder, the throbbing of his shaft wrapped in her still-convulsing pussy. Time stretched out, propelling her higher than she'd ever gone and it didn't seem to end until her body was just too weary to handle the pleasure.

Combing her fingers through his hair, she whispered his name and sighed. He tensed against her and jerked his head away. His lips had blood on them—her blood.

And she could still taste that sweet, sweet tang of his blood when she'd bit him back.

Unconsciously, she brushed her fingers against her mouth and when she brought them down, she saw the red smear of blood.

She should have been repelled.

But what she felt was satisfaction. Utter and complete.

His face had been pale, but now there was a ruddy hue to his cheeks and she knew without asking it was because he'd fed from her.

Fed *from* her—it hit her then, just what had happened to

Kel. Not in the abstract, and not that dim awareness that too often never fully formed. No, this was real, full-on understanding and her head started to spin.

Through the excess of knowledge rippling through her, she felt his body tense, felt him pulling back. Angel narrowed her eyes and wrapped her legs around his hips, hooked an arm over his neck. "Don't."

He shook his head, a panicked look on his face. "Let me go, damn it. I can't... I can't..."

"Can't what?" she asked as his voice trailed off and all he did was try again to pull away. Angel tightened her grasp.

"I can't stop!" he snarled.

She blinked, unsure at first what he meant, but the answer was already there, already forming in her mind, thanks to the bond between them. "Kel...you *did* stop."

He stilled, his big body shuddering, shaking. In a hoarse voice, he rasped, "Just let me go, Angel."

"I've done that once already, Kel. I let you go, watched while an empty box was put in the ground and dirt shoveled over it. I let you go, let it destroy me...and now you're here again. You're back. How can you ask me to let go now?"

His head drooped. He reached up, pulling her arm down and then untangling her legs from his hips. "If you don't, I'll end up destroying you for real. I can't trust myself." He shifted around and sat up on the edge of the bed, staring at the floor.

Angel shoved up, coming after him. Draping her arms around his neck, she pressed her breasts against his naked back and kissed his ear. "I trust you, Kel. You wouldn't hurt me. You *didn't* hurt me."

He snorted and reached up, touched his fingers to his lips. The sight of the red stain seemed to infuriate him. "I already did," he growled, trying again to pull away from her.

But she wasn't letting go willingly. If he wanted her to let go, he'd have to make her and he wasn't willing to do that. Wasn't willing to hurt her...and he doubted his control? She could feel the conflict raging inside him, feel the need for her tangle with the need to keep her safe.

"You don't need to keep me safe from you, Kel. You've never been a threat to me. The only thing that could hurt me would

211

be losing you again."

Kel slid her a look and shook his head. "You're wrong." Then he reached up, carefully prying her arms away from him and this time, when she struggled, he ignored her. He was off the bed in less than a second, turning to face her. "You don't know me, Angel. Don't know what I've become. What I've done."

She blinked and momentarily froze. Then fury shot through her. Coming off the bed, she stalked across the room and jabbed him in the chest with her finger. "I don't *know* you? Kel, I know you better than anybody. Better than everybody. I always have."

A mocking smile curled his lips. "Oh, baby, you have no clue how wrong you are." His gaze slid down to her neck, lingered on the spot that even now seemed to tingle and throb, almost like her body craved to feel that again.

"You just fucked a vampire—let one feed on you like a parasite."

He saw the warning in her eyes, saw it in her body as she tensed, and he could have moved to stop it. He let her hit him though, a solid jab to his jaw. If he'd still been human, it might have knocked him on his ass. Angel had always been strong. That hadn't changed. But all it managed to do was hurt her hand—his body absorbed the minor twinge like water but he could see that her hand was already swelling. Just one more little guilt to pile on him.

Staring at him with haunted eyes, she said, "I just *fucked* the man I loved. The man I've always loved. I loved you even before I understood what it really was to love anybody but my dad. I loved you when I was just a little girl and you were standing there blushing to the roots of your hair, so embarrassed by what I was telling you and even then you couldn't say anything because a part of you felt it, too. You wouldn't have done or said anything to hurt me."

Hell, she could have driven a silver dagger into his heart and it wouldn't have hurt as much as her words...or the look in her eyes.

"Times change, Angel. Neither of us are who we used to be."

"You got that right, Kel. You didn't used to be a coward."

That stung. It had nothing to do with cowardice—it had to

do with trying to do what was best for her. She wouldn't see that, though. Maybe she couldn't see it, he acknowledged. She was still so focused on who he used to be, she couldn't see what he'd become. Until she could see that, maybe she just wouldn't be able to get past this, past him.

So instead of trying to explain he wasn't acting out of cowardice, but a need to take care of her, he gave her a mean little smile and flicked the bite mark on her neck. "I didn't use to be a lot of things." Lowering his head, he murmured in her ear, "You really don't know me, Angel. Not anymore. I'm not the man you think you love...I'm not much more than a monster."

She jerked away, shaking her head. "I don't believe that."

"Oh, really?" He reached up and cupped her face in his hands, staring down at her. She stared at him with faith, a deep belief in the man she still believed existed. But that man had died long ago, before he'd really even had a chance to become whoever he might have become. It was too late for him. But it didn't have to be too late for her.

He rubbed a thumb over the curve of her lips. "My dad died a month ago. I felt it...knew it had happened, because of you." Dipping his head, he pressed his lips to her forehead and then trailed them down over her silken skin until he could murmur in her ear, "I knew. Because of you. And while you were up late that night making arrangements, you know what I was doing?"

It wasn't exactly a lie that he forced into her head. The memory he pulled up from his subconscious and forced on her *had* happened. But it had happened two days before his dad had died. The days after his dad had died found Kel locked up in his rooms and brooding, trying not to slip back into the rut of anger that had been his companion for so long.

His psychic abilities, though, rivaled Angel's now and he had no doubt he could convince her of the truth in his words as he pushed in a memory of one of the last nights he'd spent with Phoebe. He didn't leave any of it out, not the sex, not the way he'd fed from Phoebe until she'd all but blacked out, or the way that the more they hurt each other, the better it was.

Memories of that left him feeling shamed, but he wouldn't focus on the shame. Wouldn't focus on anything but convincing Angel she was better off without him. Dipping his head, he nuzzled the bite marks on her neck—odd, they seemed to be healing. Already. Not vamp quick, but certainly quicker than he would have thought.

Doesn't matter...just do it. He licked her neck and then whispered, "While you were crying over Dad, I was fucking a woman I didn't love. Fucking a woman who liked to draw blood while we did it. Every time she made me bleed, it made me feel a little bit more alive. I've spent the past year in her bed doing dirty, wicked things no decent man would do. Tell me, Angel...am I *really* the man you think you love?"

Angel tore away from him, staring at him with dark, hurt eyes. Her face was pale, ghost white. She shook her head and whispered, "You son of a bitch."

He smirked. "Sugar, you really didn't think I'd spent the past twelve years going without, did you?" He shrugged casually, forced the words out through a tight throat and hoped she couldn't hear the pain behind them. "Vamps need sex almost as much as blood. I gotta do what I gotta do."

She blinked, tears glittering in her eyes. Some of them broke free but she dashed them away. "Tell me something, Kel," she asked, her voice hoarse and shaking. "Did you feel half as alive with any other woman as you felt with me just now?"

But she didn't wait for an answer. She grabbed her clothes and bundled them against her chest, stalking out of the room. In the doorway, she paused. Without looking back at him, she said, "I don't know much about what you are now, I don't know if you have a reflection, don't know if you can't cross running water or what. But you're still a man—no matter what you say. Last night, *he* was a monster. Whether he intended to become one or not, I don't know, but he was a monster. I know what a monster is."

Finally, she glanced back at him and added, "And I know what a monster isn't. It's a pity you don't."

She left then and when he was alone, Kel's eyes closed. He'd done the right thing... So why didn't it feel like it? He grabbed his clothes, dressing in a hurry. His internal clock told him he had plenty of darkness left, but he had to get out of here, had to get away. He couldn't spend another minute this close to Angel.

If he stayed too close, feeling the echo of her pain even though both of them were desperately shielding against the other, he'd break. He would plead, beg for forgiveness, crawl at her feet, whatever it took.

Even walking out of this house was going to take more than he thought he had in him, but he needed to do it. And he needed to do it now before his resolve crumbled. A thought occurred to him and he wondered if he couldn't just dematerialize. He hadn't done it except for that one time… Shit, just a few days ago. But he had done it. He could do it again, right?

A few minutes later, he had that answer. No. He couldn't do it again. Or at least he couldn't figure out *how* to do it. And that meant he'd have to walk out.

Angel was sitting on the couch by the front door. The air in the room felt chilly and he stared at the gaping, empty window, watched as the curtains fluttered in the breeze. "You need to get that fixed."

She shot him a deadly look but said nothing.

Swearing, he turned away and started for the door. Two steps away, he paused and turned back, looked at her. She was sitting almost exactly as she had been a few hours ago, her knees drawn up to her chest, staring straight ahead as though she saw nothing around her. Even the dog was the same, sitting on the floor with his muzzle pressed against her thigh.

Might have been his imagination, but it seemed like the dog gazed at him with reproach. Even canines were giving him recriminating looks. Toronto's words came back to haunt him and he remembered that blank, empty look on her face, like something inside her had already died.

Does she look even remotely alive to you? She's been dead inside for twelve years, thinking you'd been killed.

He *had* been dead inside for twelve years. Even the few times when he'd felt some semblance of life, it had just been make-believe. The one time he'd felt alive since his Change had been tonight.

With her.

Her eyes cut to him and she demanded in an icy voice, "What is it? You got a pint of blood." She stroked a finger down her neck and smirked. "Maybe less. And considering the butcher job you just did on my heart, you must have at least a pound of flesh from me, although I'll be damned if I know what in the hell I did to deserve it. I ain't got anything left for you to take."

"Angel..." He couldn't help it. His voice softened and the guilt and grief he worked to keep trapped inside worked his way into his words, into his thoughts and he wasn't foolish enough to try and convince himself that she couldn't feel the change inside him.

She shoved off the couch and faced him. She'd dressed as well, but not completely. The shirt draped over braless breasts, clung to each soft swell, every soft curve. Her tousled hair framed her face, angry flags of color rode high on her cheeks and her eyes all but shot daggers at him. "Save it, *sugar*. You wanted me to get the point and while I don't think I got the message you were sending, I did get one. Loud and clear. Maybe I *don't* know you. And now I don't think I want to." Turning on her heel, Angel stalked out of the living room.

The dog gave him another dirty look and then padded out of the room after his mistress.

Chapter Ten

"You gave up awful easy."

Angel recognized the voice. She wished she didn't. She wished she could forget the past week of her life. Up to and including Kel. It had been exactly seven days since he'd walked out on her. Seven long days. "Easy," she murmured, shaking her head. Angel didn't even understand the meaning of the word anymore.

She turned her head and stared at Ness—no, Nessa. Toronto called her Nessa. "You know, most people don't come up to somebody sitting by a grave. It's generally recognized as private time."

The girl turned her head and studied the headstone. "Kel's father, I would guess. You were close."

Angel's mouth twisted in a bitter smile. "After Kel disappeared, his parents were pretty much the only family I had. His mom died a few years later...Jake died last month."

"I'm sorry." She said it softly, but sincerely. Nessa tucked her hair back behind her ears. All the silver rings were gone now. She didn't have a single pair of earrings on. No makeup either. A pair of baggy jeans, an even baggier T-shirt. Her eyes cut towards Angel and there was a blatant challenge in them. "You did give up too easy."

Shaking her head, Angel said, "I can't make him take something he doesn't want."

"But he does want it. He wants you. He's just afraid. Terrified. He fears he would hurt you. Or perhaps he fears what will happen when years go by, he never ages, but you do. It's a hard thing to live a long, empty life knowing the one you love is

217

Shiloh Walker

naught but dust." A haunted look entered her eyes and she added in a husky voice, "Believe me. I know."

It faded as quickly as it had come, replaced by a caustic tone. "But he's young and even if he wasn't, people often don't see the obvious until it's pointed out. He isn't what he once was...but neither are you. Not entirely."

The weird look in Nessa's eyes had Angel shifting uncomfortably. "Twelve years will change a person."

Nessa replied, "One second will change a person. One heartbeat. One moment. That, too, is something I know very well." She hunkered down in front of Angel and reached out, touched the spot on Angel's neck where Kel had bitten her.

It had healed completely. Not one sign remained. All she had left to remember that one night were her memories...and a busted window she still hadn't replaced. Boards had been nailed over it, but she just didn't care enough to worry about messing with having somebody repair it.

But when Nessa touched her neck, it burned. Throbbed. Almost like it had that night.

"People do change, girl. Some of us more than others. Some of us change in ways we don't even realize."

Angel batted the girl's hand away. "Oh, believe me. I get the fact that he's changed. I get the fact that I've changed."

Nessa smirked. "Child, you haven't got any idea on just how much you've changed—and how very little you haven't."

"Tell me something, does Kel know anybody that doesn't speak in cryptic riddles?"

The smirk on Nessa's face bloomed into an all-out grin. "Well, short, bossy, blonde brats need to have their fun somehow."

Angel cocked a brow. "Nice to know you can recognize your faults."

"Hmmm. Well, I've had a lot of years to learn that skill."

Angel frowned. "You don't look old enough to drink."

The other woman chuckled and shook her head. "And still you can't see it...things are too often more than they appear, Angel. Including me." She sighed and slid Angel a sad smile. "I look like a juvenile delinquent. But that doesn't even touch

218

what I am."

Curiosity got the best of her. "Exactly what are you? Toronto said you were a friend." Angel touched her throat, remembered how just one touch from this girl had taken away her physical pain. Remembered how Nessa had touched Toronto and Kel and the men's injuries had faded away like fog under the sun. "Some kind of... I dunno, witch or something?"

"Witch." Nessa's eyes closed and she smiled. "Aye. Or something? Aye, that, too." She shoved to her feet then and jammed her hands deep into the baggy pockets of her jeans. "Everybody makes choices, Angel. Some aren't the wisest. Some aren't the right ones. But usually, if you act on what is in the heart, you'll come out okay." She gave Angel an enigmatic smile and then murmured, "Tell me...what is in your heart?"

Then, as Angel sat there trying to find an answer, the girl disappeared.

Into thin air.

What is in your heart?

It wasn't a simple question, and Angel discovered through the rest of the night, it didn't even have just one answer.

She had love in her heart.

She had anger.

She had misery.

She had confusion.

She had doubt.

She had questions.

But above all else, there was love. No matter what Kel said, she did love him. And she didn't love some imaginary man or a boy who had long since grown up. She loved Kel. Twelve years apart, but too much of her had recognized him. So many dreams about him that weren't really dreams, but subconscious echoes of the life he lived. Echoes that showed just how much he *hadn't* changed.

In the end, the love won out. But the anger was a close

second.

Decision made, she lay down on the couch and grabbed an hour-long nap. She hadn't been able to sleep in her bed since the night Kel had left and she wouldn't be surprised if she never slept in it again. It seemed like his scent surrounded her and lying down on the bed seemed to make phantom hands course over her flesh.

Washing the sheets didn't help.

Burning the damn mattress probably wouldn't help either.

She had one chance to exorcize her ghosts. One chance. And it wasn't a good chance, either.

But Angel wasn't too concerned with odds. If she didn't at least make the attempt, she'd have the rest of her life to regret it. She'd make the attempt. And if she failed, then she failed and she would find a way to get on with her life.

Despite what that seriously strange guy, Toronto, had told Kel, Angel wasn't going to let this end her life. If Kel didn't want her, fine. One thing he'd been right about was that she'd never let herself get over him. Somewhere deep inside, maybe part of her had known he was still alive, and she'd just been waiting.

She wasn't going to wait any more.

If he turned her away, that was it. She may never be able to keep from loving him, but she'd sure as hell stop sighing and crying over a man she wouldn't ever have.

Angel would find a way to get on with her life and it wouldn't be an empty one.

She loved Kel. But she had her pride and she had a heart full of anger—and one question to ask.

She didn't bother to take anything more than a change of clothes and some toiletries thrown into a duffle bag. She wasn't exactly sure where she was going but if by some slim chance fate cut her a break, maybe it would be a while before she came back. Of course, there was a better chance she'd be heading back here within a day or so.

Once she did, she'd get the window fixed, hire a few guys to do the repairs on the house and sell the damn thing. Only one person had kept her in Greenburg all these years, only one thing. Caring for Kel's dad. But Jake was dead now...and when he died, he'd made her his sole beneficiary. A certain percentage of his estate went to the church, but the rest was hers and she was going to use it. For...something. To help her find some sort of life without Kel.

But first, she was going to get an answer to her question.

Kel lay on his narrow bed, staring up at the ugly gray ceiling overhead. One hand pillowed his head, the other was closed around the ring at his neck.

He couldn't feel Angel.

After twelve years, it was an abrupt, almost brutal absence, one he missed more than he could have expected. He was alone inside his head, more alone than he'd been in a long time. He hated it.

He'd been back in the enclave for a week now and he hadn't left his room once except to feed a few days ago. Even that had been hell—he couldn't touch a woman. No way. He'd sought out one of the werewolves who lived in the enclave—not Toronto. He couldn't look at Toronto because the shifter kept giving him censoring looks and making Kel doubt the choice he'd made.

Feeding from a male never sat well with him and he spent half that night feeling like he'd eaten bad meat or something.

His body had recovered from the injuries sustained during the fight, but his resources were drained. That quick feed a few days ago wasn't going to do the trick and he knew he needed a serious, real feed but he couldn't find the energy or the interest.

Likewise for Hunting.

Anything.

A motor sounded from outside, loud and out of place, but he tuned it out, just as he had tuned out anything and everything else.

Nothing really seemed real anymore so it was easy to ignore it all. Like turning down the volume on a radio.

So it was a little bit of a surprise when his ears picked up the sound of a fist pounding on the door of the manor. Even more surprising when he heard a voice. Easily picked it out from the others.

Angry. Demanding.

"Don't hand me that bullshit that you don't know who I'm talking about," the feminine voice snarled.

Another voice—and Kel felt the push of vamp compulsion. He recognized it, filed it away, because in a little bit, he was going to knock Josiah into the next millennium for trying to pull that mojo on Angel.

Rolling off the bed, he left his room and took off running up the steps. A woman with altered blood coming into a house full of vamps, even if they were on the side of the angels, was a bad, bad mistake.

Josiah was blocking the door but Kel could scent her—he had no doubt it was Angel.

"Leave her alone, Josiah," he said, his voice hard.

Josiah turned around and met Kel's flat stare. His eyes narrowed in understanding and he swore. "Shit. Kel, go downstairs."

Kel snarled. Striding across the room, he got in Josiah's face and dared him. "Why don't you try and make me?"

They were collecting an audience.

Toronto separated himself from the crowd, moving to stand at Josiah's side. His voice was pitched low, but the words were heard by all. "This doesn't concern you, Josiah. Just leave it."

The vamp whirled on Toronto, jerking a thumb in Kel's direction. "The last thing he needs now is to be around that girl."

"You know, *that girl* can speak for herself," Angel snapped from the doorway. Stubbornly, she crossed her arms over her chest and glared at Kel. "I'm *not* leaving until I've talked to you."

Then she sent a withering look at Josiah and added, "And whatever in the hell you were trying to pull? It won't work." Her eyes narrowed and she focused.

Every last one of them felt the force of her psychic punch as she struck out at Josiah. His face tightened but he showed no other reaction. His lip curling in a disgusted sneer, Josiah turned on his heel and stomped out. "Stubborn as he is. They were made for each other."

Rafe finally made an appearance and all the Hunters fell back to let him through. Barefoot, wearing black jeans and a plain black T-shirt, Rafe studied Angel for a minute and then he looked at Kel. Although he didn't say anything, there was a look in the Master's eyes that said, *This ain't gonna end well.*

"It seems Kel's got a guest, folks. Doesn't concern any of us." He nodded his head at Angel and then turned, left in silence.

The rest of them trickled out until Kel was left alone in the foyer, staring at Angel. She still stood on the porch, giving him an insolent glare. When their gazes locked, she angled her chin up. "What, aren't you going to try that same lame-ass mind thing?"

Kel shook his head. He reached up and scratched his chest, absently realized he hadn't put a shirt on when he had awoken earlier. Angel's eyes slid down, rested on the chain around his neck. Instinctively, he wrapped his hand around the ring, shielding it.

"I know better. If there's a vamp with the juice to force you out on mental power alone, I don't know him." He blew out a harsh sigh and murmured, "Angel, what are you doing here?"

"I had a question I wanted to ask you. That question, you answer honestly, and I'll go."

Kel shoved a hand through his hair. One question. He could handle that, right?

"You going to stand on the porch all damn night?" he asked caustically.

She frowned, glanced down at the ground. Her body shifted like she was going to move, but she didn't. She shrugged and then shook her head. "Don't worry. It won't take more than a minute."

Kel glared at her. "Get your ass in here if you want to ask me something. I don't care if it just takes two seconds."

She snorted. "So is two seconds my time limit?" she asked as she crossed the threshold and closed the door behind her.

Folding his arms over his chest, he just stared at her.

"That was a neat trick, that deal you did forcing those memories in my head. But something about them felt off." She gave him a mean little smile. "Not that I don't believe you about

223

the woman in the memories, but something about it was a lie. I'm thinking the timing..."

Vampires didn't blush. But they sure as hell could feel embarrassed and being caught in a lie would do it. He didn't bat a lash, though, as he lied through his teeth. "Got no idea what you're talking about, sugar. Is that your question?"

"No." She sauntered over to him.

As she drew close, Kel stiffened but he didn't pull away. She reached out and hooked a finger under the chain around his neck and tugged on the chain until he let go. Flashing him that insolent smile, she lowered her gaze and studied the ring. "Here's my question, *sugar*. Why are you wearing a woman's engagement ring around your neck?"

He jerked away, crossed the foyer. When he had a good ten feet between them, he turned back to meet her gaze but for the life of him, he didn't know what to say.

He'd bought it for her before his life went straight to hell. He hadn't found the right time to ask her. He'd been working on something romantic, including candlelight and roses. And although he'd told himself to get rid of it a hundred times, a thousand, he couldn't do it.

And he also couldn't lie about it, he realized as he met her blue eyes.

"You need to leave, Angel."

Her chin angled up another notch. "Sure. When you give me that answer."

He swore and turned away. He heard her footsteps, all but soundless on the gleaming wood floors, felt the warmth of her breath caress over his back as she stood less than a foot away. "You going to take off running again, Kel? That's fine. Go ahead. And I won't come looking for you again, although it doesn't matter where you go—now that I know you're alive, I could find you in my sleep."

Her hand caressed the skin of his back, leaving a fiery trail of sensation. "I won't come looking for you. If you won't give me that answer, that's fine. Once I walk out of here, I'm done."

Woodenly, he turned to face her. The words were in his throat. He wanted to tell her. Wanted to give her that answer...and more. But he couldn't.

She smoothed a hand up his chest, toyed with the ring. "And I won't be spending the rest of my life mourning you. You were right about that—I never let myself get over you. But that's done. If I leave here alone, if you let me walk out that door, I'll get over you no matter what it takes, no matter how long."

"Angel..." His voice trailed off. He didn't know what to say, other than the plain, ugly truth. "You can't be with me. I can't be trusted around you." He sighed and reached up, trailed his fingers down her neck. "Something weird happened to you that night. Not just me. He... That vamp, we call them feral, he must have wanted to Change you, make you a vamp. He fed you. It wasn't...it wasn't enough to do it, but it changed something inside you and whatever it is, it's like a drug to vampires. I'm not strong enough to resist it."

Her head cocked. "No? Doesn't seem to me like you had any trouble stopping last week. Or walking away." A conniving smile appeared on her face and she brushed her hair back, baring her neck. "And I don't see you falling on me like a raving lunatic. Neither did your oh-so-charming friend. Or any of the others...you're not the only one like you here, right? But nobody seemed all that fixated on me."

"They wouldn't dare," he growled.

Angel just lifted a brow. "If I'm some sort of drug, nobody here seems too affected, Kel."

Affected? Hell. He damn well *was* affected. Wanted to fall on her, exactly like a raving lunatic. He wanted to—he itched to do it. But even as that thought circled through his head, he realized that what he wanted from her wasn't blood. Or rather, he wanted the blood, he didn't *need* that.

He needed her.

A sad smile curled her lips and he knew without a doubt, she knew just what he was thinking.

"You're stronger than you think, Kel. I don't know what in the hell it is you're trying to tell me, but I do know that it doesn't matter. Nothing could compel you to hurt me—except your own blindness. Like pushing me away because you think you're a physical danger to me."

She shook her head. "You're wrong. And I know it even if you don't." Her hand came up and she cupped his cheek.

"Goodbye, Kel. And don't worry. I'll get okay with this somehow. I'll be fine without you in my life. I won't need you to be happy."

She pushed up on her toes and kissed him. Then she turned around and walked away.

The door closed behind her and not even a heartbeat later, Toronto appeared. "Are you really that stupid, Kel?" The shifter didn't look at him, just stared at the door.

Exactly as Kel was doing.

"I'm doing what I have to. Hell, even if I could control myself, who's to say other vamps can?"

Toronto shrugged. "Nobody. But then again...when she showed up, I didn't see every vamp in the enclave staring at her the same way I look at a hot fudge sundae." Then he grinned. "And she smells different than she used to."

"Different?" Kel asked.

There was no sound, but they both turned their heads to watch as Rafe came into the foyer, his brown eyes unreadable. "Yeah. Different."

"Different how?" Kel demanded.

Rafe shrugged. "Can't really explain it. I haven't seen her in years, Kel. I stayed away because of what I figured out that night. She's always had a witch or a shifter checking in on her. Smart vamps don't hang around vampire bait, but I can't say that's what she is exactly."

Then he closed his eyes and swore, mumbled under his breath. "*Sheila's never going to let me live this down...*" He opened his eyes, focused on Kel's face and said, "I didn't give you much credit, Kel. I don't know if anything I said is playing into this massive act of stupidity, but regardless...I was wrong. You wouldn't hurt her. You can't. And you just showed that by letting the one woman you loved walk out the door after merrily telling you she'd forget your ass and find somebody else to make her happy."

Rafe left. Toronto left.

Kel stood there alone.

Alone. In the span of heartbeats, he saw his entire damned life spread out before him. Nothing but cold days sleeping alone, and endless nights spent alone.

You wouldn't hurt her. You can't.

You're stronger than you think, Kel.

Nothing could compel you to hurt me—except your own blindness.

Outside the house, a truck engine roared to life.

Abruptly he took off running. He tore the door open and darted across the carefully manicured lawn, through Sheila's flowerbeds without a thought that the woman would kick his ass over it, down the drive as the truck drove away.

He put on another burst of speed and jumped. Angel's startled shriek didn't faze him a bit as he walked up the truck bed, climbed out and stood on the rusted-out running board as he jerked open the passenger door and climbed in.

That big-ass dog had been lying on the bench seat next to Angel but as Kel climbed in, the dog sat up and studied him with a quizzical stare.

She slammed on the brakes and he smacked a hand against the dash to keep from crashing into it, automatically grabbing the dog's collar to keep him from tumbling off the seat. The truck skidded to a halt and then he reached over, shoved it into park.

Then he settled back on the seat, reached up behind his neck and took off the chain he'd worn for the past twelve years. The dog whined, sniffed at Kel and then climbed over him, one big paw coming very, very close to a sensitive portion of his anatomy. Kel grunted as the dog poked his head outside, his massive body draped over Kel's lap. The dog sniffed, then his muscles bunched and he jumped out through the open window.

In a casual voice, Kel said, "I was working all that overtime to help pay off this ring. Talked to a few girls at school, tried to set up the perfect romantic time to propose." A smile came and went, fleeting. "Had it planned for a couple weeks after...after that night." He curled his hand around the ring and then rested his arm on the door, staring out in the dark, quiet night. The sun had just barely set and off to the west, he could see the faint pale orange glow cast by the sun. Nodding his head towards it, he murmured, "This is the closest I can get to sunlight for a long time. If ever. I may never be able to take the sun's rays."

227

Finally, he slanted her a look but she wasn't looking at him. She was staring off out the driver's window and had her arms crossed over her chest. Her heart was racing, but no matter how hard he tried, he couldn't pick up anything from her. "I've been a mess the past twelve years, Angel. I fly off the handle, I don't feed enough and when I finally do give in, it's because my body won't let me deny it."

Speaking of body... He closed his eyes. Rubbing a hand across his naked chest, he thought about what he'd done to Angel when he forced the memories of Phoebe into her head. If Angel had done that to him, he would have gone stark raving mad. Probably already had.

"The night you were up planning Dad's funeral, I wasn't with that woman. I was at home, alone. Brooding. I'd been with her the night before but when you got the phone call, I knew. I felt it and I left, went back home and wished like hell I could be there with you." He licked his lips. "I can't thank you for the way you stayed with him, helped him the past twelve years. You won't ever know how much that means to me."

Her voice was flat as she asked, "Why the hell are you telling me this? And you're sitting awful damn close, Dracula. Aren't you afraid you'll snap and attack me?"

Kel rubbed the back of his hand over his mouth. "I'm terrified I might do just that. But you keep telling me it won't happen. And others."

She snorted. "So you'll listen to others. Maybe me. What about yourself? Why don't you listen to yourself first for once, Kel? What do *you* think—would you attack me, hurt me? Do any damn thing to me that I didn't ask for?"

His voice was ragged and harsh as he answered, "Not on my life."

He closed his eyes and let his head fall back against the headrest. "I'm a mess, Angel, and I have been ever since this happened. I can't undo what I am, and I can't change what I have to do just to live."

Finally, she looked at him. "Do you think I wouldn't get that? Hell, you won't even tell me just *what* you are. There's more to it than a pretty pair of fangs and the ability to live through an injury that would kill anybody. A bit more to it than sex and the way it felt when you bit me. But you walked away without bothering to explain anything. Without telling me anything other than, *I'm sorry. I can't do this.*"

Abruptly, she grabbed the handle of the door and jerked, sliding out of the truck. Kel waited a minute and then followed, watched as she started to pace. It was growing darker by the minute and although it didn't affect him, the rocky, unfamiliar ground probably wasn't ideal pacing territory.

But her footsteps were as sure and as certain as his own, even when she paced out of the moon's rays under the canopy of leaves. Sticking to the tree line alongside the drive, she walked ten feet, turned and came back. Turned again. Ten feet, then back.

"You don't even know the meaning of *messed up*, Kel. I pretty much lost it. I was hallucinating, seeing things that weren't real..." She shot him a look over her shoulder and added, "Or so I thought. Now I don't even know if *real* exists. But I spent a month in a mental hospital after that night—I have a close, personal acquaintance with *messed up*."

"I know."

She stopped in her tracks, turned to face him.

Kel clenched his hand around the ring and had to force himself to meet her gaze. "I'm the reason. The first few months after it happens are rough. Control is non-existent. You're always hungry. You picked up what I was going through and it's stuff that a human wouldn't understand."

He gave her a thin-lipped smile. "So I'm the reason behind your personal acquaintance with messed up. Once I figured out what I was doing, once some people helped me out, I got it under control...but I couldn't ever cut you off completely. I always felt you. When you cried, I felt every last tear. When you lie awake at night hurting, I hurt with you."

He blew out a breath and lifted his hand, staring at the golden ring and the gleaming diamond. "I'm a slow study, Angel. But I finally figured it out. You can get by without me, I don't doubt that. You'll live just fine and I imagine you'll find a way to be happy."

Without lifting his head, he stared at her from under the fringe of his lashes. "But I'm not going to be able to live without you. If you walk away, my world pretty much stops."

He sighed, shoved a hand through his hair. Then, without quite realizing what he was doing, he went to her, reached out, took her hand. Tucking the ring and chain into her palm, he closed her fingers around it. "I've worn that every day, every night since the day I figured out that I'd lost you. That I'd never have you with me. But it isn't mine. I bought it for you. It's yours. Just the way I am. But I don't have the right to ask you to stay."

He cupped her face and forced her lowered chin upward until she met his gaze. "If you chose to stay with me, I'd do my damnedest to make it up to you. I'd do my damnedest to make you happy." Stroking his thumb over her lip, he said hoarsely, "But if you don't want that, I'd understand."

He let go, stepped back. Shoving his hands in his pockets to keep from reaching for her, he said bitterly, "Hell, it would be easier for me to understand you walking away than choosing to stay." The knot in his throat made swallowing sheer hell, but he had to because the words kept getting stuck inside him. "It's your choice. But before you walk away, I wanted to tell you I'm sorry. That I love you. And I do want you with me."

Then he turned and started the walk back up to the house.

His heart was pounding with an intensity that deafened him and his blood roared in his ears. The ache in his chest was huge—but he felt a little more at peace than he had in a long, long time.

At least he'd told her.

At least he'd tried to give the two of them—give *himself* a chance.

That had to count, right? He told himself that as he passed by her truck. The dog was lying by the rear tires, whining, but Kel just kept walking. Until she grabbed him.

Angel grabbed his arm and he turned, almost afraid, to face her. She jumped towards him. Thrown off balance, he caught her against him and stumbled against the truck. Her mouth was on his. Her tongue in his mouth. Her hands in his hair...and her voice whispering through his mind even though she couldn't exactly speak out loud at the moment. *You're a jerk, Kel. A class-act jerk. You think I actually want to walk away from you?*

He tore his mouth away from hers. He had to hear it. Had to. "You'll stay? Here? With me?"

"Here. There. Who gives a damn, as long as you're with me."

The relief that hit him left him weak-kneed. He crushed her against him, buried his face in her neck and just breathed in the scent of her, listened to her heartbeat pounding against his own. He stumbled around the back of the truck and ended up sitting on the bed of the truck. The tailgate was missing and looked like it had been for a while—it was a good thing because otherwise Kel would have probably ended up dropping down to sit on the ground.

"I love you," he muttered, blind to anything and everything but her.

She stroked a hand up over his bare shoulder, up his neck, and fisted it in his hair. Angel tugged gently and he lifted his head, met her gaze. She lifted her hand, let the chain dangle from her fist. The diamond ring swung back and forth between them as she asked, "Then maybe you could help me put this where it belongs."

Slowly, he reached for the ring and took it from her. Sliding the chain away, he dropped it on the bed of the truck next to him and then reached for her hand. Lowering his head, he kissed her ring finger. "I can get you a nicer one. A better one." Moving his shoulders restlessly, he said, "I don't exactly have a normal-type job but I do get paid and there's not a lot I need to spend it on."

Angel wiggled her finger demandingly. "I want the one you bought for me. And I want you to ask me the question that goes with the ring."

He kissed her finger again. "Would you marry me, Angel? Save my life?"

She smiled as he slid the ring onto her finger and then she lowered her mouth to his and whispered against his lips. "We'll save each other... How's that?"

"Good. Real good."

Her tongue rimmed his lips and he opened for her, sinking back onto the truck bed. She came with him and through the sweater she wore, he felt the soft, round weight of her breasts, felt the heat of her skin, and the rhythm of her heart. "I need you."

She shimmied her legs up and straightened up. Grabbing the hem of her sweater, she dragged it off and tossed it aside. Her bra followed suit and then she reached for his hands, brought them to her breasts. "Then have me, Kel."

Sweet and slow... That was what he wanted to give her.

But it wouldn't happen tonight...or at least not now. He grabbed a fistful of her hair and jerked her back down to him and at the same time, he rolled, placing her body under his. The smile on her lips faded, replaced by a hungry moan as he kissed her.

The rest of their clothes, her jeans and his, the lacy scrap of her panties, went flying. "Later," he rasped against her mouth. "Later we'll take it slow. Promise."

"Hmmm. Don't talk." She wrapped her legs around his waist and rubbed her sex against his cock. "Just make love to me."

Without another word, without another touch, he entered her. She whimpered and wiggled under him, working to take him inside. Through their connection, he could feel the pain edging through her and he tried to slow down. She was damp and hungry, getting hungrier by the second, but she wasn't ready for him.

Other than their one night last week, she hadn't been with a man since he'd disappeared from her life and her sheath was so sweet, snug and tight—but while that felt like heaven to him, it wasn't so good on her. He rasped, "I'm sorry," against her lips and went to pull away. "Let me..."

"Don't." Her lids fluttered down and she slipped a hand down her torso, down her belly, slipped through the pale yellow curls between her thighs.

Kel swore and straightened, leaving her body supported by the truck while he braced his feet on the ground and stared down, watched as her slim fingers stroked her clit. Her pussy convulsed around his cock and her hips undulated against his. Soft...sweet...and wet, rippling around his rigid shaft in a silken caress. "Bring me to life, Kel."

He slid his hands down her thighs and caught her behind

the knees, shoving her legs high. "You're my life." He caught her wrist and bent down, sucked her fingers into his mouth and licked away the sweet dew as he took up the teasing caress with his other hand. "You're my heart. My soul. My everything."

Lifting his eyes, he stared at her flushed, gleaming face and stroked the sensitive flesh of her pussy where she was stretched so tight around him. "Come for me. Let me see it," he ordered. Then he touched her clit, working it with smooth, quick circles. She wailed and arched, wiggling her hips, trying to take him deeper. He leaned over her, braced his hand by her head, watched her face for any sign he might hurt her. He started to shaft her, taking her with deep, hard thrusts and stroking her clit.

Her sharp, staccato scream echoed through the night. She reached down, caught his wrist and worked herself against his hand. "Come for me," he ordered. She was dewy wet, tight and swollen...and when the rippling convulsions started deep inside her, he felt it.

Growling with victory, he muttered, "That's it...come for me, sugar. Let me feel it..."

Her lids lifted, revealing dark, slumberous eyes. "Not without you." She shuddered under him, arched up and reached for him. "Never without you. Not anymore."

He hunkered over her, wrapped his arms around her slender torso. She draped hers over his shoulder and her lips touched his... The gentleness he'd wanted was suddenly there and he slowed until he was just rocking ever so slightly against her. "I love you," he whispered.

"Hmmmm... Love you...Kel." She cried out his name and bucked under him, the orgasm erupting inside her and as she clenched down around him, it set off his climax. Wrapped in each other's arms, lost in each other's bodies and thoughts, they fell...together.

Their lips met in a slow, lingering kiss and even after he collapsed against her, spent, the kiss didn't end.

There were questions. There were worries. He was no longer quite sure exactly what to make of Angel and he didn't know what the future held for them, or what awaited them... She was still mortal, right? But even as he asked himself that, a niggling little voice whispered, *Are you sure?*

She smelled different.

She moved in the night with the grace of a vampire.

Something about her simply felt different.

But none of that mattered. Not right now.

She smiled against his lips and whispered, "Kel...you're thinking too much."

Josiah came into Rafe's office and pointed out the window behind Rafe's desk. "You got any idea what's going on out there?"

Rafe smirked. "I dunno...arts and crafts hour?"

Sheila, sitting at one of the two other computers, looked up from the blog she was reading. Batting her lashes, she said, "I really like arts and crafts, baby."

Toronto came strolling in, smirking and looking entirely too satisfied. "I knew he wasn't stupid."

"I think all of you must be," Josiah snapped. "Didn't you say she was vampire bait? And you're leaving Kel *alone* with her? *Kel?*"

Sheila glanced towards the window and then sent Josiah a wicked look. "Well, as much fun as it can be to watch, I think this is one of those 'alone' kind of moments."

"But what if he..."

Rafe shook his head. "Don't. There's no 'what if', not when it comes to Kel and that girl. I never should have thought otherwise." He slid Toronto and then his wife a glance. "As I've been pointedly told."

Then he shrugged. "Besides, I'm not entirely sure what she is now. She still doesn't feel human to me, or not entirely. But she's not like she was when we first started watching her either. Who knows...maybe the effects fade."

"Or maybe she's a little more than just *altered* now," Toronto offered, giving them one of his secretive little smiles. Without bothering to explain that, he left.

About the Author

To learn more about Shiloh, please visit http://shilohwalker.com. Send an email to Shiloh at shiloh_@shilohwalker.com or join her Yahoo! group to join in the fun with other readers as well as Shiloh. http://groups.yahoo.com/group/SHI_nenigans/

An animal rights activist is about to get a crash course in werewolves. One she may not survive.

Savage Retribution
© *2008 Lexxie Couper*

Lone Irish werewolf Declan O'Connell has lost everything—his family, his clan, even his freedom—to his arch-rival, Nathan Epoc. The head of an underground werewolf clan and a brilliant scientist, Epoc plans to use Declan to create a super-wolf, a creature capable of shifting the balance of power in the lycanthrope world. But Epoc's plans are about to be thwarted

Regan Thomas, a determined animal rights activist, rescues what she thinks is an ordinary wolf from his notorious animal testing facility in Sydney, Australia. She gets more than she bargained for when the wolf turns into an extremely hunky, extremely naked man who immediately drags her into a world where the clash between two opposing werewolf clans could spell the end of humankind.

Declan has survived without a clan for more years than he cares to remember, but sexy Regan stirs up all his fierce, alpha-wolf instincts. Now Declan has one last chance at revenge. But can he keep Regan alive, and resist the overwhelming attraction between them, long enough to stop Epoc?

Summer in Australia has never been this hot...or this dangerous.

Available now in ebook and print from Samhain Publishing.

Enjoy the following excerpt from Savage Retribution...

Regan's heart hammered.

The wolf lay on its side, taking up most of her old sofa, its eyes closed, its rib cage rising and falling with rapid, shallow breaths. Dry blood smattered the grey fur on its neck, cracked and thick like black mud. The cushions of her sofa bowed and compressed under the animal's massive bulk and, as she had in the lab, Regan wondered what species it was. None she was familiar with.

How can that be?

She frowned. She was at least passingly familiar with just about every species in existence—she had to be in her line of work. How could she not—

The wolf whined again, softer, weaker, and Regan's puzzlement vanished.

In a heartbeat she crossed the room and crouched by the wounded animal, skimming her hands over its body. A wave of awe rolled through the cold worry knotted in her chest. It was unwell. Its limbs trembled and each breath seemed weaker than the last, yet its feral strength was undeniable. She'd thought it a creature of primitive power back in Epoc's lab but now, here in her room with its corded muscles under her examining fingers, its *mana* seemed almost tangible. "What genus are you, my friend?" she whispered, running her hands over steely quadriceps much bigger and longer than any wolf species she knew. Quadriceps turned to femur, femur to pelvic bone.

Regan frowned, confusion squirming in her gut. The animal's pelvis felt wrong, like some sick bastard with a Doctor Moreau complex had taken to it with a bone grinder in an attempt to reshape it into a human hipbone. "What *have* they been doing to you, mate?" she murmured, tracing the distorted bone. "My God, how can you even walk?"

She moved her hands up the wolf's spine, counting vertebrae, looking for wounds or injuries. Curiosity ate at her concern. Where had the creature come from? Wolves were not native to Australia and as far as she knew, the only ones in the country were those housed in zoos and animal enclosures. For this lone wolf to be in Epoc's lab...?

Imported illegally, perhaps?

But from where?

Her seeking fingers slid through a patch of wet fur low on the wolf's rib cage and Regan stilled her investigation. She parted the animal's dense coat, looking for... "There it is."

Fresh blood, bright red and warm on her fingers, seeped from a ragged hole puncturing the wolf's side. Regan prodded the surrounding flesh gently, worrying the bullet may be embedded in bone beneath. She'd have to get the animal to Rick. Whether the bullet was there or not, the wound needed to be—

The wolf whined. Low. Almost human.

"I'm sorry, mate," Regan soothed, removing her fingers from its rib cage. Chewing on her bottom lip, she smoothed her palms over its scapular and down first one foreleg and then the other. Both rippled with muscle and once again, uneasy wonderment wriggled in Regan's stomach. The humerus seemed too close to human in structure to be possible. She ran her hands over it and it seemed to shift. Grow longer. Straighter.

Regan scrubbed the back of her hand against her eyes. She must be sleep deprived. Bones didn't change structure. With a slight shake of her head, she went back to her examination. As soon as she was convinced the animal could be moved, she'd call Rick. He'd give his left nut to help her out, any excuse to try and impress her into his bed. But quite frankly, she had no hope of moving the animal herself, even if it would fit in her car.

Another whine whispered on the air, so soft Regan almost missed it. "Not much longer, my mysterious friend," she whispered, letting her hands settle on the wolf's rib cage again, careful to avoid its wound. Its coat felt like fine velvet under her palms and for a dreamlike moment, she felt like pressing her face to the animal's side. She leant forward, sliding her hands to its shoulder joint in search of wounds unseen and her bare nipples brushed against the wolf's chest, flesh to fur. Soft. Cool. So much more than she'd expected. So much more than any animal species she knew.

What type of wolf are you?

She returned her attention to the wolf's body. With the exception of the bullet wound, it seemed physically uninjured, but who knew *what* Epoc's scientists had been doing to it. She smoothed her hands over the silken fur, a distant more detached part of her mind admiring the wolf's superb biomechanical construct. It was a creature evolved for one purpose only—to kill—yet its beauty was undeniable. Strength, menace and deadly purpose all combined in the majestic somehow romantic form of—

The thigh muscle below her palm shifted, elongated, and Regan stumbled backward, landing flat on her bare butt with an ignominious thud. She stared at the massive, powerful and utterly lupine form. Watched it contort. Shudder.

The dense fur rippled, each strand seemingly alive with its own energy. The back legs grew long, straight. Thick, corded thigh muscles formed on bones no longer short and crooked. "What the..." Regan's stunned whisper barely left her lips.

Another shudder wracked the wolf's contorting form. Another. And another. Its fur grew thin, retracting into the flesh beneath, disappearing with each violent convulsion until its coat no longer existed and instead...

Regan's heart froze and she stared at the naked man laying full-length on her sofa.

The naked, trembling, gasping man laying full-length on her sofa.

Looking at her.

"What the *hell?*"

The man's eyes—the angry color of a stormy winter's sky—flicked over her face. Like oiled smoke, he was on his feet, hard, lean body coiling, pale flesh glistening with a faint sheen of sweat in the sun-filled room. Regan stared at him. Speechless. Unable to move.

Shaggy ink black hair fell across his forehead, brushed straight eyebrows of the same color, cheekbones high and angular. Smooth, curved pecs cut down to a hairless torso sculpted in muscle. Nothing detracted from the perfection of his body, not even the mean scar slashing his pale skin from navel to groin. Regan traced the ragged white line with her eye, her stomach clenching as it disappeared into a thick thatch of black pubic hair just above—

Oh, my God! He's huge!